By the Author

Fortunate Sum

Life in Death

Visit us at www.boldstrokesbooks.com

LIFE IN DEATH

LIFE IN DEATH

by

M. Ullrich

A Division of Bold Strokes Books

2016

LIFE IN DEATH

ISBN 13: 978-1-62639-773-6

This Trade Paperback Original Is Published By
Bold Strokes Books, Inc.
P.O. Box 249
Valley Falls, NY 12185

First Edition: October 2016

CREDITS
EDITOR: JERRY L. WHEELER
PRODUCTION DESIGN: STACIA SEAMAN
COVER DESIGN BY JEANINE HENNING

Acknowledgments

"Acknowledgments" is one of those words that starts to look funny when you stare at it for too long. Same thing goes for words like "magical" and "surreal." Speaking of, I would describe the experience of having a second book as both magical and surreal. I've been left quite speechless by the warm reception *Fortunate Sum* received, and I'd like my first acknowledgment to go out to everyone who took the time to read it. I'm grateful that readers were willing to take a chance on a new author, and I'm thankful for those of you who have jumped on board for my second venture.

The Bold Strokes team, once again, has been nothing but outstanding to work with: Sandy Lowe, who has the patience to answer my many, many questions; Jerry Wheeler, my stellar editor who helps turn my stories into the best books they could possibly be; and my fellow authors whom I've commiserated with over time—you all are invaluable.

This book, and most of my accomplishments through life, wouldn't have been possible without knowing the truest definition of motherly love. My mother is a selfless woman, one who put her children first, no matter what sacrifices had to be made. Mom, even though we're both rather bashful about you reading my books, you helped inspire the love between mother and daughter I wrote about in this one. Maybe I'll put together an edited version just for you one day—it'll be a quick twenty-five-page read.

Heather, I still haven't come up with the right words to describe how much I love you or how thankful and lucky I am to have you by my side. I'm still having a hard time coming up with an adequate thanks for those amazing koozies, never mind everything else you do for me! You are a continuous source of strength and support, and

I know that without you none of this would be possible. Thank you for helping make so many wonderful things possible.

Finally, to the person holding this book—thank you.

For Heather:
My past, present, and epilogue.

CHAPTER ONE

Everything seemed so heavy: the air, her jacket, and the way her limbs swung listlessly. The walk from her car to the front door had always seemed so short up until that day. Martha Dempsey paused for a moment and looked toward the sun. Its descent to the horizon had painted the sky a deep raspberry pink and mandarin. *Almost dinnertime*, she noted to herself before going into the house. It seemed too large at times and suffocating at others.

"Mom?" she called out, wincing as she heard her hollow voice echo through the still home. The hurt in her chest intensified, creating a dull thud of a heartbeat in the empty space. "I'm home."

"We're in the back, Marty." A ghost of a smile appeared on her thin lips at hearing the nickname her mother loathed using, only assenting to it when Martha was sick or, as in this case, had a bad day.

Without a single thought accompanying her actions, Marty made her way through the house, stopping to deposit her messenger bag on the couch and hang her suit jacket loosely on the back of a wooden kitchen chair. In less than forty steps, she made her way from the front door, through the living room, and across the open kitchen to the back door.

"Mama!" A young girl wearing a hot-pink bandana wrapped around her head jumped up from her place on a cushioned Adirondack chair and wrapped her arms around her.

"Hey, Abs." Marty held her daughter close and allowed herself to get lost in the feel of tiny arms wrapped tightly around her slim waist. For just a split second, she believed everything was right in the world. And then Denise Dempsey's voice shattered the comforting silence.

"Dinner will be ready in twenty minutes." Marty saw Denise's sharp, aged eyes judging her appearance, making her feel as small as her own child in that moment. She swallowed audibly, hoping her matching green eyes didn't hold as much scrutiny. "You should go wash up." Marty's mother turned on her heels and made her way back through the open screen door.

Marty looked down and tried to see herself through her mother's eyes. Her starched white blouse was far from wrinkle-free, and her black suit pants were deeply creased from hours of sitting. The only detail of her dress outfit that seemed unblemished were the loafers, ones that had stayed in their box since she had received them last spring for her thirty-fifth birthday.

"I guess I do look pretty terrible, huh?" Marty looked into her daughter's sparkling brown eyes and laughed as the little girl shrugged in response.

"I've seen you look worse." Her arms were still around Marty's waist, a serious expression twisting her tiny features. Marty laughed in response.

"Thanks, Abigail, I feel better already." Marty lifted her daughter over her shoulder and let Abigail's giggles improve her mood. She carried the small girl into the kitchen and sat her on the granite countertop. The deep indigo of Abigail's jeans contrasted with the creamy ivory of the expensive stone. Marty looked at the light pink schoolgirl top and eyed her daughter suspiciously. "Did Grandma dress you this morning?" Abigail nodded. "Is this a new shirt?" Marty flicked at the rounded collar, a choice Abigail would never make on her own. Abigail nodded again and started playing with one of the many buttons that lined the front of her shirt.

"Leave the girl be, Martha. She liked it this morning when I showed it to her." Denise wiped her hands on her apron. Its sunflower print was almost too cheery but did little to obscure her matching pink top with rounded collar. She looked again at Marty, this time over the edge of reading glasses she used mostly to secure her chin-length red hair off her face. Worry lines started to crease her forehead. Marty excused herself before she could ask anything.

"I'm going to go change." She turned back to Abigail. "Abs, help your grandmother set the table." She grabbed the little round face and planted a sloppy kiss on her warm forehead, lingering for a moment to inspect Abigail's temperature before releasing her and heading for the stairs.

Upstairs, Marty riffled through the drawer that held all her fluffiest attire. Every pair of sweatpants she owned, every thermal, Henley, and worn sweater was folded neatly beside the others. She ran her fingertips along each row, feeling the soft comfort of old materials tease her skin. Her awful day was worthy of her oldest, most comfortable sweats and a threadbare T-shirt with Princeton written proudly across the chest in crackled screen print.

Marty avoided every mirror in her bedroom and kept her head down as she washed her hands and face in the bathroom. She knew she looked atrocious, tired, and drawn. She didn't need a vivid reminder at that very moment. Her mother was downstairs waiting for an opportunity to do just that.

Marty moved slowly down the stairs, fatigue draining the usual bounce from her steps as she joined her family in the kitchen once again. Her appetite had been lacking, but some familiar smells from childhood caused her stomach to growl tonight.

"Chicken noodle soup and oatmeal cookies?" Marty quirked a dark eyebrow at her mother as she tied back her chestnut-brown hair in preparation for leaning over a steaming bowl. A few curls escaped and fell into her face, but Marty just didn't have the energy to care. She sat in her usual seat. Abigail lifted herself slightly onto the chair beside her.

"I figured you may want something gentle and comforting after the day you had." Marty's mother ladled the soup into large bowls.

"Can we have cookies first?" Abigail asked with the sweetest, largest smile. That grin could get her anything she wanted from her mother, but not her grandmother.

"I love you, but no." Denise pushed a bowl closer to Abigail and handed her a large spoon.

Marty looked down at her soup, moving the noodles and carrots around in search of a small piece of chicken. She brought it to her lips with a shaky hand and nibbled at it slightly. Her stomach wanted food badly, but her mouth revolted, wanting nothing to do with flavor. She knew she'd have to take it slow.

"So, did Grandma help you get all packed for our trip tomorrow?" Talking helped distract her wanting to gag. If she spoke enough, she could manage another bite or two.

"Mmm-hmm." Abigail hummed and nodded with a mouthful of noodles before filling her spoon once more and blowing on its contents. Marty watched for a moment, wishing she could muster that kind of enthusiasm for the meal.

"Did you pack her red blanket?" Marty asked her mother.

"Of course." Denise almost looked offended at the question.

"And her games and e-reader?"

"You're acting as if this were my first rodeo." The eldest Dempsey woman pierced her daughter with a chastising glare for her line of questioning.

Marty took a deep breath and looked back into her mother's deep emerald eyes. "I'm sorry."

"It's okay. You had a terrible day, I'm sure. I think it's safe to assume you're nervous about tomorrow as well?"

"The hospital is so far away. I hate having her sit in the car after her treatments." Memories of the last visit intruded in Marty's mind without permission. Abigail was sick the entire ride.

"The confrontation after today won't be easy either," Denise pointed out, even though it was far from necessary at the moment.

Marty pushed her soup away with her left hand and waved her right in a dismissive gesture, not quite ready to talk about it. She looked over at Abigail, who was chasing the last noodle around the base of her bowl. "Not now. Let's talk about anything else."

"Sweetheart, you need to talk about—"

"Not now!"

"Done!" Abigail pushed her bowl away. "Now can I have a cookie?"

Denise stood and huffed at Marty before smiling at her granddaughter. "Of course you can." She reached toward the counter and returned with a plate piled high with chewy oatmeal cookies, still warm from the oven. "Take two, one for each hand."

A bright smile lit up the little girl's face, and tears came to life in Marty's eyes. She looked so happy, her Abigail. Despite everything, she smiled just as happily at the offered cookies as she would have if it were her first time trying them.

Denise spoke to Abigail once again, sparing Marty an audience. "Abigail, why don't you take those cookies upstairs to your room and pick out a movie to watch with your mother when I leave?"

"Okay!" Her enthusiasm was contagious, and both grown women found themselves smiling as Abigail ran to the stairs and up to her room.

"She shouldn't be that happy, not with me." Marty sniffled and tried to compose herself. She had been stoic all day, and the contained emotions had started make their way to the surface. She felt it in the warmth that tickled the tip of her nose and in every goose bump that pricked at her skin.

"Parents get divorced." Denise pointed out that truth as if it were the easiest fact to accept.

"No." Marty spoke the word like acid on her tongue. "It should've never happened to us." She looked to the plate of cookies and suddenly all the scents in her home assaulted her, turning her stomach violently. "I need some fresh air." She stood abruptly, the legs of her chair crying out loudly as they scraped against the hardwood floors. Marty rushed to the back patio, sucking in air as quickly as she could. She was light-headed and heavy-hearted. She jumped when her mother's hand landed on her shoulder.

"It'll be okay."

"No, it won't." Marty looked out across her large backyard. The sun had put itself to bed and a chill accompanied the spring evening. The flowering trees that lined the perimeter of the yard were still a vibrant green with colorful petals adorning each branch. Soon enough, however, the vibrancy would fall away and leave nothing more than deep green. "I failed," she whispered. "I failed them both in the worst way." Fresh tears lit up in the moonlight, and she hugged herself in an effort to ward off a shiver.

"You could never fail Abigail." Denise pressed her hand firmly into the center of her daughter's back.

"But I failed Suzanne." She finished what she was sure her mother was thinking. She fell onto a deck chair gracelessly as the acceptance of her life from that day forward hit her square in the chest. She looked down at the hand that signed the papers. "I have an ex-wife." The words were directed to no one in particular, but the crickets chirped loudly in response.

Once Upon a Time...

Marty grew anxious at the prospect of being stood up. She checked the oversized face of her watch for the fourth time. Her blind date should've arrived nearly fifteen minutes ago and yet she still sat in the crowded restaurant alone. Two full glasses of water sat on the tabletop, condensation rolling down the cool glass. *Five more minutes*, Marty promised herself. She looked at the last few sips of red wine left in her large wineglass, wondering why she had allowed her new coworkers to convince her a blind date would be a great way to introduce herself to her new hometown.

❖

Marty could hear their conniving voices as clear as day. "Suzanne is wonderful!" Charlotte exclaimed as the plan unfolded.

"Charming and beautiful too!" Annmarie chimed in with her thoughts, her large brown eyes never leaving her computer screen.

"So why is she single?" Marty couldn't contain her curiosity. She didn't want to seem rude or offend her coworkers and new friends, but if the woman they were speaking of was so wonderful, surely she'd be paired up already.

"We never said she was single." Charlotte smiled deviously and tucked a strand of her jet-black hair behind her ear.

First impressions for Marty were a big deal. It could either make or break your future with her, but she had been wrong on both accounts with Charlotte Kingsley and Annmarie Ventuolo. At first they appeared uptight and far from approachable. Marty was the latest hire in the well-established real estate agency, and she expected to be treated like fresh meat. Charlotte was a few years older than Marty's twenty-two years and intimidating with her Morticia Addams–esque pale skin, long black hair, red lips, and a wardrobe that rarely strayed from black.

Annmarie was the complete opposite. She was bubbly and over the top from the first moment Marty walked through the door. She was closer to forty, short, and a bottled blonde. She lived by the beach, and it showed in the deep tan of her skin. Annmarie seemed like the type of woman who would encourage, help, and raise you up just to watch you fall.

The fall never came; neither did the cutthroat atmosphere Marty expected. Both women eagerly took Marty under their guidance and showed her the ins and outs of real estate at the Jersey Shore.

"Excuse me?" Marty looked back and forth between both amused women. Annmarie smiled at her screen while Charlotte moved closer to Marty's desk.

"Suzanne is sort of seeing someone," Charlotte said.

"But nobody likes her," Annmarie added.

"How do you know Suzanne?" Marty still wasn't sure a setup was the best idea.

"I was into rentals at the time, and I showed her the apartment she lives in now. After the papers were signed, we went for drinks to celebrate and we've been friends for years now," Charlotte all but bragged.

"What's wrong with her girlfriend?"

"She's rude!" Annmarie finally turned away from her computer. "She's harsh, and she obviously doesn't make Suzanne happy. Someone needs to come along and sweep that poor girl off her feet." She smiled again at Charlotte. "And you're going to get your chance this Friday."

❖

"You have got to be kidding me!" The loud voice startled Marty, and she jumped, almost spilling the last bit of wine on her crisp, floral printed blouse. The red would've stood out amongst the muted blues. When her heart calmed, Marty looked around to find the source of the rude outburst.

Behind her stood a petite blonde, no taller than five foot five. Her hair fell around her face in loose waves. The tendrils were multiple shades of blond and thick, appearing almost heavy. The stranger stood dumbstruck for a moment as Marty regarded her. She wore tight black slacks paired with a black blouse. Marty's eyebrows rose in question.

"Suzanne?" Marty stood and recalculated the blonde's height. She seemed taller now. Marty extended her hand. "I'm—"

"Not Charlotte."

"No." Marty dropped her hand and blushed slightly. "I'm not. I'm Martha Dempsey, but please call me Marty."

"Suzanne Carlson." She scanned Marty with her deep blue eyes as she spoke bluntly. "I was supposed to meet Charlotte, but I guess I shouldn't be surprised by another setup." She smiled weakly. Her lips were full and pink.

"Please, sit." Marty motioned to the empty chair across from herself. Suzanne looked as if she wanted to argue, but she was more than ready for a drink. She sat gracefully and looked to Marty again.

"I apologize for my little outburst." Suzanne couldn't hide the color that rose on her fair skin, painting her cheeks a shade of pink Marty found undoubtedly attractive. "This is the third time this month I've expected to see my friend and I walk up to a complete stranger. A surprise each time, and Charlotte knows how much I hate surprises."

Marty winced. "That sounds terrible. I'll thoroughly chastise Charlotte when I see her at the office on Monday, but until then let me buy you a drink." Marty put on her most charming smile. She knew she looked good; her choice of shirt was fitted enough to advertise her lithe build, and she kept the sleeves cuffed enough to display her early summer tan. Her hair had behaved that evening and the curls fell onto her shoulders in controlled chaos. With a hint of eye makeup and lip stain, Marty was sure to be a tempting date.

"I'm seeing someone."

Marty licked her lips and smiled again. "Then we won't call this a date, just drinks between new acquaintances."

"I don't see anything wrong with that." Suzanne matched Marty's broad smile. "I'll have a chardonnay." Marty was awestruck by the vibrant blue of Suzanne's eyes. The waiter approached the table and Marty ordered for both of them. Suzanne sat back and flashed a crooked smile.

"So, Suzanne." Marty leaned forward on her forearms and continued to speak. "Why is it that you're seeing someone and yet your friend continues to set you up?" She knew why, but she was curious about Suzanne's side of the story.

Suzanne let out a sigh. "Charlotte isn't a huge fan of my girlfriend."

"How come?"

Suzanne turned the interrogation around on Marty with a bit of heat. "Why do you let your coworker set you up on blind dates? Can't get a date for yourself?"

"I'm new to town, looking to make some friends. A blind date didn't seem like such a bad idea at the time."

"Where are you originally from?" Suzanne asked.

"Princeton."

"Fancy pants." Suzanne chuckled and sat back as their drinks were delivered. She thanked their waiter. "What brings you down the shore? Point Pleasant is more of a tourist town, not exactly known for its real estate. Princeton is surely the better place to sell homes in New Jersey."

"True, but I was ready for a change of scenery and better opportunities. Here you have homes, condos, townhomes, summer rentals, winter rentals—the possibilities are endless." Marty took a sip of her red wine. "Plus, I'm a sucker for the water. I plan on having a boat in the next couple of years."

"Oh yeah? What if you're not as successful as you think you'll be?" She was obviously a playful woman, and Marty enjoyed her company all the more for that.

"It's part of my plan," Marty said confidently.

"Do you always stick to your plans, Marty?" Suzanne leaned into the conversation, following Marty's earlier action.

"I do."

"Tell me more about your plan."

The two women talked for hours. They laughed and exchanged embarrassing stories. Marty cringed as she relived the morning of her worst hangover and how little she cared when her mother found her naked on the living room floor. Suzanne quickly countered with the unexpected wet T-shirt contest she'd participated in on a train one rainy morning the summer before. Marty never hesitated before reaching out to touch Suzanne's hand more than just a few innocent times. Once the waiter informed them of last call they realized how long they had been talking. Both women laughed in embarrassment.

"I guess that's our cue." Suzanne started to stand.

"You never told me about your girlfriend." Marty stood and stretched, her shirt lifting a bit from the waistband of her jeans.

"She's the silent type and not necessarily outgoing." Suzanne cleared her throat. "We don't go out much, but I like the quiet, strong types. The guy I was with before her was the same. Come to think of it, my friends weren't too fond of him either."

"Guy?" Marty's eyes widened.

Suzanne laughed. She was clearly used to this reaction. "Yes, guy. Bisexuals do exist, you know."

"Mmm." Marty nodded and thought for a moment. She smirked before saying, "Bisexuals who happen to go after *people* with lackluster personalities certainly do exist."

"Oh, that's just rude!" Suzanne's guffaw contradicted her words.

Marty needed to know more about this mystery woman who'd captured Suzanne's heart. She walked around the table and placed her hand in the middle of Suzanne's back, leading her from the restaurant in a chivalrous manner. "Does she make you laugh?"

"She can be funny." Suzanne's words were almost hesitant.
Marty grunted quietly.

"What? What was that for?"

"Nothing, I just…" Marty paused and met Suzanne's gaze, a playful smile pulling at the corners of her mouth. "I can't help but agree with Charlotte. You can do better."

"And you think you're better?" Suzanne crossed her arms over chest.

"I had you laughing all night, didn't I?" Just as Suzanne was about to comment, Marty continued. "But I'm just looking to make friends, remember?" Marty's breath caught when Suzanne smiled with a twinkle in her eye. She decided to press her luck. "What's your number?" She took her phone from her back pocket. "I'd like to have another friendly outing sometime soon." She didn't look up from her screen. When Suzanne gave her the number, Marty started breathing again.

"Call me soon, friend," Suzanne said.

"I will." Marty turned and started her walk through the parking lot, an extra bounce in her step as she approached her beat-up sedan. She sat behind the steering wheel and stared at Suzanne's number. She wouldn't call that night, but she would call in the morning and every morning after that until Suzanne realized that Marty was worth way more than friendship.

CHAPTER TWO

"A bigail!" Marty called from the bottom of the stairs. "You need to hurry up, and don't forget your slippers this time. I refuse to buy a pair in the gift shop for fifteen dollars."

"I'm ready." Abigail appeared and raced down the stairs toward her mother. When she stood at Marty's side, she was slightly out of breath. "I got my slippers and the fuzzy socks Grandma got me for Christmas." She held both items up high.

"Good." Marty looked around the house one last time to make sure she hadn't forgotten anything. "Ready?"

"I don't want to go." Abigail had been strong, but this was the second round of treatments, more aggressive than the first. They still had no definite answers.

"I know, sweetheart." Marty swallowed hard against the lump that formed in her throat. She hated this. She hated uprooting her daughter for endless days and nights in a hospital that would end up feeling all too much like a second home. She hated the way she couldn't tell when the days turned to nights or whether the sunset was beautiful or the sunrise brighter than usual. Hospitals changed the way she looked at life, as well as the spirit Abigail used to carry along with her. She shook her head and tried to be the optimist, a role that used to come naturally but hadn't in recent months. "You'll start to feel so much better after this. You're going to kick it for good. Thinking about that makes it a bit better, right?"

"I guess." Abigail scuffed her foot against the wooden floor.

"That's my girl." Marty ushered the young girl out to her black Subaru with a gentle hand on her bony shoulder. She had a pink duffel bag slung on one shoulder and her own tote held in her right hand.

The drive to the University of Pennsylvania hospital took close to an hour and a half. Traffic in the early hours of Friday morning was congested with businesspeople who rose with the sun. Marty shifted as she pulled into the hospital's parking garage. The denim of her worn jeans squeaked against the leather of the seat. She always wore soft jeans and even softer T-shirts for trips to the hospital. They spent long hours there, and comfort was key. That explained Abigail's colorful pajama set.

Looking at her daughter as she exited the car, Marty smiled sadly as she remembered simpler times and sleepwear decorated with Disney characters.

The pair walked in silence toward the elevators and continued that way until they entered the lobby. Suzanne and a male nurse stood at the front desk with their backs to the rest of the hospital. Marty would recognize that figure in a crowd, no matter how hectic and bustling. That familiarity made Marty's heart clench and her fingertips itch. Marty knew the bright cobalt of the polo she wore would complement her eyes, and she couldn't help but notice the way khaki trousers hugged her curves. A renewed ache thudded in her chest.

Marty wanted to disappear.

"Mommy!"

"Abigail!" Suzanne spun around and opened her arms. Marty walked slowly, allowing the pair to share in the moment without her intrusion. They embraced, and Marty dropped her head. Her emotions were still raw from the day before. When Suzanne finally stood at her full height, Marty fought to look anywhere but into the bottomless blue eyes that could so easily be her undoing.

"Suzanne." Marty nodded in acknowledgment, but she didn't look at her.

"Marty." Cold. Hard. Emotionless. Suzanne had had moments like this ever since they had received news their daughter wasn't in remission, but once Suzanne had moved out months ago, Abigail had been the only one to break through to the Suzanne Marty had fallen in love with.

The male nurse cleared his throat. "Shall we?" he said, extending his arm toward the elevators. Marty considered taking the stairs. The small group waited for an elevator to arrive and stepped through the first set of opened doors. "I'm Blake…uh, Blake Amato." The formality seemed awkward, and his deep voice sounded loud in the small space that had only been filled by the sound of whirring motors seconds before.

"I'm Marty, and this is Abby." Marty placed her hand on Abby's shoulder and regarded the man standing before her in blue scrubs. He wore thick, black-rimmed glasses and had a five o'clock shadow that appeared to be permanent. His nervous smile didn't go unnoticed.

"We've met," Abigail said as the elevator signaled their arrival.

Blake was the first to exit, followed by Suzanne, who tugged her daughter along by her small hand. Marty stood back for a few seconds, wondering why she felt like an outsider with her own family.

A middle-aged man in a white lab coat bellowed from across the small waiting area. "Well, if it isn't my favorite patient!"

A bright swath of colors swirled across the walls, and cartoon-like animals grinned from every corner. The pediatric wing of the hospital was a paradox to Marty. So cheerful and so sad.

"Good morning, Dr. Fox," Abby said brightly.

"Good morning to you, Abigail." The tall, lanky doctor moved around the small reception area to greet the family. "I see Nurse Blake personally escorted you to your treatment this morning. He'll be working in the chemotherapy room today, so if you need anything, don't hesitate to annoy him." Dr. Fox scrunched his face up goofily as he laughed at his own joke. The other three adults laughed along politely, but Marty noticed Suzanne's smile was directed at the nurse. "Let's get you into a room so we can do a quick checkup, and then we'll get started." Dr. Fox led the way toward a small examination room and spoke as he walked with purposeful strides. "And how are the Dempsey women doing this morning? I hope the traffic was kind to you."

The silence was awkward by itself, but when Blake meekly muttered, "It's Carlson now," time stood still, and the tension in the small space rose.

"Excuse me?" The doctor straightened his burgundy tie before removing his stethoscope from around his neck. "Up on the table." His large hand came down to pat the pink vinyl. Abigail launched her small body onto the table and shifted against the crinkling paper covering.

"Yeah, excuse me?" Marty didn't want to acknowledge what had been said, but the words left her mouth before she could stop them. She stared at Blake, questioning his continued presence and praying that just this once looks could actually kill.

"My last name is Carlson. We're divorced. Now can we please get back to Abigail?" Suzanne nearly barked out before leaning back against a nearby wall. Her left arm was wrapped around her body, and she covered her mouth with her right hand.

"Of course." The doctor looked around uncomfortably before continuing to take Abby's vitals.

After quick preliminaries, the small family and Nurse Blake were led to another room lined with oversized chairs. Three other children were receiving their chemo treatments that morning, each small face more pale than the next. Marty could tell by the frightened look in one small child's eyes that it must be her first treatment. She'd never forget when Abigail's face hung heavily with the same fear.

"I'm sure you both remember the drill from last time."

"She'll spend most of her time here in the hospital," Suzanne replied.

"Correct. The next two months will be rough on everyone involved, but especially Abby. We have to be careful and watch for any sign of infection."

"Of course," Marty added as she hung on to every word the doctor spoke. Her clouded green eyes never left her daughter's smiling face.

"However, I think it'd be most wise to keep her here around the clock for the first month. Last time the option of spending time at home seemed safe. This time I'm afraid it'll be too great a risk. Especially if she'll be shuffled between two homes." Marty stared at the doctor. "Around-the-clock monitoring and consistency in atmosphere—that's my recommendation." He looked between the mothers and over to the nurse. "Blake, would you mind getting everything started?" The doctor handed Abigail's chart to Blake and started to leave the room, but Marty followed closely behind.

"Dr. Fox?" she called out as soon as they were in the bright hallway. The older man turned and regarded the slightly disheveled woman.

"Yes, Mrs. Demp—um," he paused to clear his throat, "*Ms.* Dempsey?"

"I feel like there's something you aren't telling us. Six months ago we come in with a sick child and we receive a diagnosis that usually carries a ninety-five percent remission rate. Now we're right back at square one, and you're telling us we need to be careful. What's really going on with Abigail?"

Dr. Fox released a large breath before answering. "She fell into the five percent. I told you this experimental treatment would be better for her, but if her numbers aren't above borderline at the end of this month, I'm afraid they'll most likely never get better."

Marty flinched at the words, her emerald eyes shadowed by awakening tears. "So my baby will be…" Marty steadied her breath, inhaling. She sniffled once before deciding she couldn't control the emotion clawing its way up her throat. She looked to Dr. Fox, silently asking him to confirm or deny the suspicion that was turning her stomach, and he did.

"She'll be considered a terminal case."

There Were Two Women in Love

"What are you still doing here?" Charlotte asked Marty as she threw a folder onto her desk. It was late on a Friday night, and just about everyone in the office had more important plans than burning the midnight oil.

"What are you doing *back* here?" Marty retorted before spinning in her chair to face Charlotte.

"Damn clients want me to work up an offer for them tonight. Normally, I'd take all the paperwork with me to MacGregor's and have a drink while I work on it, but the buyers are such nitpickers that I need a full bottle of merlot after three hours with them." She fell back into her chair and kicked off her heels. She flexed her nylon-clad toes before continuing. "Since I'm sure my fellow agent wouldn't appreciate an offer with wine stains on it, I'm going to write it up here and then get drunk. Care to join me?" She looked at Marty hopefully.

"I'm sorry, I can't." Marty wanted to leave it at that, but she could feel the other woman's eyes still on her after she turned her attention back to the computer screen. "I'm looking for a house."

"At work? How dare you." Charlotte laughed at her own thinly veiled sarcasm.

"For myself," Marty said.

"That's right." Charlotte dug her heels into the carpet and launched her chair into the direction of Marty's desk. "Our number one agent got their bonus today."

"I did." Marty contained the proud smile begging to burst across her face. Instead, she focused on the tapping of her fingers against her keyboard.

"How was your first year?"

"Good." Marty narrowed her green eyes at the listings on her computer screen.

"Just good?" Charlotte cocked her head, her long black hair falling just to the tops of her shoulders. Marty was still unsure as to how Annmarie persuaded her to cut it.

"Record breaking." She cast a sideways glance toward her coworker and let a small fraction of that prideful smile show.

"Good for you, Marty!" Charlotte smacked her friend on the shoulder.

Sometime during Marty's first year at the local Century 21, Charlotte had become a staple in the younger woman's life. The few years that separated them allowed Charlotte to share her experience, and Marty was eager to soak up any advice Charlotte had to give. Lunch together turned to dinner and drinks. They shared late nights at local bars and summer mornings on the beach. They even went out on a few double dates.

"Suzanne must be so proud of you." Charlotte beamed. Marty turned her attention back to homes and price tags. She didn't hide her tight-lipped expression well enough for it to go unnoticed. "She is, isn't she?"

"She kind of doesn't know yet." Marty kept her head down as she broadened her search radius.

"What do you mean?" Charlotte leaned forward.

"I haven't told her anything yet. She knew I was doing well, but she doesn't know anything about the annual bonuses."

"Why not? Trying to appear modest despite the fact that we all know how conceited you are?"

"Very funny. If I told her I was getting a bonus, I'd end up telling her I'm looking at houses. If I tell her that, I'm afraid she'll think I'm going to ask her to move in with me—"

"Oh my God, she'd freak out! The two of you have only been together for what, eight months? It's way too soon for someone like

Suzanne. She loves her independence way too much. Remember how long it took her just to warm up to you and agree to be exclusive?" As Charlotte spoke, she returned to her desk and spread out several papers onto the surface.

Marty stared blankly at her hands on her keyboard. Of course she remembered those two months she'd spent trying to woo Suzanne. It was much like trying to tame a wild horse. She had used every trick she could think of, and she even bottomed out on the charm she always thought came so naturally. Finally, Suzanne got sick with the flu, and Marty spent every night taking care of her. Suzanne then realized that it was time to give in and that maybe Marty truly was the keeper she'd been declaring herself all along.

"Shit." Marty slumped back into her chair.

Charlotte looked over to her friend. "What?"

"She'd freak out."

"Yeah." Charlotte looked at Marty's sad green eyes. "Marty…"

"I was going to find the perfect house and surprise her," Marty said timidly. Her voice shook slightly, and she wiped her sweaty palm on her jeans.

"You know she hates surprises."

"I know." Marty sat forward. The silence stretched on as she struggled to recalculate her plan.

Charlotte finally broke the melancholic silence. "You'll need at least two bedrooms and a deck."

"What?" Marty's head flew up, and she looked to her friend in confusion.

"She always goes on about wanting to entertain outside, something she can't do at her apartment." Charlotte stood and walked over to Marty's desk. She took the keyboard and moved it to in front of herself. "No fireplace or pool—she can't be bothered with the upkeep." She laughed as she typed, the light from the screen brightening her already vibrant smile. "New construction, a yard, no garage, and close to the water." She hit Enter, and only one search result appeared.

She turned to Marty and spoke with a cocky smirk. "I'll waive my fee."

❖

"Open kitchen with new appliances, large deck just outside the back door, generous TV room, hardwood floors throughout the first floor…" Marty listed the home's attributes to Suzanne. "Come upstairs." She led the way up the thirteen stairs to the second floor that housed a guest bathroom and two bedrooms. "Bathroom to the right, and this is the second bedroom." Suzanne stepped around Marty and walked into the medium-sized room.

The room was bright thanks to the large windows that lined two out of four walls and looked out on a quiet yard well shaded by large trees. Just off in the distance, she could see the Metedeconk River.

"This would make a great office." Suzanne pushed her hair from her shoulders as she turned to look at her girlfriend.

"It would." Marty surveyed the space and imagined a large desk and several full bookcases. It would be a great office, but she couldn't help but think a bit farther into the future. *It'd also make a perfect nursery*, she thought. When her eyes landed on Suzanne, her breath caught at the way the sun illuminated her golden hair. She was just standing there wearing worn jeans, a plain white shirt, and a black leather jacket. Her big blue eyes were so deep and her smile so gentle, Marty was convinced they were made just for her. She didn't realize how long she had been staring until Suzanne laughed.

"What?" Suzanne checked her appearance. The zipper of her jeans was up and no bits of food hung on her face, but she wiped at it anyway.

"Nothing." Marty shook off her stupor. "You're just so beautiful."

Suzanne stepped forward and closed the distance between them. She ran her hands up the front of Marty's green cashmere sweater and wrapped them around her neck. Marty found herself being kissed fiercely. Suzanne sucked on her plump upper lip before running her tongue along its neglected lower partner. Marty moaned as she opened her mouth to take Suzanne in and squirmed as Suzanne palmed her breasts.

"Wait." Marty grasped Suzanne's wrists and put the necessary distance between their bodies to continue thinking clearly.

"Isn't this one of the perks to being your own real estate agent? Getting to take the house for a test drive?" Suzanne advanced again as Marty sucked in a sharp breath.

So many visions danced their way through Marty's mind. Some involved the kitchen counter and others took place inside the large shower tucked away in the master suite. She decided and grinned. "Let me show you the master bedroom."

"I love the way you think." Suzanne walked to the door, adding an extra sway to her curvy hips. Once she was in the hallway, she turned right.

"To the left." Marty tried not to laugh.

"I knew that." Suzanne turned toward the last room they had yet to explore.

Once Marty opened the door, they walked into the large space. Natural light flooded the room from wall to wall and up to the high ceilings. Even if the dimensions weren't as generous, the room would still feel large.

"There's an en suite and two walk-in closets." Marty stayed back and watched every reaction Suzanne had to the details like the crown molding and the nook by the window that would be perfect for a comfy chair. "What do you think?"

"I think it's great, but what do *you* think?" Suzanne walked into the large bathroom, causing her voice to echo a bit. "Ooh—a claw-foot tub!"

"Well, I think it's perfect," Marty said quietly before leaning against the bathroom door frame. She clasped her hands together to keep them from shaking.

"Then write up an offer! How much was this bonus you got after all, hotshot?" Suzanne raised her eyebrow.

"Combined with my savings, I'll have a significant down payment that'll help keep the mortgage manageable."

"Good." Suzanne stepped into the large shower. "I'd like to pay a larger portion of the mortgage, though. It's only fair since you're paying the down payment."

"*What?*" Marty spoke louder than she intended, her voice bouncing from wall to wall. "What did you say?" She walked to the shower, effectively trapping the short blonde.

"I'd like to pay more of the mor—*oh my God.*" Suzanne clasped her hand over her mouth, and her cheeks grew a shade of red Marty had never seen before. Suzanne continued to mumble through slightly parted fingers. "I thought you were showing me the house because you wanted to move in together. You're not asking me to move in. I'm so embarrassed right now." She tried to close the shower door, but Marty stopped her. Suzanne covered her face completely with both hands.

She looked so cute, Marty was sure she fell even more in love in that moment.

"Suzanne?" Marty stepped into the shower.

"Leave me here to die." The reply was muffled but clear enough to cause Marty to laugh. Suzanne was not amused. "Don't laugh at me."

"I can't help it, you're adorable." Marty wrapped her arms around Suzanne.

"I'm not adorable, I'm stupid."

"No, you're not. I *was* going to ask you to move in with me."

Suzanne peeked one blue eye out between her index and middle fingers. "You're just saying that now because I put you on the spot."

"No, I'm not. I was going to ask you today, but I was afraid it'd be too much of a surprise and I'd scare you off. I was waiting for you to approve the house, and once the papers were signed I was going to ask you."

"Really?" Suzanne looked up through her long lashes.

"Ask Charlotte. She's the one who helped me find a house you'd like and the idiot who convinced me it'd be a disaster to ask you so soon."

Suddenly, Suzanne launched herself into Marty's arms, kissing her neck, then up to her ear, over her jawline, and finally landing on her mouth. Between each kiss, just after a nibble, Suzanne continued to whisper, "I love you and that tub. It's mine, so you'll need to ask permission to use it."

Suzanne squealed when Marty lifted her off her feet.

CHAPTER THREE

Twenty-seven days in a hospital can take its toll on one's morale. Both Suzanne and Marty went to great lengths to avoid each other. When Marty was at work, Suzanne was glued to Abigail's side. When Marty came back, she'd be gone without a trace.

Abigail was much more gleeful than a child undergoing recurring chemical injections should be. Each and every time one of her mothers would enter her small, private hospital room, she'd light up and greet them as if they were home. Nothing could shatter her innocence, her gratefulness for the unfair life she had been given.

After sleeping on a lumpy cot in Abigail's room, Marty stretched her tired muscles, moving her aching bones and cracking her stiff neck. Even with the extensive decorations to cheer up the room, the morning sunshine only highlighted the institutional white walls and glinted off the machines lining the perimeter. Marty leaned closer to her sleeping daughter and watched as her eyes moved behind closed lids. She wondered what Abigail was dreaming about. Did she imagine a life without sickness? Marty would be lying if she said she hadn't shared the same dream. Did she dream of a life with two mothers under the same roof? One where her Mama made better choices?

"I'm so sorry, sweet girl," she whispered. She covered her daughter's small, cold hand with her own, being careful to not disturb the intravenous tubing. "You didn't deserve any of this." She swallowed thickly. Abigail was so pale, so fragile looking in the large hospital bed. Her red bandana drew attention to her red-rimmed eyes and the veins that ran along the thin skin. Marty blinked hard against tears that threatened to fall, her eyes burning with the need for release.

"*I* deserve this," she said shakily, the words barely loud enough to get lost in the sounds of an awakening hospital. "I deserve this." She repeated the words more firmly.

Everything had become harder for Marty as days passed slowly. She found herself staying at Abigail's bedside longer than the hospital staff recommended. Beyond the responsibility of work, she didn't care much if she hadn't slept in her own bed or showered. She was where she needed to be. Marty forced herself to ignore the voices getting louder and louder during the quiet nights, reminding her of all the mistakes she'd made and pain she'd caused.

"Mama?" Abigail started to shift beneath the thick bedding Suzanne had brought her earlier in the week after the little girl had complained about the cool temperature. "Are you crying?"

"No," Marty denied weakly as she wiped her eyes.

"Yeah, right."

"I'm not. See?" Abigail peeked at Marty through one opened eye, and Marty smiled meekly at her daughter.

"You and Mommy are always sad."

"We're not *always* sad."

"Yes, you are!" Abigail's voice was more firm, strong than it had been in recent days. Marty was both taken aback and hopeful. "If you miss each other so much, why doesn't Mommy come home?" Marty's heart hurt at the question. Abby's innocence chipped away at her false strength.

"I do miss Mommy very much, but—"

"She misses you too. She told me so." Marty watched her daughter carefully as she rubbed at her tired eyes. Did she just hear Abigail correctly?

"What do you mean she told you so?" Marty sat forward, eager to hear every word.

She pointed to the window. "The other day, we were naming the birds outside. I asked her what you'd name them, and she said something silly." Abby shrugged. "I said I wished you were here, and she said she did too." Abby's mouth widened in a comically large yawn, she closed her eyes again. Marty waited patiently to see if she had anything more to share, but Abigail grew quiet, her breathing even and deep.

Suzanne wished I was here? Marty's mind spun with desperate hope, and she unknowingly started to cry once more.

"Mama?" Abby spoke again, startling her mother.

"Yeah, Abs?" Marty wiped at the tears that still clung to her chin. "I'm right here."

"I'm thirsty."

"Do you want water or are you feeling up to drinking some juice today?"

"Water." Abigail tried to sit up but fell back against her pillow. "Is Mommy here yet?"

"Not yet, sweetheart. I'm sure she'll be here any minute." Marty went to the foot of the bed and squeezed her daughter's big toe. "Ice?" Marty waited for an answer but only got a nod in response. Abigail had closed her eyes again. She had been so tired during the past week. "Okay." Marty walked to the small bathroom in the room and brushed her teeth before stepping outside to ask a nurse for some water.

Deciding to stretch her legs for a bit, Marty took a walk to the elevator and down to the cafeteria for a cup of coffee and whatever dry version of a muffin the hospital was supplying that day. She paid with the crumpled singles she had stashed deep in the pockets of her worn jeans and turned back the way she came. When she got off the elevator, she spotted Suzanne talking to the male nurse, Blake.

Even though Suzanne was noticeably tired, she was still radiant. Marty tucked a greasy strand of her own hair behind her ear. Suzanne's azure eyes may have been clouded with sadness and fatigue, but they were still more brilliant than any jewel Marty had seen. Her short blond hair fell slightly on her forehead in a classic pixie cut and Marty thought of the days when she'd wear it up and wild. Marty noticed Suzanne's weight loss for the first time since they had separated. Suzanne was the complete opposite of an emotional eater, so her clothes hung loosely on her petite frame.

Suzanne was wearing a heavy sweater that day. *Always running cold, just like her daughter.*

At that thought, Marty smiled genuinely for the first time in days. But it froze in the next instant. A small barely there glitter from Suzanne's ring finger caught her eye. They had been separated for just over six months, divorced for almost one month, and that finger wasn't bare. Instead, Suzanne wore a sizable diamond.

All the air left Marty's lungs and she dropped her snack and the coffee. It went everywhere, but Marty was only aware of Suzanne staring at her from across the space. Was this really happening? She stepped in the puddle of coffee as she started toward her ex-wife, ignoring the dirty looks she received for leaving her mess. She also ignored the way Blake stood at his full height when she approached.

Marty used her final reserve of strength to speak calmly. "May I please have a word with you, Suzanne?" She noticed Blake move. "Alone."

"I was about to go in and say good morning to Abby."

"It'll only take a moment." Marty took the other woman's wrist and led her to a surprisingly empty waiting area. She looked down at her. "When were you going to tell me?"

"Tell you wh—"

"Don't you *dare*!" Marty pointed one long finger at the other woman. "If you're going to wear a ring, you should've been prepared to answer some questions." Suzanne broke eye contact and looked down. "Well?" Marty wasn't about to wait patiently.

"It's none of your business."

"The hell it's not! We have a kid together, a sick kid, and if you're bringing someone else around, I need to know about her." Marty took a step back and a much needed breath. She closed her eyes and counted to six, something she did every time she and Suzanne fought. When she opened her eyes again, she asked quietly, "For how long?" She watched her ex-wife's face closely. Marty could always tell when Suzanne was lying or about to.

"Two months."

Marty flinched. She knew the answer would hurt no matter

what. She wiped at her reddened face roughly with her damp palms and turned away from the woman who had once been her life. She looked absently down the hallway toward their daughter's room. "Who is she?" Marty's stomach churned in the worst kind of anticipation.

"I don't want to get into that here."

"Dammit, just tell me!" She turned with a look in her eye that was akin to a slap across the face.

"Excuse me?" a meek voice called from behind Marty.

"Blake." Suzanne lowered her head.

"What?" Marty spun around and was ready to attack the interruption, staring as Blake stood nervously before them.

"The doctor wants to see you both in Abigail's room, now." He left before the last word was finished.

Suzanne rushed past Marty, whose vision was so clouded by rage that she almost missed the way Suzanne had brushed away a tear. Putting on a pleasant face for her daughter, Marty shook off her anger and followed her ex-wife down the hall to Abigail's room. When she stepped beyond the threshold, the pitying looks became obvious, but she still looked to the doctor for hope.

"Doctor, what...?" She looked at her sleeping daughter, her glistening forehead and soaked bandana causing panic to rise in her chest.

"What happened?" Suzanne rushed to the foot of the bed.

"Abigail has a very high fever." Dr. Fox spoke quietly, calmly delivering the words in such a way that the underlying meaning was far from hidden.

"She has a fever and you left her alone?" Marty felt Suzanne's fiery blue eyes pierce her from a few feet away. Guilt seeped into Marty's heart.

"I didn't know she had a fever! She had gotten up and was thirsty. She wanted water. I just left for a minute." Marty stumbled through the excuse, and it just died in the tense space. She explained more for herself than for anyone else. "It was only a minute."

"When will she wake up? Will she be able to continue her treatments?" Suzanne fired off the questions rapidly. When the doctor met her with silence and a sympathetic look, she clasped her hand over her mouth and began to sob.

Marty felt an overwhelming need to comfort her. She started to move, but Blake stepped in and wrapped her in his arms before her foot left the ground. She lowered her head in order to escape the scene before her. It had come to this—Suzanne seeking comfort in the arms of a virtual stranger. After a minute spent collecting her thoughts and the shattered pieces of her broken heart, Marty asked, "Will she wake up?"

"There's no way of knowing if Abigail will regain consciousness. The only thing we can do now is stay by her side and keep her comfortable, monitor her condition." A silent tear ran down Marty's cheek, and she furrowed her dark eyebrows. "I'll leave you two alone. If either of you have any questions or need anything, don't hesitate to get a nurse to page me." He gripped Marty's shoulder and offered only a fraction of the comfort she needed.

Even though it seemed the world was moving in slow motion, in an instant, the family was alone in silence.

Abigail never woke up.

They Got Engaged

"How was class?" Marty sat up on the worn leather couch to peek over the back at Suzanne. The muted television flickered in the dimly lit room. Marty had lost track of time somewhere between watching a home renovation show and starting a new novel she had just purchased.

"Long." Suzanne threw her overstuffed messenger bag on the floor and walked over to collapse on the sofa. Marty laid back and let the blonde snuggle up against her chest. "I'm ready to quit."

"No, you're not." Marty kissed the crown of her head. They'd had this conversation at least once a week since Suzanne had decided to go back to school for a bachelor's in social work a year earlier. The only difference this time was that Marty was prepared with all the answers.

"Yes, I am. I'm tired. I can't keep going like this. When I'm not in class, I'm working. I miss having a life, and most of all, I miss you." Suzanne shyly buried her face into Marty's neck. She rarely admitted to such things.

As much as Marty wanted to tell Suzanne that she was right there alongside her, the truth of the matter was that she missed Suzanne too. They slept in the same bed, but they fell into it at different times and woke up on separate schedules as well. Over the past six months, Marty had been bringing more of her work home in hopes of seeing Suzanne for an extra hour or two each day, but they were only able to steal an extra few minutes before one of them had to rush out.

"What if you cut back to part-time hours?" Marty said. "You can work a few days or nights a week, and my schedule is flexible enough to be home when you are. We may even be able to work things around so we have a full day off together." Marty ran her fingers through Suzanne's thick hair, relishing the soft strength of each strand. "We could spend that whole day in bed." Marty kissed Suzanne's forehead and inhaled the decadent scent of her shampoo before she tilted Suzanne's head up. "Eat take out, watch movies." She kissed Suzanne's closed eyelids and rosy cheeks. "And we'd stay naked all day long." Marty pressed her lips to Suzanne's and kissed her sweetly at first, reminding herself of the unbelievable suppleness of the other woman's lips. Suzanne started to respond, and Marty opened her mouth slightly, tasting Suzanne's peppermint lip balm.

Suzanne tangled her fingers into the fine curls at the nape of Marty's neck and pressed her body against the long, lean form beneath her. She moaned slightly and pressed her tongue into Marty's hot, wet, and ready mouth. Suzanne started a slow rhythm, her hips against Marty's firm thigh. They separated, breathing heavily, and Marty started working at the zipper of Suzanne's oversized jacket.

"What do you think?" Marty asked casually as she pushed the coat off. Instead of answering, Suzanne threw her jacket to the floor and straddled Marty's narrow hips.

"I think." She leaned forward so they were chest to chest and looked deep into green eyes. "We should be naked now." Suzanne leaned in to kiss her, but Marty turned her head.

"I'm serious, Suzanne. Cut back at work and focus on school."

Suzanne slid from Marty's lap and over to the opposite end of the sofa, the worn leather protesting loudly against the movements. She ran her fingers through her loose waves in a frustrated gesture. "You know I can't."

"Yes, you can." Marty sat up and scooted closer, one leg curled beneath her body and her left arm extended across the back of the couch. She tried to rein in her enthusiasm and her eagerness. "Work less or don't work at all, whatever you need."

"We have a mortgage. I have bills of my own."

"With the properties I have under contract and lined up to sell within the next six months, I can take care of it. Sure, we'll need to cut back a bit. Maybe eat at home a little bit more, but we can do this." Marty reached for Suzanne's hand, but she was just out of reach as Suzanne stood and started to pace. Marty watched her move about, consumed with nervous energy.

"I'm an independent woman," Suzanne declared as she shook her hands out and started to wring them together. "My mother raised me to take care of myself and to never rely on someone else. Hell, I even tried to wrestle the tongs from the lunch ladies in middle school just so I could serve myself!"

"I know." Marty laughed lightly. "I love that about you."

"Moving in with you before I figured my own life out was a huge step for me."

Marty's eyes had softened, and every bit of gentleness she held deep in her soul was shining back at Suzanne. Marty knew Suzanne struggled to accept her unconditional support.

"I'm not your responsibility," Suzanne said with her back to Marty.

Marty reached beneath one of the sofa cushions and took out the ring box. She approached Suzanne quietly, her heart thudding in her chest. "What if I want you to be?" she asked timidly.

Suzanne turned around and yelped softly. Marty went down on one knee, wearing her oldest sweats, the jewelry box in her hand.

Marty started slowly, her voice wavering slightly. "I know how hard it is for you to allow someone else to take care of you, but that's not all I'm asking. I want you, all of you, every day and every night for the rest of my life. I want to support you in everything you do." Marty rushed through the words she had been rehearsing for the past week because she knew she didn't have long before she broke down. "I want to make your life better because you've already done that for me. So, Suzanne Carlson, will you marry me?" Marty opened the small box to reveal a simple engagement ring barely visible in the dim lighting of the room.

Suzanne got down on her knees too, kissing Marty soundly and desperately. Her fierceness burned the moment into Marty's memory. She felt as if Suzanne was finally allowing herself to accept the life she had always wanted, but never let herself imagine. Marty closed the jewelry box and let it fall to the floor.

They undressed each other slowly, taking their time to revel in each newly exposed inch of skin. When Marty tried to stand up and move to the bedroom, Suzanne tugged her to the ground. Marty covered the expanse of Suzanne's pale skin with her own body.

Suzanne spoke tenderly against Marty's moist lips. "I love you." She rolled her eyes back when Marty slid her fingernails down her spine. Suzanne moved about and Marty moved with her, making sure they each had a firm thigh between their legs. Marty started to grind her wetness against Suzanne, reveling in the feel of Suzanne's copious arousal painting her own skin.

It still amazed Marty how quickly and powerfully they reacted to each other. Without a touch, Marty was already pulsing. Now naked and under the torturous touch of expert fingertips, she danced the fine line between pleasure and pain. "I love you too," Marty replied as she filled both hands with Suzanne's luscious ass. She pulled the blonde against her, silently encouraging more pressure and spreading her lover wide open.

The couple made fast, passionate love the first time, both achieving body-shattering pleasure against the other's bare skin. But once they had calmed down and breathed deeply, Suzanne took her time loving Marty after ushering her to bed. Marty felt Suzanne counting each of her ribs with moist lips, and she giggled when Suzanne tickled her navel with her tongue. When Marty looked back into Suzanne's eyes, she saw all the promises Suzanne was too scared to make aloud.

Hours later, when both of them were finally sated and covered in a light sheen of sweat, Marty wrapped her in a tight embrace she hoped would be Suzanne's safety until her dying day.

"Yes," Suzanne whispered into the still night.

"Hmm?" Marty replied sleepily, unsure if Suzanne had uttered a word or if it was the blustering wind against their window.

"I want to marry you." Suzanne kissed Marty's hand. Marty chuckled. "What's so funny?"

"I was beginning to worry this was all just part of the kindest let-down in the history of proposals." Marty laughed again and pulled Suzanne even tighter against her. "Or that maybe you were trying to make me come so hard that I'd forget I even asked you." She bit down on Suzanne's earlobe, and the blonde squirmed.

"You figured me out." Suzanne flipped over to look at Marty. She brought her right hand up to frame her face. "But since my plan didn't work, I guess I'll just have to marry you."

"You'll have to settle for being my wife, sorry." Marty received an exaggerated eye roll in return.

"Not as sorry as *I* am."

"I'll make you suffer." Marty launched herself on top of her fiancée and smothered her loud laughter with kisses that lasted until the sun brought the black sky to life with a bright hue all its own.

CHAPTER FOUR

A bigail would've hated everyone crying. She always did hate when people were sad. She'd do anything to make someone laugh. Sadness was not allowed around her." Marty laughed slightly in spite of herself. "Just recently she came into my room after I left the dinner table crying." She cleared her throat in an attempt to let the words come out easier, more naturally. "She sat next to me and stared—really stared at me for a good minute or two before saying with a straight face, 'Knock, knock.' Of course I asked who was there and she said, 'Boo.' 'Boo who?' I replied, and she smiled this huge, proud smile and said, 'Don't cry, it's just a joke.' And just like that"—Marty snapped her fingers at her sniffling audience that lined the pews of the small church—"I was laughing, and I was wrapped in her tiny arms and somehow I felt like everything would be okay." Marty closed her eyes and stopped talking. Everything wasn't okay, but that wasn't what her audience needed to hear. "Rest peacefully, baby girl," Marty finished in a whisper before rushing back to her seat in the front row.

The silence in the church was appropriate and deafening. The service drew to a close and everyone proceeded to Marty's house for a small reception after the burial.

Marty sat on the couch and rolled the glass tumbler between her palms. She had poured herself a drink nearly two hours ago and she had yet to take a sip, but it kept her hands busy. She wasn't sure she'd be able to stop once she started to numb the pain. People were still floating through her home, chatting quietly and offering condolences when necessary. The process of a funeral was all so weird to her. Why did she have to feed people, entertain them, act grateful for their presence when she was the one suffering? Marty felt distanced and detached. Words of sorrow echoed in her mind while the thought of Abigail bounding down the stairs haunted her vision.

Marty's gut twisted when she thought of the way Blake consoled Suzanne throughout the both the viewing and funeral. *You lost your place with her. With Abigail. You don't belong anywhere.* She felt someone sit down beside her, and she stopped looking at the spot on the pale yellow wall she had been studying for twenty minutes.

"Hey." Charlotte dared to break the silence. "How are you holding up?"

"I'm fine." Marty kept her eyes on the amber liquid in her glass. She didn't dare meet her friend's compassionate brown eyes, fearing Charlotte would see the lies written across her face.

Charlotte's tone turned from soft to firm with disbelief. "Marty, talk to me. You haven't said a word since the eulogy. It's been a tough year for you. I'm afraid if you don't talk now, you'll—"

"I'll what? Get depressed?" She looked at her friend with a cold, empty expression. "I have nothing left, Charlotte, *nothing*. Suzanne and Abby were everything to me." She looked down again in an attempt to hide her tears. Two hours of contemplating her drink, and within seconds she swallowed it down without feeling it burn. Scotch was never her drink of choice, but she always kept it in the house just in case Suzanne's parents dropped by.

"You listen to me." Charlotte reached out and took Marty's left hand, her ring finger adorned with a tan line. "You are one of the strongest, most determined women I know. You'll make it through this."

"What if I don't want to?" Marty confessed quietly. "I deserve this pain."

"Stop it."

"Stop what? Speaking the truth?" Marty shook her head and looked up at Charlotte, but Charlotte was peering over Marty's shoulder. When Marty turned to see what had suddenly distracted Charlotte, she wished she had never looked.

Suzanne was standing next to Blake, his arm wrapped around her shoulders, offering a sense of security Marty once had. Throughout the entire day, Marty had stood witness to this ghost from Suzanne's past, an old boyfriend she was told, being more of Suzanne's present than she was allowed to be. It made her already twisted stomach sink deeper.

"What do you know about him?" Marty pointed her empty glass in Blake's direction.

"Blake?"

Marty nodded, her eyes never leaving the solemn couple.

"Not much really. Suzanne hasn't been answering many of our calls, and when she does, the conversation is short."

"Excuse me." Marty made her way to the stairs without looking back. Charlotte looked again to Suzanne, whose eyes followed Marty's departure.

"I can't do this," Suzanne mumbled between clenched teeth. Everyone was staring at her or standing and waiting to talk to her. There were too many questions, too much judgment, and it made her feel as if she were on display. Her chest tightened, and she fought to take in a full breath as she pulled away from her fiancé. She all but pushed the kind man toward the door.

"What do you need?" Blake asked quietly.

"I need to leave." Blake nodded and Suzanne added, "Go start the car, I'll be right out."

Suzanne made her way through the crowded space, saying her good-byes. She only stopped for a hug from Charlotte, the only person in the house she felt genuinely cared for her and wasn't just curious about her new life. Her parents sat alone in a corner. Her father picked at his third plate of finger food while her mother stared at a family portrait that still hung on the wall. The photo was taken just after Abigail's fifth birthday when Marty insisted they get unoriginal portraits taken on the beach. Every bit of the posed picture was cheesy, but the grins they wore in the picture were genuine. Suzanne approached her parents slowly.

"Mom, Dad, we're leaving." Suzanne's father scrambled to find a place to set his plate before hugging his daughter good-bye. "Have you seen Carla anywhere? I saw her before with the Dannys, but I've lost them." She referred to her brother-in-law and nephew with the plural term of endearment Marty came up with the moment they found out they were naming their son Daniel Junior.

"Oh, I'm sorry. Carla asked me to say good-bye to you for her. Little Danny fell asleep, and they wanted to leave as quickly and as quietly as possible to keep him from waking. You know how hard it is to get a cranky five-year-old back to sleep." Angela Carlson fixed the collar of her black pantsuit.

"Yeah, I do." Suzanne narrowed her eyes at her mother. She was sure she was saddened by the loss of a grandchild, but she wasn't nearly as expressive as Marty's mother. Suzanne looked over her shoulder at the woman who openly sobbed as she attempted to clean up the dining room.

"Where's Blake? I'd like to say good-bye to him." Angela craned her neck and tried to spot her daughter's fiancé.

"He's already in the car."

"Well, I hope the two of you come by for dinner soon. I'd love to get to know him better."

Suzanne regarded her mother with a look of pure confusion. Never once had the Carlson matriarch invited her and Marty over for a casual dinner. She never made the effort to get to know Marty. The most she had ever offered her ex-daughter-in-law was a polite kiss on the cheek during the holidays.

"Have you seen Marty? Her eulogy was lovely, wasn't it?" Suzanne only asked to watch her mother react.

The short, thin woman tucked her chin-length salt-and-pepper hair behind her ear before answering coolly, "Yes, Martha has quite the way with words. Jeff, dear, are you ready to go?" Angela stood and waited for her husband to join her. He looked at his daughter with soft blue eyes that held so many unspoken words.

Suzanne looked between her parents and shook her head. "Right, good-bye." She turned and made her way to the stairs.

Suzanne had told herself that once she was in her former home, she wouldn't dwell on all the memories. Up until that moment, she had managed to do so. But she couldn't leave without surrounding herself with her daughter one last time. She stared at the block lettering that spelled out Abigail's name on the wooden door. She traced the outline of an *A* and then a *B* with her fingertip before she opened the door and stepped inside. She closed the door quietly behind her before turning to look around the room. She jumped back when she saw Marty.

"Jesus!" Suzanne covered her face for a moment with her hand before looking back at Marty. "I'm sorry, I didn't know you were in here. I'll go." She turned the doorknob but Marty stopped her.

"Stay."

"I shouldn't. Blake is waiting in the car."

"Sit for a minute." Marty motioned to the empty space beside her on the twin-sized day bed. "It's nice." She sniffled and wiped her nose against the back of her hand. "And quiet."

Suzanne took a few steps forward and sat on the soft mattress. Six inches separated the women, yet it felt as wide as the grandest canyon ever.

"I don't think I'm going to change this room." Marty looked around, taking in the princess stickers they never removed from the lavender paint, the hammock filled with stuffed animals, and the small craft table tucked in the corner.

"You don't have to," Suzanne said. "You don't have to change anything until you're ready."

"I'll never be ready." Marty was quick to speak. "This is all I have left." Her eyes welled up again, and she swallowed audibly. "At least I can sit here, close my eyes, and imagine her making little monsters out of Play-Doh or drawing a picture that could be a horse, but was most likely a dinosaur or a dog."

Suzanne let out a small laugh. "She would've made a great abstract artist," she added. As soon as the words left her mouth, the smile fell from her face and her chin started to quiver. No matter how often she referred to her daughter in the past tense, she knew it would never get easier. The tears Suzanne had fought all day finally came. Being surrounded by Abigail made it impossible for Suzanne to stay strong for a second longer. She broke down into stomach-twisting sobs.

Marty swiftly wrapped her in her arms. This was the first moment Suzanne felt as if she were truly grieving her loss.

They cried together for a long time, getting lost in the familiar comfort of one another so easily. Marty's clean scent invaded Suzanne's nose, awakening all her senses at once. Marty held her just the right way, the perfect combination of softness and strength. She hugged Marty back. She wrapped her small hand around the back of Marty's neck and buried her face into her shoulder. Marty smelled of their favorite fabric softener and the body wash Suzanne bought in bulk every month. Marty tightened her grip around Suzanne's slim waist, and Suzanne found herself pressed firmly against her ex. To her surprise, she tightened her own grip in return. It brought her back to a time when this embrace could solve all of the problems in her world. A time that felt so long ago.

She wasn't sure if it was Marty's hot skin beneath her palm that startled her back to reality or the unexpected and woefully inappropriate flicker of desire she felt. Suzanne pulled back suddenly and pushed at Marty. When Marty didn't let go soon enough, Suzanne balled her hands into fists and slammed them against her chest to gain some distance. Marty relinquished her hold and moved away from the abrupt, violent outburst.

"I'm sorry." Marty held up her hands in a gesture of surrender. "I shouldn't have done that."

"No, you shouldn't have! You have no right!" The fury that had been building within her had finally reached its boiling point, and she had a hard time sitting still. She was finally ready to fire off all the things she should've said over six months ago. "You do not get to touch me, you do not get to tell me it'll all be okay! You gave that up the night you destroyed us!" Suzanne's voice cracked. She was sure the guests below them could hear her every word, but she couldn't muster up the necessary energy to care.

"We both destroyed us. I just gave you a good enough excuse to walk away!" Marty responded loudly.

"Excuse me?"

"You were gone, Suzanne! When Abby was in the hospital the first time, you wouldn't even look at me." Marty stood toe-to-toe with Suzanne, her nostrils flared.

"You mean when you finally decided to grace us with your presence? You were so busy with work that we barely saw you."

"I had to make sure we didn't lose the house or the cars, and I had to be prepared to pay any hospital bills the insurance wouldn't pick up. You knew that."

"Was that my fault too because I didn't work?" Suzanne asked, stepping even closer and looking into Marty's eyes. She wanted to see the moment her next words made impact. "Tell me this, Marty, were you really working or was she not your first?" Each word was delivered through a venomous smirk.

"Fuck you."

"Ladies!" Both women looked at Marty's mother standing in the doorway shaking her head. "This is hardly the time or place for this. You both should know better."

"I'm sorry, Mrs. Dempsey. I was just leaving." Suzanne rushed past the older woman and fled the house.

After the front door had slammed shut, Denise looked back to her daughter. "We'll talk about this later." She turned and went back down to the first floor, which still held a few guests.

"Son of a bitch!" Marty kicked at a cardboard box that sat on the floor at the foot of Abigail's bed. The box was filled with everything she had with her during her final stay at the hospital. Marty wasn't ready to unpack it yet. She wiped her face in frustration and looked down to see a battered teddy bear staring back at her. She remembered giving it to Abby when she was two and had a bad respiratory cold. Somehow, she and the two-year-old had decided to name him Ripley. She picked up Ripley from his resting spot and sat him on the edge of Abigail's bed. She looked intently at the plush bear. She fingered his frayed ears, held him up to her nose, and closed her eyes. He smelled of Abigail. When she opened her eyes again, she started sorting through the rest of its contents.

She pushed aside books and magazines Abigail never got the chance to read along with various sweaters and hats, several bandanas and fuzzy sets of socks. Something beneath all the novelties caught Marty's eye. The corner of a bright blue envelope stuck up, one that didn't belong to any stationery Marty was familiar with. Marty turned it over and read the front. In Abigail's bubbly, large print was *Mama* followed by several hearts and a lopsided smiley face. With a trembling hand, she opened the envelope and pulled a small sheet of paper from it. Before she read the first line, her eyes had welled with tears, obscuring the rest of the words but not making them any less clear.

> *Dear Mama,*
> *Why do cows have bells? Because their horns don't work!*

Marty laughed and wiped her nose before continuing to read the short but sweet letter.

> *Thank you for being such a great mom. I love you.*
> *Love,*
> *Abigail*
> *P.S. I'm sorry you're so sad.*
> *P.S.S. Mommy's sad too.*
> *P.P.S.S. And she loves you too.*

Marty stared at the last line for what felt like forever. The memory of her last conversation with Abigail had been buried so deeply beneath grief, she had almost forgotten about it. She reread the words over and over, letting them sink in, stick out, and touch her heart each time. She thought back to the earlier incident with Suzanne and allowed herself to believe for just one minute that what Abigail had written was true. Maybe Abby's last words to her weren't wishful thinking. Maybe Suzanne loved her, still loved her. Maybe she hadn't lost everything after all.

They Had a Wedding

The happy couple swayed in time to one of their favorite songs. Marty beamed down at her bride, sparkling with a happiness so immense it was blinding. She gripped Suzanne's left hand before twirling the gorgeous blonde. Marty was rewarded with Suzanne's belly laugh, a sound she knew would make her heart stutter for the rest of her life.

"Are you enjoying yourself, Mrs. Dempsey?" Marty asked when she pulled Suzanne close once again. She kissed the back of her hand softly before nibbling gently at the soft skin. Suzanne let out a girlish giggle.

"I am, Mrs. Dempsey. This has been one of the best days of my life."

"One of? What's another?"

"The night I met you." They turned at the sound of silverware tapping against crystal.

"If everyone would please take their seats," the DJ said softly. "We have a few people who'd like to say a few words to this lovely couple."

Suzanne's sister was the first to speak. Carla wasn't one for public speaking. She sounded rushed and shaky, but as Suzanne's maid of honor she was obligated to say something. She finished the short speech with kind words that took her sister by surprise.

"Suzie," Carla said, raising her glass. The deep magenta of her gown highlighted the blush on her cheeks and the nervous flush across her chest. "I can only hope I find a love like you have with

Marty. She brings out a side of you I've never seen, and it's beautiful. You both bring out the best in each other. And, Marty, please don't hurt her because then I'd have to kill you and I don't stand a chance in jail. Cheers to Marty and Suzanne." Carla swallowed her champagne in one gulp.

"That was sweet," Marty leaned over and whispered in her wife's ear.

"She's not kidding." A devious smirk curled up across Suzanne's mouth before she kissed her new wife softly. They separated with a quiet pop.

"Good to know."

"Up next, Mrs. Carlson, the mother of one of our beautiful brides, would like to say a few words." The announcer handed Angela the wireless microphone.

"Oh, no." Suzanne shrank into her chair.

"It'll be fine." Marty gripped Suzanne's hand on the tabletop and hoped she believed her words, even if Marty didn't believe them herself. The newlyweds looked at one another with alarm in their eyes when they noticed Angela stagger.

"Hello." Angela looked around the cozy space. "Doesn't Suzanne look stunning?" A round of applause resounded in the room. "Like mother, like daughter." Angela cackled, and a few guests laughed as well. "But seriously," She held the microphone with a steady hand as she twirled a tumbler of scotch in the other. "This isn't exactly what I had envisioned for my oldest daughter when I dreamt of her wedding day." Angela took a sip of her drink.

Suzanne looked to her sister with a panicked expression. Carla placed her hand on her mother's wrist and tried to stop her subtly, but was brushed off.

"I had pictured a normal life for Suzanne, one with a handsome husband and biological children, but she decided to be a lesbian." She waved her hand toward Suzanne, a small bit of liquor spilling over the edge of the crystal glass. "I suppose she could do worse than Martha."

"I can't listen to this anymore." Suzanne moved to stand but was held in place by Marty's strong hands.

"Hey." Marty locked her eyes on watery blue and smiled reassuringly. "Today is our day," she said. "You can curse about this all you want later when everyone has left." Marty laughed in an attempt to bring the mood back to the wondrous feeling that engulfed them moments before. "Right now, just be my bride on our wedding day."

Suzanne took a deep breath and visibly relaxed. "Okay, but only if you promise my family baggage won't scare you away."

"I'm already under contract. I'm not going anywhere." Marty held up her left hand and pointed to her wedding ring.

"That's enough of that." A firm voice echoed around the guests and both brides. Charlotte had the microphone and Angela was walking away with her head down like a child that had just been reprimanded. "I think it's time for Marty's best friend and maid of honor to get us back on track, what do you all think?" The crowd responded with a robust *yes!* in unison. "We should all be proposing a toast to two very important, very beautiful women in this room." Charlotte raised her glass into the air, one black eyebrow quirked up. "That would be myself and Annmarie, for introducing these two." The crowd erupted with laughter, both brides joining in.

"It's a tale of deception, intrigue, and tomfoolery, but we don't have time to go into all of that right now. What I do have time to say is: Suzanne, boy am I glad this one stuck!" Suzanne wrapped herself around Marty's arm and placed a kiss on her shoulder. "And Marty, I'm still mad at you for making me wear purple."

"Magenta!" Marty called out.

"It's purple," Charlotte said with a chuckle. "I've been so lucky to be part of such a beautiful love story, one that has many more chapters left to live, with the kind of happy ending two wonderful people truly deserve. A toast," her glass was in the air once again, this time with finality, "to what destiny and true love looks like."

While everyone finished their champagne, the DJ hid the microphone back at his station, ensuring the speeches were finished for the night. As the first course was being served, he played a list of ballads both brides had requested. Several couples rose and made their way to the small dance floor.

"I'd love to dance with my wife again," Suzanne said. She rose from her chair and smoothed the front of her cream-colored suit. Her long, thick blond waves were pulled to the side and secured with an antique silver comb, the length cascading over her right shoulder. The matching cream silk blouse she wore under her suit jacket was left unbuttoned just enough to showcase a tantalizing hint of cleavage, enough skin to distract Marty from time to time. Marty followed her wife to the center of the floor.

They were lost in one another and the rhythm they moved to. The flash of cameras did little to distract the wordless communication in their gaze and between their bodies. With every pass of Suzanne's fingertips over the bare skin of her shoulders and arms, Marty's knees would weaken with desire. More than once Marty would look at Suzanne's pink lips and be overcome with the urge to taste them. Every time she got that urge, she'd dip her head and kiss her bride tenderly.

Marty touched Suzanne's cheek, tracing the outline of cheekbones and eyebrows with a whisper of a caress.

"You are gorgeous," Marty said. Suzanne lowered her head and tried to hide her blush, but Marty captured her chin in her hand and forced her eyes up. "I love you." She kissed the tip of Suzanne's nose. "Only because you're so beautiful." Marty smiled when Suzanne let out a loud guffaw, one that rose above the chatter and music that floated around them.

"I better make sure I maintain myself, then."

"You better," Marty agreed.

"You can let yourself go, though." Suzanne ran her hands up Marty's bare arms into her loose brunette waves. She combed her fingers through Marty's hair, scratching along the back of her head. The taller bride nearly purred at the ministrations. "I don't mind being the better-looking one," Suzanne said.

"And let you get all the attention? Never!" Marty lifted her wife off the ground and spun her in a circle before releasing her and kissing her soundly. They danced and laughed into the night, only separating long enough to refill a drink or to seek out a second slice of decadent wedding cake.

Once the newlyweds had made it back to the honeymoon suite they had booked at a local resort, Suzanne sat on the edge of a large bed covered with rose petals, awaiting her wife's return from the bathroom. She had forgotten all about her mother's drunken offenses.

None of that mattered anymore.

All her attention and thought went to the woman who was showing her just how much love one human being was capable of having for another. With each kiss, she echoed the vows she'd spoken earlier in the day and made a promise to embrace this new life with her whole heart and being. This life was no longer just hers. It was *theirs*.

CHAPTER FIVE

Marty stared at her reflection and a tired woman stared back. It had taken her twice as long to shower, dress, and brush her teeth that morning. Everyone at the office told her a week off wasn't enough, that she needed to take her time and get back to work when she was ready. But every night her empty house echoed with regret, failure, and despair. She had no choice but to be ready because staying home and being reminded of everything she lost sounded a lot worse than going into work and staying distracted for a few hours. Marty stared blankly into her own eyes. The darkness was calling to her. Maybe she should stay in bed a bit longer, rest her tired limbs along with her heart. Maybe she should think a little harder about what part of her life was worth living anymore. Marty shook her head.

She smoothed her palms down the front of her black skirt one more time before leaving the house.

Marty was overwhelmed being back at work, feeling everyone's eyes on her and listening to their hushed whispers about "the woman whose daughter died." Only Annmarie and Charlotte managed to talk about mundane topics after an initial check-in with their sullen friend. The dark circles under her dull green eyes and the state of her frizzy hair gave away her real state, but she assured the two women she was something less than fine but still alive.

Three picky, unrealistic clients kept Marty busy that Monday afternoon. She needed rapid-fire showings and complete strangers to keep her mind and heart from dwelling on what she should've done differently.

"Were you not listening when I said that we wanted a finished basement?" a particularly demanding client barked at Marty.

"Vince…" The man's embarrassed wife tried to calm him.

"Why did we go over a list of things we wanted if you were just planning on showing us whatever you had handy?"

"Mr. Talerico, basements in this area are hard to come by. The closer you get to the beach, the rarer they become due to flood risks. We discussed this when you first mentioned wanting to live by the beach. We even went over damage reports from Hurricane Sandy."

"The basement isn't the only problem with this house." The tall, tanned man ran his hand over his slicked-back black hair. "For a million dollars, there's only three bedrooms. Do you have any kids? Because we have two. You must have none, otherwise you would know how much space children need. Bedrooms, play rooms, TV rooms…" The gruff voice trailed off as Marty's attention turned to thoughts of Abigail. She only had one bedroom, and they'd had plenty of fun in that home. At least until she'd destroyed their family.

But her client was right. She didn't have kids. Not anymore.

"We're done for the day." Marty looked at the keys in her hand, red indentations marring her palm from holding them so tightly.

"What? You said there were four properties you wanted to show us, and this was the first," Mr. Talerico called after her. Marty waited for them to meet her at their cars before responding. She took a deep, necessary breath and steadied her voice.

"After this," Marty searched for the right word, "*discussion* we just had, I'd like to do another search and get back to you tomorrow with the results."

"I'd like to see the other three today." He crossed his arms over his broad chest and stood defiantly. His wife looked toward Marty apologetically.

"Trust me, none of them will meet your standards. I'll contact you tomorrow morning." Before he had the chance to respond, she opened her car door and climbed into the safety the Subaru offered. She didn't wait until the couple were in their own car before starting the ignition and pulling away. "Asshole," she muttered to herself as she pulled onto the quiet road.

Against her better judgment, Marty took the time during her drive to think about what she was going to do next. Depending on what voice in her head was in charge at the moment, her options went from moving to a new state to driving off the nearest bridge. She pushed the darkest of those thoughts out of her mind and focused on the former. She could move. If not to another state, then back up north to Princeton. But that would mean giving up Abigail's room and the memories it held, not to mention uprooting her mother once again.

Her mother.

Marty picked up her phone and dialed her office. After two rings, Charlotte answered. "Hi, Charlotte. Listen, can you let everyone know I'm not coming back to the office? I'm going to take the rest of the day off."

"Sure. Is everything okay?" Marty could hear Charlotte's concern. She hated to worry her.

"Yeah." A long stretch of silence filled the car as Marty navigated local, familiar streets. "I'm heading to my mom's."

"That's good, very good."

"Thanks." Marty fell quiet again and rolled her eyes at her own awkwardness. "I'll talk to you later."

"Take care, Marty."

Both women hung up as Marty pulled up in front of her mother's condominium. She rushed up to the front door and rang the bell. No one answered right away, so Marty rapped her fist against the oak door three times.

"Hold your horses!" the muffled voice called out from inside. When Marty's mother opened the door, her annoyed expression quickly faded to worry. "Is everything okay?"

"Yes, I'm fine," Marty repeated for what felt like the hundredth time that afternoon. "Can I come in?"

"Of course!" Denise stepped aside and allowed her daughter to enter. "Why don't you just use your key?"

"Because you're entitled to your privacy. What if you had a

man over?" Marty meant it, but she barely hid her amusement at such an idea.

"Nonsense! If that day ever came, I can promise you that'd you know about it well before you'd be planning any surprise visits." They both laughed, and Denise led Marty to the kitchen for a cup of coffee. "Have you eaten?"

"I had something small at the office."

"Have a small piece of coffee cake. I baked it fresh this morning."

"What makes you decide to bake in the morning? I always found that so strange." Marty took a small piece of cake.

"You always liked sweets." Marty's mother fixed a cup of coffee just the way her daughter liked it and placed it next to the cake. "By baking for you, I figured it'd keep you from eating whatever god-awful sugary treats your friends were bringing to school."

"Twinkies are not god-awful."

"They could survive an apocalypse. The only other thing that could do that is cockroaches, now what does that tell you? Now what really brings you around here on a Monday afternoon? I haven't heard from you all week."

"I know." Marty poked the cake with her fork, never once looking up at her mother. "I'm sorry."

"Don't be sorry, just tell me what's been going on in that head of yours."

"Suzanne and I got into a fight at the funeral."

"Tell me something I don't know. Tell me something everyone who was in your house that evening doesn't know."

"God." Marty dropped her fork and covered her face with her hands. "I'm so embarrassed, but we needed to have that fight." At her mother's glare, she added, "The timing could've been better." She put her elbow on the table and held her head in her hand.

"What do you mean when you say you *needed* to have that fight?"

"There was no fight, no semblance of finality before the separation." Marty sat back. "When I got home that night…" Marty looked at her mother, shame written across her face. "There was no conversation. She never asked about what had happened. She wouldn't let me speak. Every time I tried to bring it up, she just shut me down. Eventually she got so tired of me trying to contact her that she did all her communicating through a lawyer."

"So you never had the fight you expect to have at the end of a marriage?"

"No." Marty cleared her throat, trying get rid of the gravel that had settled there. "I never got to fight for her."

"And you thought you could do that in Abigail's room on the day of her funeral?"

"Of course not, Mom. That was just months of hurt letting loose at once." Marty shook her head at the memory. "This is going to sound crazy." Marty laughed hastily and blinked back tears.

"What?"

"I think I have a chance to fight for her now." Marty grabbed her purse and fished out Abigail's letter. She placed it on the table and slid it across to her mother. "I found that in the box of Abby's things from the hospital." She watched in silence as her mother's eyes scanned the paper, a small smile accompanying her quivering chin.

"She was always such a bright girl, but this is just a letter."

"Abigail told me Suzanne missed me. We were in the hospital, and Abby told me a story about them naming birds and how Suzanne wished I was there with them!" Marty looked at her mother earnestly, desperate for her to see it all too. "Read the last line again," Marty tapped her foot, eager to hear the words she had read over and over at least a hundred times, she needed to know she wasn't imagining them.

"'She loves you too,'" Denise read.

"If Abigail thought Suzanne loved me, then maybe there's a chance she still does."

"She's with Blake now, Marty." Denise said, shoving reality in her daughter's face. Marty felt the words, but she knew what her mother was doing. She was afraid a false glimmer of hope could damage her fragile heart more than the sadness that had already burdened it.

"I know, but if there's the smallest chance of fixing this, I owe it to myself and to my daughter to go after it." Denise obviously didn't agree with her, but Marty knew she'd have her support no matter what she decided to do. "Even if I can manage a friendship with her, I'd be happy. I just need her in my life."

"I know, sweetheart." Denise covered Marty's hand and gave it a reassuring pat. "I'm just afraid you're using this as a distraction."

"What do you mean?"

"I don't want you to cling to this and have it keep you from properly grieving."

"I've been grieving for months now." Marty pulled her hand away and stood. "I was grieving my lost marriage, my sick child," she said softly. "I'm still grieving, but I'm barely surviving. I think I need Suzanne in order to do that. So if shifting my focus from wanting to stay in bed all day to patching things up with Suzanne is not the *healthiest* thing to do, I don't really care."

Denise followed Marty to the door. "Do whatever you need, dear. I'm just worried about you."

"You're making it sound like I need to be protected from Suzanne." Marty opened the door and looked to the setting sun. "She obviously needed to be protected from me. Bye, Mom." Marty kissed Denise's cheek and left.

When Marty got home that night, she spent over an hour just staring at her phone. Several times she got as far as dialing Suzanne's number, but just after eight o'clock she finally built up the courage to hit the green button that would put her in contact with the love of her life.

"Hello?" Suzanne sounded confused, which hurt Marty more than a curt greeting could. Confusion meant that when she looked at the caller ID, Suzanne wondered why Marty was calling, simply because they no longer had anything to talk about.

"Hey, Suzanne, how are you?" Marty didn't try to hide the hope in her voice. She paced her living room and ran her fingers through her hair nervously. She flinched when they got caught in a knot.

"What do you want, Marty?" Indistinct noises clattered in the background before the familiar sound of a closing door.

"I was hoping we could talk?" Marty didn't mean for it to be a question, but for some reason, she couldn't keep the inflection from the last word. "I wanted to apologize."

"We have nothing to talk about." Suzanne spoke as if she were reading her cold, empty words off a piece of meaningless paper. "You said your piece and I've said mine. I think it'll be best if we don't say any more."

"I hear what you're saying, but I feel—"

"Jesus Christ, Marty! This isn't a therapy session!" Suzanne took a deep breath and released it into the phone. "I'm moving on with my life and you should too. So please don't call me again." She hung up before Marty could utter another word.

She dropped the phone to her side and closed her eyes.

I'm moving on with my life. The words echoed in Marty's head. *You should too.*

"I'm trying," Marty mumbled to herself. "I'll never stop trying."

❖

Suzanne left the bathroom quietly and wasn't surprised to see Blake standing on the other side of the door. He followed her into her bedroom.

"What did Marty want?" Blake asked.

"I guess you heard all of that?"

"The doors aren't exactly made of steel."

"She wanted to talk." Suzanne threw her phone onto the bed.

"About what?"

"I don't really know. I told her I didn't want to talk to her." Suzanne's nostrils flared slightly. She wasn't in the mood for an interrogation.

"Hey, come here." Blake gently led her to the bed. He sat her down and knelt before her. "Are you okay?"

Suzanne looked at him incredulously. She really didn't want to tell this brilliant man he was stupid, but… "Did you really just ask me that?"

"You know what I mean, Suzie. I know you're not okay. You haven't been sleeping well, and you've been so quiet lately. I'm just checking in."

Suzanne looked into Blake's eyes and considered all the ways she could answer him, but nothing really felt like the truth. She hadn't expected to hear from Marty. It shook her up and pissed her off, but what agitated her more was how naturally reluctant she was to discuss any of it with the man she was looking at now. "I'm fine. I'm going to get dinner started."

She focused on method, routine, and the small tasks at hand. Preparing dinner had become a vice for Suzanne as of late. Her concentration would rarely wander during preparation. If Blake had noticed how each meal had become increasingly more time consuming, he was kind enough not to mention it. Suzanne was grateful because these small things kept her from drowning in her thoughts.

"I wish you would talk to me." Blake's voice startled Suzanne from behind. She put down the pepper she was about to gut and turned to him.

"I talk, plenty." She stood with one hand on her hip and the other on the counter.

"Not about the big things." Blake walked slowly toward Suzanne.

"I'm not ready," Suzanne replied quietly. "But when I am, you'll be the first person to hear what I have to say." Suzanne watched as Blake's eyes brightened at her words. She hoped with all her heart what she had just promised was true.

They Wanted a Child

W e'll get there." Marty spoke those three words so confidently.
"What am I doing wrong?" Suzanne asked between
angry sobs. After a tirade of curses and tears, she collapsed onto the
foot of the bed. Her shoulders slumped and she shook as she cried.
Marty sat beside her and took her hand.

"You're not doing anything wrong." Marty shrugged. "The
doctors told us it could be hard to conceive after the miscarriage,
but they didn't say there's any reason why you wouldn't be able to."
She wished she had a better explanation, or any explanation, for that
matter. She turned slightly so she could run her hand up and down
Suzanne's hot back. Suzanne had been crying hard so long, she had
started to sweat. "Please, sweetie, try to calm down."

"Calm down?" Suzanne looked at her with red-rimmed eyes.
"It's easy for you to be so calm when you're not the one who can't
get pregnant again!" Suzanne was shouting. Marty tried her best not
to react to the small bit of spit that landed next to her eye, knowing
the slightest motion would turn a medium-sized breakdown
catastrophic. "Maybe the miscarriage was a sign I'm not meant to
get pregnant."

"Don't say that." Marty knew how desperately Suzanne wanted
to carry their child. "This is only our third try. In the grand scheme
of things, that's nothing." She regretted the words the moment they
left her mouth.

"Nothing? Are we looking at the same 'grand scheme' here?"
Suzanne made air quotes with her fingers.

"I think so?" *At least she's not crying anymore*, Marty thought.

"Between the sperm and the doctor visits, this is costing us six hundred dollars a pop. Every time I fail to get pregnant, that money goes right down the drain." Suzanne pulled the damp tank top away from her stomach. "And don't even remind me about that first vial we wasted trying at-home insemination."

Marty didn't need reminding. She had never scrubbed a carpet so hard in her life.

"Maybe that's the problem?" Marty pointed out in a higher voice than usual. When she knew she had Suzanne's attention, she continued. "Maybe all the added stress of money is making it hard to conceive."

"So, it *is* my fault. Is that what you're saying?"

Marty knew she was going to have to tread lightly. "No!" Marty raised her hands and held them out. For some reason, she thought it'd keep her wife calm. When she spoke again she used her softest, most gentle tone. "I'm just saying that perhaps we should be a little more relaxed about this. Let's try one more time during your next cycle, and if it doesn't take, we forget about it for a bit. We're still young. There's no need to rush this."

"I thought you wanted to have a baby." Suzanne looked as if she were about to cry again, and Marty jumped in.

"There is nothing more I want in life than to have a baby with you. And if it doesn't work this time, and you're not ready to try again, I'll do it."

Suzanne looked at her wife, shock evident across her face. "But you always said you never wanted to carry a child."

"I'd do it for you," Marty said softly. Suzanne melted against her wife and started to cry again, this time without anger. "If I can't carry, then we'll adopt. Whatever it takes to start a family with you, I'm willing to do it."

"I love you so much."

Marty spoke between short kisses. "I love. You too. Always." She pulled her wife's tank over her head and took off her own T-shirt. Suzanne's nimble fingers made quick work of her tight jeans before she sank her teeth into the sensitive skin at the center of Marty's throat. The brunette maneuvered herself and her wife toward the bed, and they fell against the plush mattress together.

Marty kissed her way down Suzanne's body, stopping at all her favorite spots to nibble, and she paused for a moment just above the womb she hoped would soon carry their child. She said a silent prayer to a God she was skeptical of to give them that child. They had nothing but love to offer a baby. Later on that night, as they lay spent in each other's arms, Suzanne stroked between Marty's breasts.

"Do you want a boy or a girl?" Marty asked. Suzanne was on her side, tucked under Marty's long arm with her right leg thrown lazily over Marty's hips. Marty's breath rustled Suzanne's blond tendrils when she spoke.

"I'd be happy with either, as long as they were healthy."

"That's cheating. Everyone has a preference."

"Well, I don't."

"I see myself with a girl. Baby stuff for girls is so dang cute. There's bows and ruffles on everything, and you can wear matching outfits." She finished her daydream with a kiss to the top of Suzanne's head.

"Why not you?" Suzanne's poked at Marty's bare ribs, causing her to pull away and protect herself with both arms.

Marty grabbed a pillow and shielded herself. "Because you could use more ruffles and bows in your wardrobe. Ah!" Suzanne poked her cold toes into Marty's calves, and Marty fell out of their queen-sized bed. "Ow!"

Suzanne looked over the edge of the bed down at her naked wife. "You okay down there?"

"I think I got rug burn on my ass."

"Serves you right."

"Kiss it and make it better?" Marty stood and pressed her small bare behind in Suzanne's face, waiting for a pair of lips. She got a slap instead. "Jeez!" She rubbed at the tender spot. "Will you be spanking our daughter too?"

"Only if she takes after her mother," Suzanne said with a raised eyebrow. "Now get your rug-burned butt back in bed. It's cold here all by myself." Marty slid beneath the covers and gathered Suzanne in her arms. After a beat of silence, Marty spoke again.

"I agree with you. I'd be happy with any healthy baby we get." She nodded, approving of her own statement.

"But a girl would be cute," Suzanne added.

"Oh, the absolute cutest." She peppered Suzanne's face with small kisses. "Because she would take after you." Suzanne started giggling uncontrollably when the kisses grew unrelenting and spread across her sensitive chest. Their future was clear to Marty in that moment. No matter where life took them, they'd go happily as long as they were together.

❖

It had been three days since that devastating day. Three days spent talking casually of Suzanne's next cycle and their plans for it. Marty walked into their bedroom after a morning meeting to find Suzanne sitting on the bed surrounded by what looked like at-home pregnancy tests.

"Suzanne?" She dropped her briefcase just inside the entryway and discarded her heels beside it. "What's going on?"

"Seven." Suzanne's wide blue eyes looked around, unfocused.

"Seven what?"

"I took the first one and it said positive." She shook her head and her hair, slightly knotted, hung loosely in front of her face. Marty reached forward to tuck a few wayward strands behind her ears. "So I took another and another and another…"

It didn't take long for Marty to catch on to what was going on. "Suzanne, are you pregnant?"

She nodded timidly at first, but the nod became firmer. "Yes, I'm pregnant. I'm pregnant."

"You're pregnant!" Marty said loudly enough for her neighbors to hear. She hugged her wife and kissed her soundly enough to stifle the gleeful laughter she felt bubbling inside at the good news. When they separated, both women's eyes were filled with happy tears that continued to fall into the night.

CHAPTER SIX

*I*t's a girl," the doctor announced happily as he held the crying newborn up for all to see.

Marty stared in awe. The little face, scrunched up and red, was perfect. Ten little fingers and ten little toes, legs kicking furiously as the nurses wrapped the baby up and got her to her mother. Marty looked at Suzanne and beamed wildly. They had spent the last nine hours experiencing things no pregnancy book or website could've prepared them for, but it was all worth it in the end.

Suzanne lay exhausted, propped up against damp pillows as she waited anxiously for her daughter to be placed in her arms. Her blond hair was plastered to her sweaty neck and her face was still blotchy from exertion. Marty's breath was heavy with the beauty of it all.

Another shrill cry startled Marty, and she snapped into action, moving quickly to Suzanne's side, grabbing her hand and speaking softly yet emotionally.

"You did great." Marty's eyes started to well with tears of pride. "So, so great."

"Here's your daughter." The head nurse of the maternity floor handed the pink bundle to Suzanne. "Have you picked a name?"

"Abigail." Suzanne spoke in wonder. "Abigail May." Suzanne looked up into Marty's watery emerald eyes. "She's beautiful."

"Just like her mother," Marty was quick to add.

"Thank you, Marty."

"For what?" Marty laughed. She'd done nothing special. She'd barely even reminded her of the many breathing exercises they had practiced together over the past two months.

"For being here. You didn't have to do this."

"Yes, I did."

"Blake will be happy to know I wasn't alone." She touched the tip of her index finger to the baby's perfect button nose.

"What?" Marty looked around the delivery room frantically, hoping one of the many strangers milling about the room could clarify the situation. She started to worry something was wrong with Suzanne.

Just then a disheveled man burst through the door. "Oh thank God! I'm so sorry." He rushed to Suzanne's side and froze the moment he saw the newborn. A tender smile lit up his bearded face, and his eyes softened with wonderment.

"Hey, Daddy," Suzanne said happily. Blake leaned in and kissed the blonde's forehead before doing the same to his daughter.

"Now that the father is here, we need you to step outside. Give the family some alone time." An older nurse started to gently pull Marty toward the door.

"Wait," Blake called out, walking over to Marty. "I need to thank you. You've been a wonderful friend to Suzanne through this whole pregnancy. After today, I don't think I can thank you enough." He stuck out his left hand, white gold band wrapped snugly around his ring finger, and waited patiently for Marty to accept his thanks.

When her own hand extended, Marty looked down and lost the ability to breathe. The ring on her finger was gone. She was not married to the woman cradling a dozing Abigail. Her Abigail.

"She's my daughter."

Blake dropped his hand. "Excuse me?" he said with an amused smirk.

"Abigail is my daughter." Marty spoke loudly, her voice rising well above an appropriate volume for a hospital room. "She's mine and Suzanne's." Desperate tears made their way down her red cheeks. She could feel a fire building inside, one born of jealousy and rage. This man was taking her life away from her and assuming

it to be his. A life he was not worthy of. "Suzanne?" Marty looked past Blake and stared into the other woman's eyes.

Suzanne stared back with no recognition.

"Come on. You can wait outside until we get her in a room." The nurse pushed again and Marty tried to resist, gaining the attention of a much stronger male nurse. Both hospital employees took an arm and guided a hysterical Marty to the hallway.

"That's my family!" she screamed. No one believed her. No one seemed to have heard her. The only sound that filled the space was a happy couple laughing together over their newborn.

Marty sat up and struggled for air. She gasped, searching desperately for oxygen. She glanced at the bedside table to check the time. The large red numbers that read three o'clock in the morning taunted her. In the weeks since Abigail's passing, sleep had eluded Marty. More often than not, she'd find herself dozing on the sofa after work, but in bed, her eyes would be wide open and her mind riddled with thoughts she could never seem to put to rest either.

Four weeks of Marty trying to reconcile with Suzanne, and she hadn't made much headway. The most progress she had was recently when Suzanne didn't immediately hang up or ignore her calls altogether. She had managed some small talk about the weather and even heard about Suzanne's full-time job at the local library. When Marty tried for more personal details, Suzanne would end the call immediately. Marty would chastise herself for pushing too hard too fast. She knew Suzanne better than anyone, and she knew she didn't take kindly to being forced into anything.

Marty looked at the clock again and sighed deeply. When she closed her eyes, short, sporadic clips of her dream and other nightmares haunted her. She often dreamt of Abigail standing over her paralyzed body, asking her why. Other times her dreams felt more like fantasies, of enjoying a beautiful day on the beach with Suzanne when suddenly an enormous wave washed ashore and took Suzanne from her. Every dream, each with its own thinly veiled message, was more vivid than the next, driving Marty to avoid slumber altogether.

She opened her eyes again and stared at the ceiling. Shadows danced along the textured surface and drew her into a hypnotic state. There, somewhere between conscious and sleep, Marty's next move became clear to her.

❖

"Sometimes, Rosemary, I swear you stick me in the Reference section just to keep me close enough to listen to your gossip." Suzanne smiled warmly at her elderly coworker. She was convinced the library had been built around Rosemary Smelson.

"It's not gossip if it's factual." The short, gray-haired woman looked at Suzanne over her eyeglasses. "I do not lie."

"If you say so." Suzanne stacked the rest of the returns onto a large metal cart she pushed to the opposite end of the long aisles. She wasn't in the mood for factual gossip that morning, no matter how juicy.

The best part about working at a library was the peace Suzanne found there. The job didn't pay well, but it kept her busy. After her divorce, she had felt as if she no longer had a life of her own. The entirety of her world was with Marty. So she slowly started to rebuild. Suzanne got a job she knew she'd be good at, and when she ran into Blake the simplicity of the relationship was appealing. She even surprised herself when she willingly changed the nature of their relationship from friendship to more.

Suzanne placed several books on a low shelf and pushed the cart forward.

Blake. Suzanne thought of her fiancé. He was a kind man, a handsome man, and his job paid well. Suzanne's mother had always told her to look for those three things in a future husband. *Happy, Mother?* Suzanne mused to herself with a sigh as she pushed a particularly thick book between its neighboring volumes.

As the quiet surrounded Suzanne, she recalled the past few nights and all the ways Blake had been caring and kind—so caring and kind she felt suffocated by his very existence. He followed her around, catered to her, and asked about her well-being every time she was quiet for a moment too long.

She felt guilty for being annoyed by his behavior, but she was. The final straw was the night before when he'd overheard a curt conversation with Marty and offered to talk to her on Suzanne's behalf and ask her to back off. Suzanne snapped. She had never yelled at the man before. After she was done, he'd left the room like a scolded puppy. Blake had no place in that part of her life.

Marty. Suzanne stared at the worn cover of the encyclopedia in her hands, fingering the dented corner. Marty was a kind woman, a beautiful woman, and she had a job that paid well—but she was a woman nonetheless, one thing her mother never encouraged her to go after. *Happy, Mother?* She sighed again, this time out of anger, and dropped the thick volume onto the cart. The thud echoed throughout the quiet space.

"Is Suzanne Dempsey working today?" she heard someone ask from the opposite side of the shelves.

"I'm sorry, who?" Rosemary asked. Suzanne inched closer to the corner of the bookcase.

"Carlson, Suzanne Carlson. Is she working today?" The louder the voice got, the more familiar it became.

Suzanne scrambled back to her cart and checked her appearance. Her violet polo was bright beneath a black cardigan, and she knew her jeans were worn, but they fit her well. But why did she care what she looked like?

"Hey."

Feigning surprise, Suzanne spun around and placed her hand over her heart, which was beating quickly, but not from shock.

"Marty." She ran her fingers through the short hair at the back of her head. "What are you doing here?" Suzanne struggled to keep her tone neutral. She had no in between with Marty. She was either too happy to see her or ready to scream at her.

"I'm sorry to just show up like this, especially at your work. I just needed to see you." Marty's eyes held such desperation, such hope for consolation, that Suzanne couldn't be angry.

"Marty…"

"I know, you don't want to talk to me so I'm sure you don't want to see me, but…" Marty paused and looked around awkwardly. She swallowed hard and looked down at her hands. "I keep having dreams about Abigail."

For whatever reason, Suzanne ignored her better judgment and succumbed to her need to comfort the taller woman. "It's kind of funny that you're here, I was just thinking about you." She whispered the small confession. Marty lifted her head at the words, a cocky smile on her gorgeous face. "Not like that." Suzanne corrected her sternly but couldn't suppress a giggle.

Marty shrugged nonchalantly. "A girl can dream."

Why was it so easy to flirt with Marty? Why did they stop so long ago, and why did she have an overwhelming desire to start again now? Suzanne shook the thoughts from her head. Marty's voice cut through the thick silence.

"Please have lunch with me?"

The earnest look on her face was the only push Suzanne needed to answer yes.

They Faced Challenges Together...Mostly

Marty still couldn't find what she was looking for, no matter how many times she scanned the paperwork fanned out before her. Being a real estate agent had its perks, like working from home. With Suzanne being five months pregnant, they found themselves in full-blown nesting mode, and preparing for a baby took up a lot of time. So only having to spend morning hours at the office came in handy.

"Dammit," Marty mumbled under her breath as she pushed aside the stack of two-bedroom listings within a five-mile radius. Her clients were searching for a palace, and all she could come up with were bungalows.

"Tough day at the in-home office?" Suzanne stood, resting her head against the doorway. Marty spun in her chair and looked at her wife's protruding belly, making her way up to her humored, calming blue eyes.

"My clients are a major pain in the ass, but the commission will be worth it." She rose from her cushioned office chair and stepped closer to Suzanne. "You cut your hair." Marty moved closer and kissed the corner of her wife's plump mouth before running her fingers through her new style.

Now Suzanne's gorgeous face, enviable bone structure, and large blue eyes were no longer hidden. Her hair was cut short, clipped closely around her ears and at her neck. The top was a bit longer so it could be styled playfully up and away from her face. Marty appraised her new look and kissed her soundly.

"I love it. I was sure it was impossible, but you look even more beautiful."

"Oh stop!" Suzanne blushed and dropped her head. Marty caught her chin and raised it again, looking at her with sincerity.

"You're stunning." Marty kissed her again after she knew her words were absorbed. She sat back down at her desk. "How was class?" She pulled a new stack of listings from a worn red folder, leaning back and stretching her sore back before slumping forward again.

Suzanne stepped into the room and started to move the cardboard boxes about aimlessly. They had everything they needed to turn the office into a nursery. Each piece of furniture was boxed up except for the antique rocking chair Marty's mother gave them. The blonde sat, rocked one time and then once more before answering.

"I didn't go to class."

"Why not?" Marty didn't turn to look at her wife, who was seated behind her. She flipped a sheet of paper and drew a large, angry X across the back.

"I wasn't feeling very well." That got Marty's attention. She turned slowly toward Suzanne, her thin eyebrows high, pinning her with her stare. Silence grew thick and awkward in the room.

"What was wrong?" Marty was concerned, but she couldn't shake the hardened tone out of her voice. This wasn't an abnormal occurrence anymore. Since the pregnancy had been confirmed by their doctor, Suzanne started to tread carefully through life, taking care to eat right and rest. Marty encouraged it all, but also noticed Suzanne got anxious about every small feeling. She couldn't help but mentally note all the complaints from the past week alone: heartburn, gas, back pain, knee pain, headaches, and a vaginal discharge that made her feel wholly unsexy. All completely normal, but Suzanne nearly panicked each and every time.

"I had cramps…"

"You had what?" The shock on her face would've been comical if it weren't for the flames in her eyes.

"Cramps," Suzanne mumbled, clearly uncomfortable with this confrontation.

"Why didn't you call me? I was home all afternoon, I could've—" Marty stopped abruptly, piecing more details together. Suzanne didn't go to class, but Marty had been home since noontime and it was now after four o'clock. A haircut, no matter how drastic, would not take four hours. "Where were you if you didn't go to class?"

"I got my hair cut—"

"Suzanne," Marty warned.

"I went to the hospital. It turned out to be nothing!"

Marty ran her fingers through her long, curly hair and scratched harshly at her scalp. She clamped her eyes shut for a moment before opening them and locking onto Suzanne.

"Why didn't you call me?" She spoke through a clenched jaw. Marty didn't wrestle with her temper often, but when she did her temper often won.

"I didn't want to worry you."

"Did you really just say that?" Marty pushed back her chair and slammed it into the wall. Suzanne flinched. "Were you worried?" Marty asked. Suzanne nodded, keeping her eyes on her hands folded on her lap. "Then I should be worried too! Dammit, Suzanne! We're married. That means we sleep together, live together, and worry to-geth-er!" Each syllable of the final word came out separately. "Will you call me when the baby's born to spare me the worry of you being in labor?" Suzanne had yet to look up, which infuriated Marty even more. "Jesus Christ." She left the room, taking the stairs at a rapid pace.

Suzanne sat quietly for a few moments collecting her thoughts and controlling her emotions. She got up and followed Marty to the kitchen, but instead of stopping as Marty got a glass of water, she walked by briskly and went out on the deck.

It didn't take long for Marty to follow. Suzanne sat on the steps of their large deck, her legs spread slightly to make room for her growing belly. She wiped roughly at her tears as Marty approached. She grew rigid when she felt her settle next to her. As much as Suzanne wanted to, she would not look at Marty. Her eyes remained on the full moon above their yard.

"I know you prefer to deal with some things on your own," Marty said quietly with an even, gentle tone. "And you know that I don't handle fear very well." She took Suzanne's hand, and Suzanne gripped back tightly. "We both need to work on that." She stroked her thumb across Suzanne's knuckles. "When something worries you, tell me. And when that worry scares the shit out of me, I won't fly off the handle." Suzanne chuckled lightly. "I'm sorry for yelling at you." Marty turned toward Suzanne and rubbed circles over her back, taking extra care of the sore lower half. Suzanne could feel the tense muscles there relax beneath the touch.

"I'm sorry I didn't call you." Suzanne tucked her head into Marty's neck and continued to cry. Her hormones prevented her from stopping the tears as they fell.

"Just promise me you'll call any and every time something bothers you, no matter how insignificant. I want to know about it." Suzanne nodded and felt herself being pulled into a tighter embrace. Marty kissed the top of her head. "Come on, I'm going to start dinner."

Suzanne gripped her forearm. "Wait." She swallowed thickly against her tears. "There's something else I need to tell you." Marty blanched and fell back onto the step. Suzanne felt instantly guilty and gripped her wife's hands before looking into her worried eyes. "I'm quitting school."

Marty sighed and laughed with relief. "Oh thank God!" She hugged Suzanne tightly and kissed her. When she finally pulled back, Suzanne stared at her with confusion.

"You're not mad?"

"Mad? No." Marty smirked. "Curious? Yes."

"I just want to focus on the baby and our family. I have my associate's, so I could still get a decent-paying job—"

"If you want to stay home with the baby, I won't stop you." Marty interrupted.

"You won't?" Suzanne stared up at Marty dreamily.

"No, I won't. I'd love nothing more than for one of us to be home with this little munchkin every day." Marty splayed her hand across Suzanne's pregnant stomach. Suzanne felt warmth and love in the touch. "I'll be home as much as possible, of course, and when you need time to yourself we'll make it happen."

"Are you sure?" Suzanne cupped Marty's cheek. She ran the pad of her thumb along her high cheekbone and then down to her full bottom lip.

"I'm positive. This will be good for our family."

"I love you."

"I love you too." Marty kissed Suzanne's thumb before standing once more. "Is it okay to start dinner now, or do you have any more bombshells?" Marty already started toward the house.

"I know the sex of the baby."

"You what?"

"Just kidding." The blonde bit her lip and kicked at the wooden planks of the deck.

"You're not funny," Marty said while shaking her head. Suzanne knew her scowl was fake.

Suzanne sauntered forward, wrapped her arms around her wife's waist, and leaned in to whisper in her ear. "I'm hilarious, and you know it."

Marty spent the rest of the evening trying to pay Suzanne back for her little trick, but she never succeeded.

CHAPTER SEVEN

Marty sat awkwardly at the small table and pulled at a loose string on her cloth napkin. With all her might, she tried not to focus on the tardy blonde. Instead, she forced her mind to stray to wonders of the food industry. How many napkins they had, how many they went through on a daily basis, and how many they knew to order in the first place. It couldn't be an exact science.

"I am starving!" An overstuffed messenger bag hit the aged wood floor with a thud that startled Marty.

"Hey!" Marty sat up straight and welcomed a frazzled Suzanne.

"I haven't been here in forever. Do they still have huge salads?" Suzanne asked with a casual ease about her.

"They may have gotten bigger over the past year." Marty joked, feeling somewhat giddy at the thought of Suzanne never sharing their spot with anyone else. "The Cobb salad is still ridiculously large. It may even come with a whole dozen hard-boiled eggs on top now."

"Sold." Suzanne closed her menu and pointed to the iced tea on the table in front of her. "Is this?"

"Unsweetened raspberry. Still a favorite?"

"Of course." Suzanne took a sip and closed her eyes. "It's surprisingly hard to find. Everyone wants to sweeten it, which is completely unnecessary." Marty watched as Suzanne savored the beverage with her eyes closed. When Suzanne reopened her eyes, Marty was smiling. "What?"

"You gave me the same speech on our first date."

"I drank wine on our first date."

"That wasn't a date. That was simply a drink between new acquaintances." Marty's cocky smirk brought out her dimple.

"Uh." Suzanne cleared her throat. "How's work going?"

"Same as always, I guess." Marty shrugged, slightly deflated by Suzanne's quick exit of the personal conversation. She reminded herself she couldn't expect an immediate fix. "I'm thinking about going for my broker's license soon, maybe opening up my own office."

A waiter approached and asked for their orders. Marty ordered for both herself and Suzanne, giving the young man a polite smile as he left them alone once again.

"That's good. It's something you've always wanted." Suzanne took another sip of her tea and folded her hands atop the linen tablecloth.

"It's a lot of work. I know it'll take time, but I figure I've got plenty of that now…" She let her words trail off, not needing to elaborate. Marty decided to turn the questioning on Suzanne. "What about you? Tell me about the library." Marty sat back.

"Honestly, there's not much to tell. I needed to get out and do something, and the library was one of the first job listings that popped up when I searched. I went there in person to drop off my resume, and I started the next day."

"You seem to really like it." Marty tilted her head and watched as a small smile lit up her ex-wife's face.

"I do." Suzanne stared at her hands as she spoke. "I didn't think I would at first. It's so quiet, you know? All that quiet can make a person go crazy." She laughed lightly. "But it turned out this particular type of quiet is good for me. I can work and think at the same time, which has helped me remain sane over the past few months. I can't get lost in myself." Her voice grew quiet as she finished. Marty wondered about all the implications of that short sentence.

A silence fell over the table, and Marty shifted uncomfortably. She was overwhelmed with the urge to apologize, explain, beg, and grovel, but one look at Suzanne told her that was the wrong approach. She knew if she opened her mouth and anything more than casual small talk and pleasantries came out, she'd risk losing Suzanne forever.

"Five years ago, you would have said you wouldn't be caught dead working in a library. It's funny how life takes us places we never expect to go."

"You're talking about Blake, aren't you?" Suzanne crossed her arms over her chest defensively and sat up straighter.

"No." Marty mirrored the other woman's position. "I'm referring to your hatred for books and talking quietly." That earned a hearty, genuine laugh from Suzanne, the first Marty had heard in over a year. If she could go back in time, she'd be happy just to relive that sound over and over again.

"I don't hate books," Suzanne replied once she recovered from the fit of laughter. "I hate reading. There's a difference."

"I'm so sorry." Marty bowed her head.

"You should be."

The waiter brought two large plates for Suzanne and Marty. One salad overflowed with every accompaniment one could desire, and the other plate was barely visible beneath a large, juicy burger and several handfuls of fries.

"You always have to order something unhealthy," Suzanne said as she mixed the creamy dressing into her leafy greens.

"Oh please, like you're not going to eat some of these fries."

Silence fell once again, this time comfortably, as Marty and Suzanne busied themselves with eating. Every so often, one of them would make a noise as she enjoyed a particular bite. More than once Suzanne reached across the conveniently small table for a fry without as much as a glance at Marty for permission. As the generous amounts of food dwindled to a little more than a few bites remaining, Marty started the conversation up again.

"Since you brought him up, tell me about Blake." She felt an imaginary pain in her chest at the mention of the man who managed to mend the woman she had broken. Suzanne's fork stilled.

"I did not bring him up." She pointed the utensil at Marty.

"Yes, you did. Now tell me about him."

"I don't think that's a good idea." Suzanne put down her fork gently and wiped at her mouth with her napkin.

"Listen, Suzie, after today I'd like to work on having a friendship with you, and in order for that to happen, I need to be comfortable talking about the guy who's going to be your husband someday." That wasn't a complete lie. Marty did hope for friendship at the very least, but ideally they'd end up as much more.

Marty waited nervously as Suzanne sat and looked at her. She'd put her intentions out there, and now Suzanne would decide whether they were to proceed or not. Suzanne fixed the collar of her polo and took a sip of her near-empty iced tea before finally responding.

"We dated in high school," Suzanne started but abruptly stopped as Marty choked on her water and droplets sprayed onto the table. "Are you okay?"

"I'm fine," Marty croaked out and patted her chest. She had heard they had a past, but she had no idea he was a high school sweetheart returning to sweep Suzanne off her feet. "Please continue." She waved her hand in what looked like encouragement.

"We dated in high school and even managed to keep in touch through college, but after graduation, life got too crazy between nursing school for him and my less-than-innocent social life." Suzanne looked down in embarrassment. Marty knew all about that time in her life. No specifics were needed.

"And you got back in touch recently?"

"We ran into each other at the hospital one day. I was going to introduce you but…"

"I know." Marty didn't need to hear it. She wasn't there.

"We talked a lot when there wasn't much else to do but talk. He became my cafeteria buddy and the person who'd help me understand what the doctors were talking about."

"That's, um," Marty cleared her throat, "that's good." She was absent so damn much during Abigail's earlier treatments and then again during the second round that she'd been oblivious to her wife reconnecting with someone who'd pick her up from the wreckage of their marriage. "Is he good to you?"

"Very." Suzanne smiled but it never reached her eyes. "It's very simple."

"Simple can be good, I guess." *Simple is boring*, Marty thought.

"After the past year, simple is exactly what I need. He's a good man, and he was very good with Abigail. So when he proposed, I made the right choice." Suzanne paused and nodded to the waiter as he cleared their dishes.

"Any dessert?" The young man reappeared stealthily.

"No, thank you." Suzanne directed her response to the waiter and then an explanation to Marty. "I have to get back to work." The check was placed between them. Suzanne sighed heavily when Marty grabbed the check. "You don't have to—"

"I know, but you didn't have to come to lunch with me and you did. It means more to me than you'll ever know." Marty turned sheepish as she stood and prepared herself for the inevitable good-bye.

"I actually enjoyed myself." Suzanne retrieved her bag and got up.

"Don't sound so surprised." Marty laughed awkwardly and scratched at the back of her neck. Suzanne just gave her a sideways smile. When neither woman made a move to leave, Marty decided to press her luck. "Can I hug you?" She grimaced at how stupid the request sounded. "I'm sorry."

Suzanne stopped Marty's attempt at an apology by doing just that.

Marty was quick to return the embrace, but she was also quick to turn her head and bury her face in fragrant hair. That feeling was the closest to comfort Marty had felt in too long. But Suzanne didn't relinquish her hold quickly. In fact, she stepped closer when Marty tightened her grip. Suzanne's phone rang. She looked apologetically at Marty and swiped across the screen to answer.

"Hey." Suzanne spoke quietly into the phone. "I'm just finishing up lunch now." Silence fell again as she looked at Marty and turned away slightly. "Just a salad with a friend from work." Marty cocked her head and wondered if she should leave now or wait. Whoever

Suzanne was talking to was not allowed to know she was with Marty. "I'll see you later. Oh, and Blake?" Marty perked up. "Give me a call when you're done with your shift, I'll start dinner. You too." Once Suzanne ended the call, she turned back to face Marty fully. "Thank you for lunch."

"Thank you for the company." Marty felt the warm smile spreading millimeter by millimeter across her face, the smile that only the woman she loved could put there. "If you're available, I'd like to go through some of Abigail's things soon. I wouldn't feel right going through all of our family's stuff without you."

Their family.

Suzanne froze with an indescribable look on her face, and then she all but ran out the front door. As much as Marty wanted to go after her, she knew it'd be more like chasing. Something told her to stay where she was and give Suzanne her space. What gnawed at her mind was not knowing what giving Suzanne space meant for the progress they had made.

They Had a Beautiful Baby Girl

Did you give her anything for the pain?" Marty looked at the fresh-faced nurse entering the delivery room with panicked eyes. "We're not planning a natural birth!"

"Marty—" Suzanne started to chastise her frantic wife, but she clenched her jaw in pain. She growled and reached for Marty's hand.

"Ah!" Marty's mouth was wide open in a silent scream when Suzanne bore down on it. Every knuckle and joint cracked in unison. *No better place than a hospital to break some bones*, she mused. "Seriously, where are the pain meds?"

"Sweetheart, I'm fine." Suzanne fell back against her pillow as the contraction subsided.

I wasn't asking for you. Marty kept the thought to herself and wiped the sweat off her wife's forehead instead of arguing. "You're sweating like a beast."

"How sweet of you to notice." Suzanne chuckled and shifted in the hospital bed even though she'd exhausted all the comfortable position options. In fact, any and all comfort had been gone from the beginning of the seventh month.

Marty, for her part, was as supportive as a spouse could be. She'd delivered anything and everything Suzanne needed since day one of her pregnancy, becoming even more attentive as the months continued. She did all of her work from home once the doctor showed concern about Suzanne's swelling. She shopped, prepared meals, and massaged Suzanne's plump feet every night. Suzanne wasn't ashamed to admit she was going to miss the pampering.

She reached out, and grabbed the collar of Marty's pale blue blouse, and pulled her close. "Promise me one thing after all of this is over with."

"Anything, always." Marty's green eyes softened with honesty.

"If I ask for one…" Suzanne clamped her eyes shut and brought her free hand to her large belly. She panted as she tried to control her reaction to the pain. "The foot rubs," she said between clenched teeth. "Promise they won't stop."

"I promise I will rub your feet every time you ask me to."

"And surprise me even when I don't ask?" Suzanne looked hopeful as she released Marty's shirt.

"And surprise you even when you don't ask." Marty leaned forward and kissed her damp forehead. "Any other requests while I'm at my most vulnerable?"

A young male nurse laughed as he overheard the conversation.

"No." She took a deep breath. "But you should probably stay away from grocery shopping in the future."

"Gladly," Marty agreed, smiling down at Suzanne, whose cheeks were rosy, her eyes clear and bright. "You look gorgeous."

"Save the compliments for a few weeks from now when I hate my body. I'll need them then."

"I'll tell you every day." Marty moved in to kiss Suzanne's parted, dry lips but was interrupted by the doctor entering the room.

"How are we doing in here?" The question seemed to aggravate the unborn infant, and Suzanne screamed out during the most painful contraction yet. "Before you answer, let's get her something for the pain." Dr. Reynolds spoke directly to Marty.

"Thank you!" Marty sighed in relief, looking forward to having her forearm back.

"You're about six centimeters dilated, and your contractions are more frequent."

"And real *fucking* painful!" Suzanne added colorfully.

"That too." The doctor, a gentleman in his mid-fifties with a rounded belly and gray beard, nodded at a nurse. He was giving her the go-ahead to position Suzanne for an epidural. The nurse busied herself with syringes and preparing a catheter for the patient. "We're going to give you an epidural, but first we need to insert a catheter."

Marty blanched at the word. She was normally so sure-footed and confident even in unexpected situations, but now she looked like she was about to pass out.

"I'll be fine, and in no time we'll be a family." Despite the shaky tone of Suzanne's voice, confidence shone within the words, which helped clear the clouds from Marty's eyes. "Okay?"

"Okay." Marty shook her queasiness off and kissed her before moving back enough to let the staff work.

Marty found it difficult to stand back and be an onlooker as several sets of hands manipulated Suzanne. Various items went into her pale skin and came back out, other objects went in and would stay until after the baby was born. To Marty, Suzanne was the most fragile, special thing on earth, and watching her be handled in such a way set her on edge. She tapped her right foot and kept her fists clenched at her side. Finally, twenty long minutes later, the pain had left the blonde's features.

"You're doing great," Marty whispered to her.

"I know." The response came quickly, but the words were sluggish. Hours on a roller coaster of pain and being pumped full of medications was beginning to take its toll on Suzanne. Marty heard the snap of rubber gloves.

"Ladies, it's show time. You're just about nine centimeters dilated, and the baby is descending. Let's push." Dr. Reynolds sat on a stool at the end of the delivery bed and moved into position. "This won't be comfortable for either of you," he said in a calm tone, but that didn't keep Marty from tightening her grip. "But once you hear your baby cry, it'll all be worth it." Marty could see the smile reach his gray eyes over his blue hospital mask. "Ready, Mrs. Dempsey?"

Both women nodded.

Childbirth wasn't a quick process, but it was definitely a whirlwind. Medical staff moved around as the doctor barked out orders, but Marty was oblivious to everything except Suzanne. The awe she felt at watching her wife deliver their child was shattered by an earsplitting cry.

"Congratulations, it's a girl." He held up the reddened, slimy, wrinkled being for Marty and Suzanne to see. Marty wasn't embarrassed when she started to cry. "Would you like to cut the cord?" Just the thought caused Marty to turn green, and the doctor didn't even bother to tamp down his laughter. "Don't worry, most new fathers can't do it either."

That didn't make Marty feel any better about her weak stomach getting the best of her, but she didn't regret her decision. She'd rather tell the story of how Abigail's mother couldn't handle cutting the cord rather than when Abigail's mother threw up all over the doctor and a few nurses in the delivery room.

Their daughter was taken away to be cleaned up and swaddled, the tiny cries never subsiding. The doctor finished up with Suzanne, and stable vital readings were echoed among the staff.

"She's perfect, did you see her? She's absolutely perfect," Marty said to anyone who'd listen. She wiped at the tears on her chin with the sleeve of her visitor's hospital gown. With wide eyes, Marty watched a nurse approach with her daughter.

"Congratulations, Mrs. Dempsey." He handed Marty the bundle and left her to share the moment with her slightly dazed wife. Marty looked down into the scrunched face of her child, and in that instant her heart swelled enough to make room for both her wife and daughter.

"Here she is, Suzie." Marty leaned forward and laid their squirming child on Suzanne's chest. "Abigail May Dempsey."

"Abigail May." Suzanne's voice was weak and tired, but still amazed. Marty's heart swelled. In a split second, her small world had just got a whole lot bigger and even more perfect than it already was. Dr. Reynolds was right. Nothing before that very moment mattered anymore.

CHAPTER EIGHT

Marty spent her Saturday evening buried beneath new listings and potential clients with impressive properties they were looking to sell. Even with the headache she quickly numbed with a tumbler full of scotch, Marty was grateful for the company work provided. She fell asleep on the couch in her jeans and a wrinkled white tank top. An incessant ringing tore Marty from her fitful slumber. As the fog lifted from her brain, she started to recognize the familiar chime of her phone. Misjudging her distance, Marty rolled off the sofa and landed on her knee.

"Dammit!" She stood quickly and hustled with a limp toward her phone on the kitchen countertop. She slid the green bar to answer the call before looking at the ID. "Yeah." She spoke gruffly, her voice deep from sleep or lack thereof.

"Good morning to you too." The voice on the other end was playful, chipper, and welcome. The moment Suzanne's voice registered in Marty's addled brain, she perked up.

"What time is it?" Marty pulled the phone away and squinted at the display. She could barely make out a nine before she heard Suzanne speak again.

"It's almost ten." Suzanne didn't try to mask her amusement. "Let me guess, you fell asleep on the couch, didn't you?"

"I have no idea what you're talking about." Marty stretched her cramped limbs, wincing at the twinge of pain between her shoulder blades.

"Did the chiropractor send you a Christmas card again this year?"

"A card and a cookie platter." Hearing Suzanne's hearty laugh soothed Marty and alerted her all at once. It was Sunday morning, and Suzanne was calling her for the first time since their shaky reconciliation. Despite the odd tension at the restaurant, Suzanne seemed as devoted to remaining in touch as she did. Marty breathed a sigh of relief. She was unsure of how to proceed after her ex-wife's hasty departure at lunch and had just decided to leave the ball in Suzanne's court. She was glad she did.

"What are you up to besides being lazy?" Suzanne asked. Marty could hear a faint crunching sound on the other end of the phone, telling her that Suzanne was indulging in a late breakfast. She could almost smell the coffee as Suzanne slurped quietly.

"I have to head to the grocery store in a bit." Marty took a few steps into the kitchen and reached for the closest cabinet. A small smile of satisfaction spread across her full lips as she spied a small jar of instant coffee. She couldn't be bothered with making a pot today, not just for herself.

"Have your skills improved, or are you still a disaster when it comes to food shopping?" A low chuckle warmed Marty's ear.

"Well, I had to adapt or starve." Marty laughed along with Suzanne and left out a few select words that would hint at just how much of disaster Marty was at the store still. If she needed milk, she'd leave with only cereal, and she always bought side dishes without a main course. Some people had a knack, and she wasn't one of them. "Today's trip will be pretty straightforward, though. I just need a few things for a barbecue later." When she was met with nothing but silence, Marty continued. "I'm having a barbecue later. I'm having it here."

"What's the occasion?"

"There isn't one."

"You just decided to throw a party?" Marty couldn't blame her for sounding skeptical.

"It's not a party. My mom and Charlotte keep asking me if I'm okay, and they don't believe me when I say I am."

"Should they believe you?" Suzanne asked. Marty froze at the question. She almost said no.

"Spending so much time alone gets to me after a while, so I figured a small get-together would be good for me and it'd get those pesky women off my back." Marty felt so many more words line up on the tip of her tongue. She wanted to tell Suzanne about the voices she heard late at night and the dreams that haunted her even after the sun rose, but she kept those burdens to herself. "I'd love it if you could stop by."

"You don't have to do that."

"I insist!" Marty declared a bit too quickly, her excitement getting the best of her. "Bring Blake along. I'd like another chance at meeting him. The last few times weren't exactly under the best circumstances, and I know my mother would love to see you."

"Okay."

"Great!" When Marty spoke, her tone was surprised and relieved. "Everyone's coming over around four. All the usual suspects will be here."

"Annmarie and Charlotte?"

"Of course," Marty laughed warmly, "like they'd say no to free food."

"Good point." Suzanne said. "Should we bring anything?"

"An appetite would be good, but other than that? No, thank you."

"If you think of anything, call me. I can stop on my way over."

"I will."

"I guess I'll see you later, Marty."

"Later, Suzie." Marty ended the conversation and stared at her phone. She had a feeling that the casual barbecue amongst family and friends she'd just planned would be anything but.

❖

"Shit!" Marty dropped a bag of ice on her foot for the third time, and that was after four trampled hamburger buns, a well-shaken case of beer, and a near-sprained ankle after tripping over a garden hose. She bowed her head in defeat. Guests would start to arrive in less than an hour, and she had barely managed to set up the backyard, never mind fill the coolers or prepare the food.

Knowing she'd be playing hostess to Suzanne and Blake, the happily engaged couple, proved to be a crippling distraction. Along with that came the worry of what her mother might or might not say to her ex-wife. If Marty was being honest with herself, she was starting to regret extending the invitation.

Slowly, carefully, she tipped the ten-pound bag of ice toward the open mouth of a large red cooler. Sweat started to bead along her hairline as she concentrated on the small task. One cube hit the plastic with a sharp sounding thud. The rest of the cubes started to follow in a frozen waterfall. The doorbell rang, breaking Marty's concentration. She spun around and threw the cubes onto the lawn.

"Perfect," she muttered before dropping the half-empty bag at her feet. Marty ran toward the house, mindful of the coiled garden hose, and made her way to the front door. She hoped to see her mother on the other side—she could use all the help she could get. When Marty opened the door wide, she was surprised to see Suzanne fidgeting with a bottle of wine.

"You're early." Marty stated the obvious. She was in shock.

"I am." Suzanne looked from the wine's label to Marty and back again. "I thought maybe you could use some help." Marty still blocked the doorway, frozen in surprise. Suzanne cleared her throat. "I remember how you used to have a hard time—"

"I'm terrible at managing parties. Just say it, Suzie." Marty watched as the blonde fought to form a defense.

"Just the preparations, you're terrible at setting up." Suzanne grimaced. "But you manage the rest wonderfully!"

"Yeah, yeah." Marty stepped aside and motioned for Suzanne to come inside. "The kitchen is the biggest disaster area." She took the bottle from her guest and knew it was merlot before she read the label. "Where's Blake?"

"He has work, so he'll get here a little later." Marty turned the small gift in her hands. "I'm not sure if you still drink it."

"I do." Marty traced the script on the label with her thumb. She lied, albeit unintentionally. The merlot was still her favorite wine, but she hadn't enjoyed a glass since she and Suzanne had split. The flavors always reminded her of her former life. When she looked at Suzanne again, her sapphire eyes sparkled with genuine happiness that was hidden partially beneath apprehension. Maybe Marty would finally be able to enjoy a glass that evening.

Once Marty shut the front door, every action that followed seemed automatic and ritualistic. Suzanne hung her light jacket in the closet nearest the living room and went straight for the kitchen. Marty looked on with keen eyes, appreciating the sway of Suzanne's womanly hips. She wore a polo shirt the color of lilacs and tucked it neatly into her jeans. Suzanne knew how to wear preppy clothes well, and it always gave her tomboy look a classy edge.

"What in God's name has gone on in here?" Suzanne's loud voice brought Marty back from the brink of inappropriate thoughts.

"Party preparations?"

The countertop was riddled with miscellaneous items and most of the food was still in the refrigerator or cabinets. The closest Marty had managed to get to cooking was separating hot dog and hamburger buns.

"Let me—"

"No." Suzanne raised her right hand and kept Marty from entering the kitchen. "You go outside and stay out there. Leave this to me."

Suzanne opened the cabinet above the stove, where they kept the largest serving bowls, but several plastic containers rained down and scattered across the floor. When she turned to chastise Marty, she was already out of the back door. Suzanne shook her head and took a deep breath.

She moved about the kitchen easily, comfortably, with the knowledge of where everything was or where it should be. She fixed the salads and filled bowls with snacks, thinking of parties they had thrown and small get-togethers they'd hosted for their friends. While she rinsed her hands, Suzanne looked out the window and watched

Marty light the grill. At any minute guests would start to arrive and put an end to their time together. Suzanne leaned against the counter and looked on, relishing those final moments.

Suzanne watched Marty move with precise, relaxed movements. She poured charcoal from a heavy bag into the grill base, each muscle along her back, shoulders, and arms flexing as she worked. Her royal blue blouse was sleeveless, and the material was thin enough to showcase each ripple of her lean body. Her knee-length khaki shorts hugged her thighs, and her bare calves looked strong as she walked back and forth methodically.

Suzanne knew what it would feel like to step behind her ex-wife and wrap her arms around her trim waist. She knew if she kissed the back of Marty's neck, it would taste moist with a salty trace of sweat. The blonde shivered at the thought of Marty's natural musk, and how she'd be able to reduce the other woman to whimpering mess just by running her nails along her lower abdomen. Suzanne lost herself in all the fantasies Marty could star in, easily and dangerously distracting her from the task at hand. And just as easily, she missed the sound of the front door opening and the sound of approaching footsteps.

"Suzanne?"

"Denise!" *Act natural.* "I didn't hear you come in!" *Real natural, it's like she caught you with your hand in the cookie jar.* "So quiet!" *Or down her daughter's pants.* "How are you?" Suzanne ran her hand across her forehead and smiled the best she could once she realized she hadn't dried her hands yet.

"I'm fine." Marty's mother narrowed her eyes at Suzanne before looking her up and down. "I wasn't expecting to see you here."

The two women looked at one another as the statement and all its implications hit home. Denise had always been a blunt, honest woman, and Suzanne gave that right back to her.

"I wasn't expecting to be here either." The tightness around her lips eased, and Suzanne resumed her casual stance against the counter. "I called Marty this morning and she invited me." She shrugged. "I miss a lot of people, you included." She finally approached her ex-mother-in-law and wrapped her arms around her. She closed her eyes when Denise hugged her back robustly.

"I miss you too, Suzanne." When they separated, Denise looked around the kitchen and back to Suzanne with an amused smirk. "You must've been here for a while?"

"I knew she'd need help."

"So did I, but I was curious how it'd turn out if Martha was left to her own devices."

Marty interrupted from the doorway. "Well, too bad. Your awful plan was foiled." The sun was shining behind her, illuminating her chestnut hair in the most angelic way. Suzanne struggled not to gape.

"Why must you always save the day?" Denise said to Suzanne.

"Hey!" a loud voice called out from the front of the house.

"More guests, how delightful." Denise's wise eyes held something that frightened and confused Suzanne as Denise walked away to greet the newest arrivals. This was the first confrontation since the divorce, and Suzanne was sure Denise had her own thoughts on the matter.

The latest guest entered the kitchen with a covered bowl in hand. No matter how many years passed, Tess Dwyer would always be stunning. Her auburn hair was pulled back and meticulous, her toned yet perfectly curvy body hugged by tight denim and cotton.

"I wasn't sure what to bring, but I remembered how much you enjoyed my guacamole." Tess handed the bowl to Marty with a wink. Suzanne filed through countless memories in her mind, and she knew for sure Tess had never brought guacamole to a party they hosted.

"You do have a knack. You're going to love it, Suzie." As the name registered with Tess, she looked between Marty and Suzanne with shock.

"Suzanne! How are you?"

"I've been doing okay." She moved to the other side of the kitchen counter in order to avoid any awkward hug. "Yourself? How's Jennifer?"

"She's wonderful!" As soon as the words left her mouth Tess cringed. "I'm so sorry, I didn't mean to—"

"It's okay." Marty was quick to smooth over the discomfort. "She's a good kid. You should be proud. Where is she?" Marty looked around, expecting a little girl identical to her mother to come running around the corner.

"She's spending the weekend with her father. I figured I could indulge in some adult time."

"I bet you did." Suzanne's grumble was quiet enough to go unheard by her ex-wife and neighbor, but Denise snorted before leaving Suzanne to finish her preparations. The doorbell rang, and she sighed in relief at the promise of new faces to distract her.

An hour later, the barbecue was in full swing and people were mingling with plates full of food. Marty stood by her mother's side, casually talking and watching her guests and keeping a keen eye on the bowls full of snacks. She heard Suzanne's laugh from the opposite side of the yard.

"Marty?" Denise followed Marty's gaze. "Did you hear what I said?" Marty merely hummed in response. "Blake's here."

"What?" Marty scanned the small crowd and found him quickly. He was approaching her.

"Hey, Marty." Blake extended his hand. His smile was bright, and his brown eyes were soft as he greeted her. She took his hand and shook it firmly. "Thank you for inviting me."

"I'm glad you could make it." Marty almost choked on her words.

"I'll admit I was a bit surprised when Suzie told me we were both invited."

Marty bristled slightly at the use of her ex-wife's nickname. She knew she'd have to get used to that if Suzanne was to marry him. *If.*

"Listen, Blake, Suzanne is very important to me and you seem like a nice guy. I want to be friends with both of you, and I want to avoid any potential animosity there could be between us."

"I appreciate that," Blake said.

"Now please, make yourself at home by going and eating as much as you possibly can." Marty pointed toward a long table set as a buffet. "Beers are in the cooler and any liquor, soda, or juice you could imagine are in the kitchen."

"I am starving." He looked like he was about to drool as he stared longingly at a pile of cheeseburgers.

"Then why are you still standing here?" Marty laughed and gave his broad shoulder a gentle shove. She watched as he walked away. Her happy visage fell when she looked back at her mother.

"I'm impressed and worried." Denise crossed her arms over her chest, an action she'd perfected during Marty's teenage years.

"By what?" Marty gulped her beer and concentrated on resisting the urge to look behind her and watch Blake greet his fiancée.

"Your ability to lie so well."

"I didn't lie, not completely, anyway." Marty looked around to make sure all the guests were involved in conversations that would cover her words. "Suzanne is important to me, and he does seem like a nice guy. The friendship part was a bit far-fetched, though."

"I'd say." Denise chuckled and moved to slyly look around her daughter at the couple in question.

Marty looked too, against her better judgment. Suzanne wrapped her arm around Blake's as she stood stiffly at his side. Marty noticed she said very little as he conversed with her old friends, but she kept casting short glances in Marty's direction.

"I should be discouraging you, you know?" Denise looked her daughter in the eye once again. "The last thing a mother should do is support her child in trying to steal someone's fiancée away."

"Then why are you?" Marty was genuinely curious.

"Because I believe Abigail was right."

No more explanation was needed. Marty saw the little girl's written words when she closed her eyes.

She loves you too.

❖

Suzanne pulled back the comforter of her king-sized bed with a flourish, allowing the sheet beneath to get caught up and float freely in the air for a moment. She carefully analyzed each of the muddled thoughts from that evening.

"Did you have fun?" Blake asked from across the bed. He was already stripped down to his boxer briefs and climbing into bed.

"I did." Suzanne tugged at the hem of her oversized T-shirt before joining Blake between the covers. She shifted around and settled her back against the front of his body. Blake held her in place by wrapping his arm around her waist.

"You seemed like you did." He kissed the side of her neck gently. His stubble scraped against her skin, causing Suzanne to flinch. "It made me very happy to see you like that." He kissed the back of her neck again, and this time the stubble didn't bother her as much. She even leaned back to find more contact.

"Did *you* have fun? I know Annmarie can be a bit much sometimes," Suzanne said with a smile.

"I had a wonderful time because I was with you." Blake tightened his grip around Suzanne and drew her closer into his embrace.

Suzanne smiled contently as she basked in this feeling of intimacy. It was nice to feel loved and protected. Sleep started to take her when she felt Blake toying with the bottom of her shirt. His touch moved from material to her skin, he traced her upper thighs and over to the side seam of her underwear. Suzanne pulled away. "I'm sorry."

"Don't be sorry." Blake sighed and rolled onto his back. Suzanne turned to look at him. "I just got my signals mixed up, that's all."

"Signals?" Suzanne asked.

"You were very touchy-feely all night, especially later on. I thought you were trying to tell me something." Blake winked.

Suzanne tried to remember what Blake was referring to, and she felt ashamed when she recalled it. Marty had walked off to join Tess in the far corner of the yard away from any curious ears and had engaged in what looked to be a rather intimate conversation. Tess was leaning in close, and once Marty had reached out to take the other woman's hand, Suzanne wrapped herself around Blake and peppered his neck with kisses. "I suppose I could blame the alcohol for that." Her face reddened with embarrassment.

"You had one beer! You don't have to blame anything." Blake laughed. "It was nice. And if you're not ready, I'll wait. I have no problem waiting for you." Blake reached out and brushed his thumb along Suzanne's cheekbone.

Suzanne looked at the man before her. His eyes were soft with kindness, and he lay with a smile regardless of the history that weighed her down. She took in his physical presence, his well-muscled chest with a spray of fine hairs across it and defined abdomen that had once captivated her with its peaks and valleys. Blake was a very attractive man. So why was Suzanne struggling to keep her focus on him? She'd told Marty to move on because she had done so herself, and it looked like Marty was heeding her advice with Tess Dwyer.

"I'm ready." Suzanne shifted to lie atop a very surprised Blake. "I'm ready," she whispered again and told herself she truly meant it.

And Suddenly They Were Mothers

Five months had passed since Abigail was born. She'd brought such joy, such challenge to their everyday lives that Marty and Suzanne never knew what to expect each morning when they awoke hours before their alarm. Marty had noticed a change in Suzanne, but she'd also noticed it in herself. They weren't playful wives and romantic partners anymore. They were mothers.

Marty dug another burping cloth out from between their couch cushions. "I'm so glad my mother agreed to take Abigail today."

"It hardly took convincing."

"True." Marty smiled at Suzanne and looked back to the pile of toys at her feet. Their kid wasn't even six months old, and they had already spread out every last gadget and gizmo they had received at their baby shower. They wanted to make sure Abigail knew she had options when it came to entertainment. Her life didn't have to revolve around peek-a-boo.

"I feel like we haven't been able to really clean in forever."

Marty stared at her.

"What?" Suzanne asked.

"I never thought I'd see the day where you got excited over cleaning."

Suzanne had grown the most over the past few months. She had matured in ways Marty didn't even consider, and she had grown substantially as a person. Suzanne was a natural mother. Marty was so proud of her wife, but she was also observant enough to pick up on new insecurities and distractions. Marty twisted the small cloth around her fingers as she watched Suzanne buzz around the kitchen. A baggy gray sweatshirt hung from her frame, the title *Jersey Girl* was scrawled proudly across her breasts, and matching pants completed the outfit along with whatever mismatched socks Suzanne had chosen that morning. She hadn't strayed far from that uniform since Abigail's birth, and that was very unlike Suzanne Dempsey. And it wasn't like Marty found her unattractive—Suzanne found herself unattractive.

Marty moved quickly, her cotton pajama pants not making a sound as she made her way into the kitchen. She stood in front of Suzanne. She looked at her face, taking in her tired features and the beauty she had memorized over the years. A beauty that filled her heart completely.

"I love you." Marty stepped forward and trapped her wife between her lean body and the kitchen counter. She ignored the surprised look on Suzanne's face, but she also saw Suzanne formulate her escape plan. She wasn't getting away this time. Marty grabbed the shorter woman's wrists and brought them behind her back. With one hand, she held them firmly. "Trust me?"

Suzanne nodded.

Marty leaned in slowly, bringing her lips within millimeters of Suzanne's, close enough to feel her small exhale. Just as she was about to close the distance, just as Suzanne puckered in anticipation, Marty ran her tongue along the bow of Suzanne's upper lip. Marty moved to her lower lip, biting down gently before kissing her. Once Marty felt her actions being mirrored, she pushed further. What started as a gentle kiss turned quickly to a burning flame of forgotten passion. Suzanne parted her lips parted eagerly, and Marty moved in to taste her. Marty kissed her, pulling back as Suzanne groaned in displeasure.

"You're so beautiful." Marty brushed her moist lips against Suzanne's ear. She spoke barely above a whisper, too afraid to break the sensuality of the moment.

"No, I'm not." Suzanne's firm response caused Marty to pull back and look into doubtful indigo eyes.

"You are." Marty kissed Suzanne before continuing. "You're

beautiful and so *fucking* sexy." She released Suzanne's wrists and gripped the counter while she felt beneath her sweatshirt. Suzanne jumped at the first caress across her soft belly. She may not have been as toned as she once was, but Suzanne was womanly. Just the feel of such femininity beneath her fingertips made Marty wet.

"You don't see what I see," Marty said quietly, making sure her hot breath ghosted across the sensitive skin behind Suzanne's ear. "You don't know what you do to me." She scraped her manicured nails along Suzanne's ribs before palming one of her heavy breasts. Despite Suzanne's recent aversion to intimacy, her body responded to the touch instantly. Her nipple hardened against the center of Marty's palm. It took all Marty's willpower not to pinch and pull and rush them along to the oblivion she knew they both missed desperately. Instead, she traced the material of Suzanne's worn bra in lazy, indistinct patterns. Suzanne whimpered whenever Marty drew closer to her straining nipples. Suzanne put her head on Marty's shoulder.

"How?" Suzanne's question was nearly lost in a panting breath.

"How what?" Marty released the counter and ran her fingers through the short hairs at the back of Suzanne's head. She still marveled at the softness of her golden locks. Her other hand dropped to her wife's lower back.

"How could you want me?" Suzanne asked in a small voice, shaky with disbelief.

Marty kissed her temple. "How could I not?"

"I'm still fat and I have stretch—" Marty put her finger on Suzanne's lips.

"I'll always want you." Suzanne shook her head, which would have frustrated Marty if it weren't for the lust clouding her mind. "Don't believe me?" Marty gripped Suzanne's right hand and put it down the front of her pants. Suzanne didn't need any direction from the there. The blonde gasped the moment her fingertips came into contact with her drenched skin. Dormant, familiar sensations crawled their way along Marty's spine as she fought against the urge to grind against Suzanne's hand. She wanted Suzanne to explore and really feel the evidence of her desire.

"Shit, Marty, you're so wet." Suzanne pressed into her, rubbing herself against the back of her hand as she ran her fingers through delicate folds.

"And all I did was grab your boob." Marty's small chuckle died the moment Suzanne circled her fluttering opening with her fingertip. Suzanne slid her finger in easily, pulling the trigger on Marty's cocked and ready passion. Marty palmed both of Suzanne's breasts roughly, scraping her thumbnails over sensitive, turgid nipples. Suzanne continued a steady, quick pace of in and out with her finger for a moment before pulling out and rubbing tight circles around Marty's throbbing clit.

The amount of pleasure thrumming throughout Marty's body was sinful, and she wanted to share it with her lover. She felt along Suzanne's soft belly and down to the waistband of her sweatpants. Just as she dipped the tips of her fingers beneath the elastic and teased top of her perfectly trimmed hairline, the front door swung open and a loud cry filled the quiet home. The women separated hastily and tried to straighten their appearances. Suzanne started washing her hands at the sink while Marty leaned against the counter and tried to catch her breath.

"We're back!" Denise entered the kitchen, bouncing Abigail against her chest in her best effort to soothe the upset infant. "She's fed and changed, but I think she's missing her mommies."

Suzanne dried her hands and took her daughter in her arms. As she passed Marty, she whispered, "We'll finish this later."

Marty looked on with love-filled eyes as Suzanne lifted Abigail to the sky. In the blink of an eye, she stopped crying and a smile lit up her chubby face.

Later that night, seconds after Abigail had finally settled in her crib, Marty walked into the bedroom to find Suzanne spread out naked on their bed, sound asleep. They didn't make love then, but they awoke before the sun and relished the quiet intimacy only a still world could provide. They indulged and they worshiped their bare skin until Abigail woke up. The balancing act wasn't easy, but they were finally figuring out how to be mothers and be themselves at the same time.

CHAPTER NINE

Suzanne finished rubbing the sunscreen onto the rim of her right ear just before Blake emerged from the bathroom all smiles. His mood had improved significantly since the physical shift in their relationship, but this smile was different. "You're really excited to play golf today," she said, observing his almost giddy state.

"It's been a long time. Even longer since I managed to get my brother to tag along!" Blake tugged on the brim of his baseball cap. He appeared thoughtful for a minute before sliding it to the side and leaning in to kiss Suzanne lightly. "I see you're preparing for a day out. Where are you heading?"

Suzanne fought a grimace. There wasn't much internal debate before answering, "Marty's taking the boat out and asked me to join her." She forced a laugh. "She probably wanted to ask someone else, but I'm the only person she knows that has sailing knowledge." Blake finished getting ready and walked to the front door in silence. Suzanne's heart was beating anxiously. Should she say more? "I don't have to go," she whispered.

"Yes, you do." Blake looked into her eyes. "I've been telling you to go out, to not sit home if you don't have to. A day out on the water will be good for you."

"But…" Suzanne wanted to argue, but why would she? She didn't want to turn down Marty's invitation. She missed the boat, and Blake was right. A day out on the water would be good for her.

They stood together in front of the door, neither adding to their conversation but not making an effort to end it, either. Blake finally made a move once his brother drove up and honked his horn. Blake opened the front door for Suzanne. She grabbed the bag she had packed earlier and walked out to the car.

"Hey, Suzanne!" Blake's brother called out from his idling SUV. "When will you come play with us?"

"Never!" She chuckled and turned back to Blake. "Have fun."

"You too." He kissed her again, this time with the brim awkwardly between them. "Not too much, though."

Suzanne wanted to dish out a comeback, but he was in the car and on his way already. His words echoed in her head and settled like lead in her gut. She got in the car and started to drive, all the while analyzing her thoughts and motivations.

"What are you doing?" Suzanne didn't answer her own question. "You know this is a bad idea." The sun was shining beautifully, and the temperature was surprisingly warm for the tail end of a New Jersey summer. But the weather didn't surprise Suzanne. Neither did Marty's early morning invitation to go out on the boat. But Suzanne was definitely surprised by her own eager acceptance. "A really, *really*, bad idea." Suzanne reprimanded herself aloud.

The whirring sound of her car's air-conditioning surrounded her as she drove the well-known route to the docks. Blake was enjoying the beautiful day, why should she feel guilty for doing the same? Suzanne's logical reasoning had come easily as she picked out a bathing suit and packed up a few essentials into her small messenger bag, but as she parked and got out of the car, she couldn't help but mutter one last time, "Bad idea."

She walked the planks of the dock confidently despite her anxiety-ridden legs. She knew their boat—*Marty's boat*—was in the same slip year after year, and she found it easily. The large sailboat moved gently with the calm waves that splashed below. Suzanne froze for a moment as she watched Marty from afar milling about on the deck of the boat. Suzanne inhaled deeply, the earthy scent of the bay calming her jittery nerves. She moved forward and called out.

"Permission to come aboard?"

Marty spun around in search of the voice. "Hey!" She extended a hand. "Come on up." Her bright smile was all the encouragement Suzanne needed.

"How's *SAM* been doing?"

"She's been doing well, I guess." Marty cleared her throat and took Suzanne's bag from her, placing it next to a cooler. "It's late in the season for a first run, but I didn't want to leave her wrapped up for another full year. Plus, it's a good reason to get out and enjoy this weather. Ready?"

The routine was always the same: untying the boat, starting the engine, steering, and prepping the sails. Suzanne remembered what a great team they made whenever they took *SAM* out, even if they hadn't done it in years.

Suzanne would never forget the day they had purchased the boat the summer Abigail was born. Marty had wanted one for so long, and Suzanne was nearly speechless at the excitement her wife exuded as they shopped around. Choosing a name was the hardest part, but when Suzanne noticed the way Marty's eyes lit up after opening a congratulations card from one of her coworkers, she knew they had found it. Listed in the top left corner were the names of their small family members: Suzanne, Abigail, and Marty. *SAM* was adhered to the arch board the very next day.

"How long has it been since the last time we did this?" Suzanne asked as she stood beside Marty in the small alcove that held the steering wheel. The hum of the engine and the sound of water rushing around them soothed Suzanne more deeply than it ever had. Marty didn't answer.

Once they had reached the middle of the bay, Marty dropped anchor and called out for Suzanne to bring out the blanket she had stowed away. Together they laid out a small meal of sandwiches and beer, with two chilled bottles of water to combat the sun. And Suzanne enjoyed sneaking glimpses of Marty as she relaxed with a beer in hand, smiling toward the sun. They sat in peace and enjoyed their lunch as boats and Jet Skis passed in a hurry.

"I forgot how beautiful it is out here."

"It's been a while." Suzanne handed over her crumpled wax paper to Marty as she startled to clean up.

"When was the last time just you and I came out here?" Suzanne asked again. Try as she might, she was unable to recall that memory.

"The summer right after Abigail was born," Marty said, still looking away to the distant horizon.

"We celebrated our anniversary on the boat that summer." Suzanne said. She bit her lip slightly.

"We did." Marty stood up and pulled her black tank top over her head, dropped her simple cotton shorts to the floor, and kicked them aside. "That wasn't the last time we were on the boat, however. That was just the last time we took it out alone." Marty stretched her long, tanned limbs and lay back across the blankets. Suzanne stood and followed suit, quickly disrobing. "I'm still convinced that party boat saw your tits that night."

"They did not!" Suzanne threw her top at Marty and laughed as it covered her face. Suzanne was grateful for the mirrored lenses of her aviator sunglasses so she could look unobserved at Marty's breasts glistening in a tiny black bikini top. She swallowed thickly and forced herself to lie beside Marty with a feigned casualness.

"Nice bathing suit," Marty said. "Teal is definitely your color."

Suzanne blushed at the compliment.

The two women stared up into the clear blue sky and enjoyed the peaceful calm. Close to twenty minutes passed before either of them spoke. They were lost to the warm sun and cool breeze.

"We took Abigail crabbing," Marty said. The recollection was so quiet the lapping waves almost washed it away.

"Hmm?"

"The last time we took *SAM* out was when Abigail wanted to go crabbing."

"That's right!" Suzanne shielded the sun from her eyes with her right hand and sat up. "She was terrified when we finally caught one." She laughed at the memory.

"And you got so sunburned you couldn't move for days." Marty poked at Suzanne's exposed shoulder. "I hope you slathered up today. You're already pink."

"I put on a sufficient amount, thank you." She pushed Marty

playfully. "We should do this more often. I'd hate for *SAM* to feel neglected."

"I'm thinking about renaming her."

Suzanne's smile fell. "To what?"

"I'm not sure yet." Marty looked into the murky water. "It's not the family boat anymore." Suzanne knew it was the truth. Her name no longer belonged in the acronym scrawled across the boat. The same sick feeling that had twisted her gut in the restaurant weeks before was back. Talking about their family would never get easier.

"Whatever you choose, I'm sure it'll be perfect." Suzanne was surprised by how emotional she felt in the moment. She'd signed divorce papers, spoken to a lawyer about handling a marital split, and had even been able to look Marty in the eye when she told her it was over. Why was something so seemingly insignificant in the big picture making her chest heavy with anxiety? Why did she feel as if reality was finally hitting her?

"I was going to name it after Abby's favorite purple rhino," Marty said. If she was aware of the turmoil Suzanne was dealing with, she didn't let on. "But I don't think Archibald is a good name for a boat."

"Only if it were a yacht."

"Maybe Ripley, then? I don't know." Marty shrugged, her eyes still closed.

"Ripley would be nice." Suzanne needed to breathe, and in order to breathe, she needed to move. Suzanne jumped to her feet and walked over to the cooler. "Beer?" she asked over her shoulder.

"Water, please."

Suzanne wrestled with ice and freezing water, digging to the bottom of the drink cooler in search of a water bottle. Her fingertips just grasped the prize when something dawned on her. "You haven't touched the water from earl—" Just then, Marty splashed water across her face and chest and into her mouth. Suzanne froze with her eyes closed.

"It got a little too warm, don't you think?" Marty bit back laughter as water dropped from Suzanne's chin.

"Not funny," Suzanne warned as she opened her fiery blue eyes wide.

"Very funny."

"Not funny at all." Suzanne bent back toward the cooler for a handful of ice.

"Hilarious!" Marty finally let herself go into a fit of laughter. She guffawed until a shower of ice cold water shut her up. Silently, menacingly, she narrowed her sparkling green eyes and started her advance.

"Stay back!" Suzanne warned, but her wide grin did little in the way of a threat. She raised her other hand, the ice cubes dripping from her small fist. They reflected the bright sunlight. She watched as Marty's lean muscles coiled, her thighs defined as she bent her long legs and came closer. Marty reached out and grasped Suzanne's wrist.

As Suzanne moved away, trying to save her ammo from winding up in the enemy's hands, her heel hit in a small puddle on the deck of the boat, causing her to lose traction. She started to fall back toward the cooler, but Marty jerked her forward, and Suzanne landed on top of her, sprawled out across the smiling brunette.

They heaved with laughter, and Suzanne's chest was tight with anxiety, surprise, and something that hit her with a surprising force—happiness. Against Suzanne's better judgment, she didn't pull away immediately. She looked down into Marty's face and gave her a rakish grin, as if to ask whether it had been on purpose or not. Suzanne couldn't keep from looking at Marty's moistened pink lips. She froze as Marty started to lean up so slightly, just enough for her breath of anticipation to ghost across Suzanne's mouth, effectively jarring her from the trance.

"We should head back." Suzanne felt dizzy when she sat up. She wanted to blame the movement for the way her head spun, but she knew it was the desire she saw in Marty's green eyes that was to blame. "Blake should be home soon, and I want to get dinner started." *Blake*. She wondered if she was reminding Marty or herself of Blake.

"Of course." Marty hopped to her feet casually and made her

way to raise the anchor. Suzanne opened and closed her mouth in an attempt to say something, anything, to alleviate the new tension that settled around them, but as the engine roared to life, she figured this misstep might be better left unacknowledged.

"He spent the day with his friends," Suzanne added unnecessarily while readying the boat for its return.

"That's good." Marty spoke with her back to Suzanne.

"We're good about having time to ourselves." Suzanne continued to talk, unsure as to why. She was just making an awkward moment more uncomfortable, and she was sure Marty didn't need any more reminding about her fiancé. "You know how I am when I lose my autonomy."

"Yeah, Suzie. I know," Marty said tersely.

The ride back to the dock was spent in silence, Suzanne's mind preoccupied with imaginings and scoldings of what could've happened in the privacy provided by the center of the bay. Her cheeks were rosy from the sun and her close proximity to a surprising temptation. And why had she rambled on about Blake? In retrospect, it looked like she was bragging about the guy just to bother Marty. When she looked over, Marty's face was stoic and unreadable, leaving her alone in her turmoil.

"I had a great time." Suzanne leapt onto the wooden platform and looked back up to Marty, who was still on the boat. "Thank you for the invitation."

"*SAM* missed you." Marty patted the railing she was leaning against a few times. Despite Marty's casual remark, Suzanne could tell how much Marty missed her.

"Let's do it again soon, okay?"

Marty nodded and said, "Tell Blake I say hi."

"Okay, sure." Suzanne tilted her head slightly. "Good-bye, Marty." And with that, she turned to leave.

They Took It All in Stride

I don't wanna go!" the five-year-old wailed for the twentieth time that evening, but at least this time she didn't smash her small fist against her mother's chest.

"I know you don't, baby girl, but you have to." The first day of kindergarten had crept up a little too quickly. Marty buried her nose in the sandy-blond hair just below her nose. She and Abigail were sprawled across the sofa, Marty on her back and her daughter lying atop her. An innocuous cartoon played on the television.

"Why?" Abigail asked again, around the thumb in her mouth.

Marty huffed. "So you can learn all kinds of fun things and grow up to be super smart." She kissed the crown of Abigail's head.

"But I'm already smart," Abigail removed her thumb from her mouth. A small spot of spittle soaked through Marty's gray tank top. "A-B-C—"

"I know you are, Abs." Marty wrapped her arms around the small child, holding her tightly against her chest.

The mothers found it much easier to soothe, console, and convince Abigail that going to school would be fun and for the best, all while both women were more emotional than Abigail. They just kept it a secret.

"It'll be fun," Marty continued. "You'll make friends and play fun games."

"But I have fun and play here, and you and Mommy are my friends." With a shaky breath Marty collected herself. She couldn't help but wonder if Abby would feel the same way when she was fourteen and listening to her mothers as they forbid her from seeing that boy or girl she felt she was ready to start dating. *One year at a time*, Marty reminded herself with a small chuckle.

"And we'll be here when you get home from school tomorrow, ready to hear all about it." When Abigail looked up at her mother, Marty smiled at her blue eyes. They looked more and more like Suzanne's with every day that passed. "Your mommy and I love you very much, Abby, and we want you to have the best life possible."

"'Kay!" The small, surprisingly loud voice rumbled against Marty's chest before Abigail shifted into a more comfortable position. End of conversation.

❖

Marty and Suzanne clasped their shaking hands together while Abigail picked the dandelions withering away in the grass by the bus stop.

"She'll be okay." Suzanne squeezed Marty's hand. They watched as Abigail ran her small fingers through the green blades. Her pink dress was perfect for the first day of school, but her backpack was too large for her small body. She crouched close to the ground with her back to her mothers, her pigtails remarkably even despite the wrestling match Suzanne had with them that morning.

"But will *we*?" Marty asked with a tremor in her voice. "How did we get here so quickly?"

They were encircled by more small children and drowsy parents. Abigail was the youngest of the flock, and Suzanne and Marty were surely the most emotional. They heard the telltale sound of school bus brakes squealing in the distance, and they looked down the road.

"Abigail?"

"Abigail, come here!" Marty didn't mean to shout. The people surrounding her, her neighbors but still strangers, eyed her curiously. "Listen to me, Abs." Marty knelt and looked her daughter in the eye.

Suzanne was at her side immediately. "What did we tell you last night?"

"Always say please and thank you." The child nodded.

"That's right." Suzanne grabbed Abigail's tiny hand with her left and placed her right on Marty's shoulder to steady herself. "And what's your teacher's name?"

"Mrs. Ford."

"Very good." As the loud rumble of the bus grew closer, Suzanne looked positively panicked. "Now remember, if you get lost on your way to the bathroom or on your way back to class—"

"Don't be scared and find a teacher to help me." Abigail looked nonplussed. Where was the clingy, desperate child from the night before?

"You're going to do great, baby girl." Marty stood as the large yellow bus came to a stop in front of the small crowd that had formed. The bus driver was a bit too bright and cheery for Marty's liking. This was a devastating day, why did that middle-aged woman enjoy it so? The metal doors swung open.

One by one, the children climbed onto the bus, all giggles and excitement. Abigail was the last to join them because Marty still had hold of her hand. Abigail tugged, and then she was free, moving away from her forlorn parents.

"Your day will go the way your mouth turns!" Suzanne called out. Abigail turned and looked at her with a comically large grin, the corners of her cherub mouth turned up as high as they could go.

"You have two ears and one mouth, use them proportionately!" Marty's added advice fell like a weighted burlap sack. Her daughter's smile turned into a confused scowl before she climbed the steps to the bus. To her left, Suzanne stared at her quizzically. She could almost hear her wife wondering what the hell that was. Truth be told, she had no idea. Marty shrugged before looking at the cloudy square windows of the bus.

Abigail found a seat quickly, and the bus started to move. It inched away from the mothers. Their daughter waved excitedly. Both women raised a motionless hand in the air as the vehicle departed. As if on the count of three, tears welled the moment the bus turned the corner.

"I thought the kid was supposed to cry!" Marty wiped at her stubborn tears and tried her best to hide her glower.

"I'm guessing this is your first?" A tall redhead approached the women from behind. She was young and beautiful and seemed quite amused by the emotional display playing out before her. She extended her hand to Marty. "I'm Tess Dwyer, Jennifer's mom."

Marty sniffled and gently took the offered hand. "Marty Dempsey, Abigail's mom." She didn't let on that she had no clue who Jennifer was, nor did she introduce the woman at her side. "Are you new to the neighborhood? I haven't seen you around."

"Guilty." Tess looked at Marty with delight. "We just finished unpacking, actually."

"Where are you from?" Suzanne said.

"Linden. After my divorce, I wanted to get away. The shore seemed like the perfect place."

"How are you liking it so far?" Marty asked.

"I'm liking it better and better every day."

Marty felt Suzanne's muscles tense. She grabbed the blonde's hand and chafed it between her own. "My wife and I couldn't imagine a better place to raise our daughter."

Suzanne had a tamed case of bed head, and she was wearing a worn T-shirt. Marty held her closely with an arm around her shoulder. She felt a genuine smile of pride because she still enjoyed introducing Suzanne as her wife. Marty was surprised when Suzanne wrapped a possessive arm around her trim waist.

"So this is your wife?"

"Suzanne Dempsey." She extended a hand to Tess.

"Nice to meet you." Tess looked from one woman to the other as she shook Suzanne's hand. "Very nice to meet you both." An awkward silence engulfed them following the introduction. "Well, I have to get going. A six-year-old's laundry won't do itself!" The pathetic joke earned stiff giggles, and Tess walked away. Suzanne turned and looked at Marty with a teasing smirk.

"That was interesting."

"Yeah." Marty tugged at her collar. A turtleneck was perfect for the frigid air-conditioning in her office, but it was suffocating her right now.

"I guess I won't be able to let you out of my sights when we bring Abigail to the bus stop." Suzanne wrapped both arms around Marty's waist and pulled her close. She looked up into her eyes innocently. The embrace was returned immediately.

"Oh please, like I have eyes for anyone but you. Besides, she's not my type. Ah!" Marty jumped when Suzanne pinched her side.

"Gorgeous redheads aren't your type?" Suzanne arched an eyebrow and looked at Marty incredulously.

"Nope." Marty bent slightly to place a tender kiss on Suzanne's forehead. The fringe of her short bangs tickled Marty's nose. "I prefer pinchy, stunning blondes with a wicked sense of humor and shockingly impressive skills in the bedroom." Suzanne giggled against her chest.

"Come on," Marty said as they pulled apart. "I still have another hour before I have to be at the office, the perfect amount of time to sulk about my baby girl being all grown up."

"I can't wait to see how you act when she starts dating." Suzanne smiled and took Marty's hand as they walked home.

"All the boys will be scared of me."

"Or girls." Suzanne pointed out the obvious.

"Oh God." Marty's mind hurt from the overwhelming thought of Abigail's teenage years. "Just keep her away from girls like me. We're nothing but trouble."

"You're telling me!" Suzanne swatted Marty's backside before ascending the steps to their front door.

CHAPTER TEN

"I cannot believe how big Danny is getting." Suzanne looked at her nephew in awe. She could still remember the day he was born.

"Tell me about it! He's walking and talking now—the kid rambles on and on! He rarely makes sense, but he's still more talkative than me." Suzanne's sister laughed lightly and continued to watch as Danny sat raptured by his grandfather's storytelling. She pushed her long blond hair from her shoulders. "I'm just glad Dad has a new audience for his tales."

Suzanne held up her glass of wine. "Cheers to that." Their crystal glasses clinked quietly. "When we were little, Carla would go days without saying much more than yes and no." Suzanne leaned into Blake as she spoke.

"Not like I could manage much more than that with you, Miss Chatterbox!"

"I do remember Suzanne getting detention more than once for that motor-mouth," Blake said.

Suzanne smiled at how effortless it was for him to settle in with her family. Their past together certainly helped that along.

"So, what have you been up to lately?" Carla asked her sister casually. "It's been a while since the last time we've seen you. How are you? I don't want to pry, but I want to know if you're okay."

"I'm fine." Suzanne paused in order to listen in on her mother talking to her brother-in-law about how hard the business world used to be on women, and how it still is. "I'm doing much better than Daniel is right now." The two women giggled conspiratorially.

"But seriously, I'm hanging in there. I'm keeping busy with work, and Blake has been a good support system." Suzanne gripped Blake's hand and looked sadly at little Danny. "Some days are harder than others. Some mornings I wonder if it's even worth getting out of bed." Her voice dropped to a whisper. She hadn't shared these thoughts, these feelings with anyone until now. Suzanne figured she needed to keep it a secret, a cross she had to bear in silence. Blake held her hand tighter. She looked at him guiltily.

"It is worth it because we love you. Especially Danny. He adores his aunt."

"And I am absolutely crazy about him." She looked tenderly at the boy, who was now bored by his grandfather and trying to stand on his chair.

"He's been asking for Marty."

"Has he?" Suzanne relinquished her hold on Blake's hand before returning her attention to her full wineglass. She looked at the crisp liquid as she swirled it around.

"How is she doing? Have you talked to her?" She grinned delicately.

"If you asked her, she'd tell you she's doing as well as can be expected." Suzanne wanted to end the conversation when she felt Blake shift uncomfortably beside her, but Carla wasn't having it.

"But…"

"But she's not. I can tell she's not." Suzanne recalled the morning her ex-wife had arrived at the library searching so desperately for her. "I don't think she's sleeping very well. And she has that look in her eye, that hard one like she had after we lost the first baby, you know?" Suzanne waited for Carla to nod. "I don't know if it'll go away this time, though."

"I've wanted to call her, but I wasn't sure if that'd be weird."

"She would like that. She'd really like to hear from that little guy too."

"How are the wedding plans coming, dear?" Angela scooted her chair closer to her daughters and looked at Suzanne expectantly.

"They're not. I'm not quite ready for a ceremony yet." Suzanne sighed. "Blake and I are happy to enjoy a long engagement." She smiled at her silent fiancé. His eyes were on her, but he looked distant. She wondered if they were really on the same page.

"I'm so glad you could make it tonight, Blake. I'm sure a man with such an honorable job is a busy man," Angela said with her most charming smile.

"I have long hours, sure, but I get time off just like anyone else." He cleared his throat. "Which is nice because that means I get to spend more time with Suzanne."

Blake looked at Suzanne, and her heart sank slightly. He looked so proud, so content, and all she could think about was how she couldn't wait to set up a play date between Marty and their—*her* nephew.

"You know, Suzanne, you should be very grateful that he's as crazy about you as he is," Angela said. An air of unease settled over the table. Even Jeff Carlson shifted uncomfortably.

"And why is that, Mother?"

"Considering your past? You should be eager to marry a man who's so forgiving."

"I don't think—" Blake's reply got shot down by Suzanne's instant reaction.

"Forgiving? What is it that I need to be forgiven for exactly?" Suzanne didn't even try to tamp down her rising voice. "Being married once before, or being married to a woman?"

"Who's ready for dessert?" Daniel stood and tried to offer a distraction. The only attention he got was from his five-year-old son.

"If Suzanne wants to take her time getting married, that's her choice, Ma, not yours."

"But thanks for your permission!" Suzanne snapped at her sister.

"Our decision really." Blake sat back, ignored.

"That's not what I meant, and you know it." Carla inhaled deeply and looked from her mother to sister. "Let's just change the subject. You've got some great color," she said as she looked Suzanne over. "Have you been to the beach?"

"No, I was out on the boat." Suzanne was ready to fight. Her mother always brought that side of her out.

"Oh man, I miss that boat!"

"Martha doesn't mind you taking the boat?"

"We took it out together." Suzanne squared her shoulders.

"And Blake?" Usually stoic, Angela looked shocked at her future son-in-law.

"I—"

"Was playing golf with his friends," Suzanne answered for him. Her fury gave her tunnel vision, making her oblivious to the man next to her.

"He was fine with you spending time with your former partner?"

"Wife!" Suzanne shouted and slammed her palm down on the table. "She was my wife, Mother, the woman I raised my child with." Even though she willed herself not to cry, she couldn't help it. "My marriage failed, and I lost my daughter, and you can barely acknowledge either simply because Marty is a woman." Her eyes bore into Angela. "I need some air."

Suzanne pushed back from the table and went out the back door, waiting until she was outside before letting out a growl of frustration. The night was cool and quiet. Her parents' deck offered the perfect sense of solitude for the kind of introspection Suzanne's mother always forced upon her. With a graceless thud, she sat down on one wooden step and held her face in her hands.

When she looked up again, her childhood backyard seemed less magical. She searched her mind for memories to distract her, memories of their shed and the tire swing that hung from the large tree in the back. But none of those memories were able to drown out thoughts of Marty. Thoughts of how good it felt to be with her, to laugh along with her, and especially how good it felt to touch her. The almost kiss was something she had fought hard to forget, but it still burned beneath her flesh. When the wind picked up through the yard and brushed against her face, it felt like Marty's breath crossing her lips. Suzanne jumped when the back door opened.

"Approach at your own risk," Suzanne warned, assuming it was Blake.

"I've dealt with you in worse times." Carla took a seat beside Suzanne and looked at her. "I'm sorry about all that."

"You don't have to apologize for her." Suzanne looked at Carla thoughtfully. "Where's Blake?"

"I told him to let me handle this one. It seemed more like a sisterly situation."

"Thanks." Suzanne sighed in relief. She was embarrassed and angry. Blake didn't deserve to be on the receiving end of that.

"Of course. I know I don't have to apologize for her, but she was never fair to you, and she was especially never fair to Marty. She was just never comfortable with the idea."

"And that makes it okay?" Suzanne was exasperated, but all the fight had left her tone.

"No, but she thinks it does. She loves you unconditionally, but when she's not comfortable with something she's not even willing to try to be." Carla shrugged. "If only she were more like Dad."

"Has anything fazed him since we were teenagers?"

"Not since you dyed your hair purple and came home with a nose ring." Suzanne snorted at the memory. When the laughter died down and nothing but crickets filled the air once more, Carla finally asked, "Will you tell me about your sailing session? Keep it PG rated, please."

"Nothing happened." Suzanne pushed at her sister's shoulder with her own. "Marty was taking the boat out and invited me. Since I wasn't doing anything, I took her up on her offer."

"And nothing happened?"

"Nothing."

"That's surprising."

"We're just friends, Carla, nothing more. We're trying really hard to rebuild something that'll allow us to be in each other's lives without any grudges."

"How's that going?"

"It's hard. It's very hard."

"Because you're holding a grudge?"

"Because I'm *not* holding a grudge and I feel like I *should* be!" Suzanne ran her fingers through her short hair and scratched at her scalp. "I feel like I should be mad at her. I should blame her for this constant pain in my chest, but I don't. I'm not mad at her. This pain won't go away because it's from missing Abby and the life we had with her."

"You do realize how crazy that sounds, right?"

"What?"

"You're trying to hate your ex-wife when your first instinct is to not hate your ex-wife. You're missing a life you had with Abby and Marty. You will always carry Abby's memory with you. That pain will never leave your heart, but do you really think a friendship with Marty will be enough to make you happy again? Really, truly happy?"

"It'll have to." Suzanne looked at her sister, defeat weighing down her body and shimmering in her eyes. "I'm with Blake now."

"You could break up with him," Carla said casually.

"I can't, not after everything he's done. He's been so supportive, and he was so wonderful with Abigail. I can't hurt him." Suzanne stood and straightened her jeans and button-up blouse. "We can be happy together." Her voice was unconvincing. "We have to be. I might be pregnant." Carla stood quickly and made it to the door first. She held the knob securely to keep Suzanne where she was.

"You *might* be pregnant?" Carla's eyes widened. "What the hell does that mean?"

Suzanne's heart sped up. "I don't—it's not…" Suzanne took a shaky breath. "We haven't been very careful, and I know how these things work."

"Are you late? Did you take a test?"

"No!" Suzanne looked through the window and spotted Blake talking to her brother-in-law. "I'm due any day now, and all I can think about is what if I'm pregnant? I'm not ready for another child. Marty and I were parents together. I managed to raise a child because of a partnership. We were a team, and I don't want that with—" Suzanne stopped abruptly, and her face flushed. She was ashamed of what she was about to say.

"You don't owe him anything, you know?" Suzanne looked at Carla with large, glistening eyes. "Listen, I've been in a room with both you and Marty and you and Blake." Suzanne narrowed her eyes at her sister, wondering where this was going. "I've never seen two people look as in love as you and Marty. You two looked at each other like no one else in the world existed. It was disgusting for the longest time, and then I realized that I wasn't disgusted by it. I envied it. You and Blake? He may look at you like that, but you sure as hell know there's someone else in this world when you're looking at him."

Once her speech was finished, Carla bounded into the house and scooped up her son.

Suzanne stood stunned in the doorway. *Since when is Carla the smart one?*

❖

"So, how was your day with Suzanne?" Denise Dempsey was bursting with curiosity. Marty had decided to enjoy Sunday dinner with her, the first Sunday dinner since Abigail had passed. Marty hadn't been ready to continue that tradition without the most crucial player in her everyday life. But over the past couple of months she had been trying to resume a life Abby would be proud of her for living. "Did you have a good time?"

"Yeah." Marty was tempted to drown out her mother's question with the hand mixer she had poised over a bowl of boiled potatoes, cream, and butter. She gave into that temptation. *The potatoes won't mash themselves.* That only bought her a few minutes of distraction.

"Did you two talk?" Denise looked over the rim of her glasses as she dished out a spoonful of peas next to a healthy portion of roast beef.

"Of course we talked. Did you think I took her on a silent boat ride?" Marty chortled and poured them both a glass of red wine.

"You know exactly what I mean, and I do not appreciate your sarcasm."

"I'm sorry." Marty allowed herself to think as she chewed. There really wasn't much to tell, and she surely wasn't going to tell her mother about how Suzanne wound up on top of her. She swallowed. "We talked some, but not about anything important. Mostly about the past."

"Reliving memories is a good start. She'll remember how good her life was when she was with you."

Marty nodded gently. "It felt good. I know we haven't been apart for a long time really, but when I look at her, I feel like it's been much, *much* longer."

"That's because it has been. I told you we needed to talk, and this is exactly why. Ever since Abigail got sick, you two hadn't been the same."

"Of course not, we were helpless."

"And it is understandable how two parents change once their child is diagnosed with such a serious illness, but you two acted as if you had separated then. Like your plan was to divide and conquer."

Marty resigned herself to the truth. Her mother was right, and she saw it then too. They had never faced the obstacle together. The way Suzanne accused her of never being around at the hospital haunted Marty every night when she struggled to sleep.

"I didn't mean to upset you."

"You didn't." Marty felt the tear on her cheek run toward her chin, "I just didn't see it until the end. By then, it was too late." She sat back in her chair.

"Neither of you saw it." Denise reached across the table and gripped Marty's hand.

"I was so blind—"

"No, you weren't!" Marty's mother shut her down immediately. "Your sole focus was on your child, just like any good parent."

"But if I had just been there more, called a couple more times, maybe if I had told her I loved her more…" Marty looked down at her mother's hand and swallowed the pain in her throat. She took a deep, shaky breath through her nose. "We could've been okay."

"Did Suzanne try? Did she reach out to you and ask for or offer help through all of this?"

"No, but that's Suzie. She doesn't ask for help or talk about things when she's really upset or scared. She prefers to hide them until they go away or work through it herself. I was her wife. I should have made her talk to me, and I should've done everything in my power to give her the help she needed." Marty started to sob.

"Martha, look at me," Denise demanded gently. When Marty looked at her with watery jade eyes, she set her posture firmly. "You will not cry over the past, do you hear me?" Marty nodded. "You will carry Abigail in your heart as you find happiness in the future. Her memories will assist you and Suzanne as you rebuild what has only been fractured, not broken. You two are far from broken."

"I hope you're right, Mom." Marty lowered her head and rested it on their joined hands. "God, I hope you're right."

And Lived Happily Ever After

The road seemed more like bumpy, patchy pavement. Unusual for their neighborhood, but they had only been driving for five minutes. How far and in what direction did they go? Suzanne kept her ears open in hopes of catching a telltale sign of their surroundings, but Marty was careful to keep the radio turned up. Normally, this would annoy Suzanne. She hated being clueless, and she really wasn't a fan of surprises. But when Marty and Abigail woke her up that morning with bright smiles and breakfast in bed, Suzanne was ready for any plans on the horizon. She just hadn't expected the blindfold.

"Are we there yet?" She spoke loudly enough to be heard over the constant strum of a guitar and pounding drums. "This blindfold is making me dizzy."

"No it's not." Marty placed her right hand on Suzanne's thigh. "You're just anxious because you hate surprises."

"Says the woman insisting on surprising me."

"It's our wedding anniversary, the first anniversary we're actually celebrating since Abby was born. It should be special."

"It'd still be special without making me blind."

"Hush." Marty took the next turn a bit sharper than necessary, causing Suzanne to topple slightly to the side. Just as she opened her mouth to scold Marty, the car came to a stop. "We're here."

Suzanne waited impatiently for Marty to exit the car and come around to open her door. Once Suzanne had both feet on the ground, she started speaking again.

"You know I can still hear and smell, right? I know we're at the docks." She felt Marty grab on to her bicep and pull her gently forward, and let Marty guide her down the familiar planks, the sound of small waves crashing against wooden piles surrounding her.

"Your detective skills never cease to amaze me, Suzie. Here we are." Marty stripped away the blindfold with a flourish and looked triumphant when Suzanne's blue eyes flew open and sparkled with surprise.

SAM's deck was lined with white Christmas lights, with a large blanket spread out in the center, covered with plush pillows. Next to the makeshift bed was a bottle of champagne on ice and cooler with what the blonde could only assume was some sort of delectable goodies.

"Martha Dempsey! This is beautiful," Suzanne said.

Marty grinned wildly, an almost shy expression taking over as she dug the heel of her stiletto into the dock. "Jeez, we've been together for years, and it's weird to hear you call me that." She scratched at the back of her neck as Suzanne chuckled. "You really like it?"

"I love it." Suzanne stepped forward and looked up into shimmering green eyes. "And I love you." Tilting on the toes of her black loafers, Suzanne kissed Marty softly and wrapped her arms around her lithe waist, reveling in the smooth material of the little black dress Marty had chosen for the occasion. She let the kiss deepen as she continued to feel along the curves of Marty's sides down to mid-thigh, where the telltale signs of a garter belt lay. She swallowed hard. "I like this dress too." She spoke against Marty's smiling mouth.

"I imagined you would." Marty's voice was deep, smoky, and arousing as she pulled away. She extended her left hand. "Shall we?"

Suzanne laced their fingers together and the two women ascended the boat, both filled with excitement for the evening to come.

❖

"I expected the strawberries and chocolates when I saw the champagne, but the macaroni and cheese with cut-up hot dogs was a surprise."

"Well, I do know the fastest way into my wife's pants is by cooking her favorite foods and making sure she's liquored up." Marty took another sip of her champagne and settled against the mountain of pillows beside her wife.

"So, this whole evening is about sex?"

"No!" Marty's eyes grew wide. "I wanted this evening to be about us and the love we have for—" Suzanne cut her off with a kiss. "Mmm." Marty's gentle hum of approval vibrated against Suzanne's smiling lips.

"I know we love each other." Suzanne paused to take the champagne glass from Marty and placed it to the side. "But let's focus on how hot we still are for each other after marriage and a baby." She turned her body and pressed her full length against Marty.

"I am still quite enamored by you."

"Yeah?"

"Yes."

"Tell me more."

Marty met Suzanne's demand with a tender, nearly salacious look. This had been a common occurrence since the birth of their daughter. Though most of her insecurities had been banished, Suzanne reveled in Marty's superior way with words when it came to describing the passion that continuously burned between them.

"Even though we often fall asleep with a child between us, it doesn't stop my mind from wandering." As Marty spoke, she traced the outline of Suzanne's jaw with the tip of her index finger. "Being at work and dealing with clients doesn't distract me from thoughts of you either." Marty ghosted the pad of her thumb over Suzanne's full lips. "Sometimes all I can think about is how you taste."

Suzanne couldn't contain herself as Marty's words caused her hips to jerk forward and she ran her tongue along Marty's thumb. Marty's nostrils flared, and she inhaled sharply.

"I love you, Marty." Suzanne rested her weight on one elbow

as she raised her free hand and cradled Marty's cheek. "I don't tell you that enough."

"You show me every day." Marty beamed.

"I know," Suzanne rolled her eyes at the sudden emotion causing her voice to waver, "but I need to tell you more. I don't think you realize what your eyes do to me, or that crooked smile you love to flash so often."

"My smile is crooked? I thought that was the only straight thing about me." Marty feigned shock, and Suzanne pushed at her.

"You're funny, but you need to shut up and let me say this." Suzanne looked at Marty as she mouthed a silent apology and then smiled. A torrent of butterflies let loose low in Suzanne's belly. Even a breath full of therapeutic bay air did little to calm her racing heart and quivering insides.

"It took me a long time to get comfortable with the idea of essentially belonging to another person, but I think that's the greatest lesson I've learned from being married to you. Marriage isn't about belonging to someone, but belonging *with* someone." Suzanne laced her fingers around Marty's. "I was so stubborn, and you pushed right past it."

"I demolished your stubborn walls."

"You did," Suzanne agreed before swallowing against the lump that had formed in her throat. "I love you so much. I love waking up to the sound of you getting ready in the morning. I love listening to you as you read a book that's particularly frustrating or suspenseful. Your breathing changes, and you shift around like you have ants in your pants." They both giggled lightly. "You're so strong in all the ways I'll never be, and you never hesitate to show me your weaknesses. I love that." Suzanne leaned forward and kissed her gently.

"I love your scent. Especially right here," Suzanne traced the delicate skin where Marty's neck met her shoulder. "Your skin is so soft, I could get lost in it for hours." She trailed her fingers down between Marty's breasts. "But most of all, I love your heart because it chose me for some strange, unbelievable reason. Out of every person in this world, you fell for me. I don't know what I did to deserve you, but I am so, so lucky to call you my wife." A tear slid down the side of Suzanne's face.

"Since when are you the wordy one?" Marty said before she pressed her lips to Suzanne's.

"I say all that, and you had to be a smartass and make a joke?" After one more firm kiss, Suzanne pulled back to give Marty a chastising look.

"Of course," Marty said before lowering her hand to the button of Suzanne's dark wash jeans. "I know how uncomfortable you get when I put too much focus on your emotional moments. So instead of talking, I'm going to show you just how much I love you back by worshiping every inch of your gorgeous body."

"Oh. *Oh!*" Suzanne gasped as Marty targeted the damp patch on her panties and applied just the perfect amount of pressure to the spot. Her eyes rolled back slightly before closing completely.

"Look at me. Before I lose you to my impressive talents, I want you to listen. Are you listening?" She punctuated her question with a pinch to Suzanne's engorged clit.

"Yesss," Suzanne hissed.

"I fell in love with you, but you took a chance on me. You could've had anyone. *I* am the lucky one." Whatever words Suzanne could conjure up died on her moist lips as Marty pushed her cotton panties aside and sank into wet heat. Suzanne's inner muscles contracted immediately around the pleasurable invasion.

Marty's pace was slow and languid, torturous for Suzanne. She couldn't move her hips fast enough, and the little room available in her jeans made it hard for all of her target spots to be reached in unison.

Suzanne growled in frustration. "Fuck this." She pulled Marty's hand from the front of her pants and stood. Within seconds, she'd stepped out of her jeans and underwear, straddling her motionless, and slightly surprised, wife. "Give me your hand." Without any more instruction, Suzanne sank down on Marty's two fingers and perfectly positioned palm.

She started moving slowly, but that pace only lasted momentarily before her movements became more erratic. Suzanne was about to ask for more—more fingers, more pain, more pleasure—but her wife already knew exactly what she needed. Marty bit Suzanne's breast through her thin linen shirt. It wasn't enough. Suzanne pulled back and haphazardly unbuttoned the blouse before pulling down the cup of her bra. Marty bit down again, sinking into creamy flesh and swirling her tongue around one stiff nipple. Suzanne stopped moving.

"God, yes." She ground her hips down into tight circles, Marty applying just the right amount of pressure to her throbbing clit. Suzanne's stomach started to tighten, a coil of earth shattering pleasure wound tightly, low in her belly. "God, right there."

"You know, if you keep calling me that—"

Suzanne silenced her with a kiss. "Don't stop!" She gripped a fistful of Marty's hair and gave it a hearty tug. Kissing was nearly impossible at this point. Suzanne breathed raggedly into Marty's mouth.

Suzanne's orgasm was fast approaching. Every sensation that had been clawing its way beneath her skin was settling in the small area of engorged, sensitive flesh between her quivering thighs. She was ready to be overcome with not just pleasure, but love and security and everything else that went hand in hand with being loved by Marty Dempsey.

"*Yes!*" The word echoed out across the bay as the water rippled along with her constricting inner muscles. Wave after wave shook through Suzanne and finally she collapsed against Marty, sated and ravenous all at once.

Marty stopped peppering small kisses along her damp hairline as Suzanne stood up. "What're you…?"

Suzanne stood within a foot of Marty, discarding first her blouse and then the bra they had managed to work their way around earlier.

Suzanne was completely naked, illuminated by nothing more than the early evening moonlight and string lighting, and she had never felt more beautiful than she did in that moment as Marty gazed at her hungrily. They had seen each other naked thousands of times, and Marty still looked awestruck. She strolled over casually to where they had initially dropped their bags and coolers and picked up the blindfold Marty had used on her earlier. Suzanne laced the silky material between the fingers on both of her hands and pulled it taut.

"I think it's time for payba—"

"WOO!"

Both women jumped as a loud cheer and a low air horn echoed in the distance. Suzanne dropped to the deck gracelessly, a loud thud and smack accompanying the movement. "It's too dark. They couldn't have seen me." Marty lay back beside her wife and pulled a blanket over both their bodies while her laughter slowed to a steady chuckle.

"Judging by the thumbs up you received, I'd say the moon is brighter than you think."

"No!" Suzanne's head whipped up, and she stared at Marty's playful grin. "You're just messing with me." She narrowed her eyes dangerously.

"Am I?"

"You better be."

"Or what? Will it be time for payback?" Marty started to lean in for a kiss, but Suzanne's warm lips were nowhere to be found.

Suzanne didn't get her payback that night, but an unsuspecting Marty was a wonderful subject to prey upon for the whole following week.

CHAPTER ELEVEN

Suzanne tossed another shirt to the side, writing it off as imperfect for the occasion. A night out at a bar was far from formal, but it still mattered to her that she looked good. Other than Marty's barbecue, Suzanne hadn't spent time with anyone outside of family or Blake. She wanted to avoid others questioning her well-being and emotional status, something she always found funny. People could be so invasive if they thought you were on the brink of an emotional breakdown.

"Are you sure you don't want me there?" Blake asked from the doorway of Suzanne's small bedroom. Why did he have to phrase it that way?

"It's not about wanting or not wanting you there." Suzanne stared at her open closet.

"I can drive you and pick you up, in case you have a few drinks."

"I don't plan on drinking." She pulled out a blouse and appraised it for a moment, imagining herself in a bar wearing it. It didn't work.

"Are you pregnant?" Blake's question caused Suzanne to drop the hanger she was holding.

"What? Why would you ask me that?" Suzanne's mind reeled. Was Blake listening in on her conversation with Carla the other night?

"I don't know, I mean," Blake scratched at his chin, "your mood has been all over the place lately, and now you're heading to a bar with no plans of drinking."

"Blake, a lot of people go to bars and don't drink." Suzanne laughed at his idea of pregnancy symptoms and nearly asked if that was what he had learned in nursing school. She spared him the sarcastic quip, not wanting the conversation to escalate into an argument.

"And I found the tests under your bathroom sink." When Suzanne looked at Blake, his arms were crossed over his chest. He looked cocky, like he had her right where he wanted her. "Are you pregnant?" he asked again.

Suzanne was at first annoyed, feeling like her privacy had been invaded, but she had told him to treat her house like his own when he stayed over. That's what engaged couples did. But this was unexpected and something she had planned on keeping between herself and her sister.

"No, I'm not pregnant." At his blank stare, Suzanne knew he needed more of an explanation than that. "I had a brief irrational moment, so I took a test."

"You should've told me."

"There was nothing to tell! Can we please just drop it?" Suzanne stripped off her shirt and tossed it in the direction of a laundry basket, missing. She grabbed the first tank top she saw and pulled it on.

"Will Marty be there?" Blake questioned meekly. Suzanne looked at him, but he was looking at the floor.

"She will be, yes."

"That's good."

Suzanne narrowed her eyes. "It is good."

"You two have been talking a lot lately."

"Just say what you're thinking, Blake," Suzanne said in a huff. *What's his problem tonight?* She crossed her arms and stood defiantly, ready for this tense conversation to go another round.

"I'm not thinking anything really, I'm just making an observation. That's all."

"Sounds like more than an observation."

"And you're getting very defensive." Blake's voice started to rise. He wiped at his face roughly and adjusted his glasses before approaching Suzanne. He placed his hands on her shoulders. "I'm not starting a fight, I'm just trying to figure out a way to ask if there's anything I need to worry about."

Suzanne pulled back. "Like what?" Blake's jaw tensed and released a few times. Suzanne wasn't sure how to read that.

"I love you and I trust you." Blake grabbed Suzanne's hand and held it to the center of his chest. "But you've been spending time with Marty and talking to her a lot. Now you're insisting I stay home when you're going to meet a group of friends at a bar…" Blake let his sentence drop off. He already said the minimum needed to insinuate *everything*.

Suzanne looked deeply into his chocolatey eyes and saw no malice, just a hint of jealousy laced with insecurity. She didn't intend for the next words out of her mouth to be a lie, but she didn't want anyone getting hurt. "It's a girls' night."

Marty had been both anticipating and dreading this night out for a while. She didn't feel right celebrating anything, let alone one of her friends gaining another year to her life. Having a small get-together at her own home to prove to her friends that she was, in fact, surviving was completely different. This was cheery music and laughter and smiling. It all made Marty feel guilty, but Annmarie wouldn't accept no for an answer.

The loud music was thoroughly distracting. The thundering bass and the loud clatter around Marty had pulled her attention in fifteen different directions since she had walked through the worn wooden door an hour earlier, but that was two beers ago. Before she saw Suzanne walk up to the bar.

"Marty?" Hearing her name jostled Marty back to her present company. She turned and looked at Annmarie. "Did you listen to a word I said?"

"Of course!" Marty's features twisted comically, as if she was offended by such a question.

"So, has that ever happened to you?" Annmarie's dark eyebrow raised sharply. Marty knew she was caught, so she might as well play along.

"Yes?"

"You've found a dead body in a vacant home before?"

Marty choked. "You what?"

"I knew you weren't listening to me. I can always tell when you check out." Annmarie chortled lightly before turning to see what she was looking at. Suzanne was standing just on the outskirts of their small group, waiting patiently for the bartender to pay her the appropriate amount of attention. "Speaking of checking out…"

Marty scrunched her nose at her friend's implication. "I wasn't checking anyone out."

"Don't lie to me." Annmarie bit into her martini olive. She chewed slowly, and Marty wondered if she was expecting more of an explanation or if the subject would be dropped. "You look worried." Annmarie sipped her drink. "I thought you said you two were in a good place."

"We are."

"Then why do you look terrified?"

"Look around us! It's been a long time since we've been out like this."

"Well," Annmarie slid a bit closer and continued in a voice that could barely be heard over the music, "it's a good thing you came separately, then." Marty shot her a confused look. "If things get awkward, you can make a quick exit without doing any harm." Annmarie shrugged and finished her drink. "I'm going to the bathroom." Marty was left alone.

Suzanne was thirty feet away. Marty stood still, the bottle of beer dripping condensation along her numb fingertips, and gathered her waning courage. Why was she so nervous now? Why did she care so much about what her friends would think if they saw them talking? These were people she barely heard from after the divorce and only received sympathy cards from in the mail after Abigail's passing. Charlotte and Annmarie were the only friends who checked on her regularly, and Marty knew they did the same for Suzanne.

So why did it matter what Bonnie and Steve or Carol and Teresa thought at all?

"This is ridiculous," Marty grumbled under her breath and set her beer down on the bar before advancing on Suzanne. As she approached, she noticed Suzanne eyeing up a full shot glass. It looked like it could be tequila, but Marty wasn't sure. "Hey."

Suzanne threw back the shot like the experienced drinker she wasn't, turning and smiling bashfully though a disgusted grimace. "Hey, yourself." Suzanne's voice was deeper thanks to the burn of the alcohol. A few droplets glistened on her lower lip, and Marty watched transfixed as they gathered in the middle. Suddenly, those lips were moving again. "I wasn't sure if you were going to be here," Suzanne turned her attention to the full pint of beer the bartender handed her. "Thank you."

"I wasn't sure if I would be either, but you know how persuasive Annmarie can be." Marty flashed a sideways smirk. Before Suzanne could agree, Marty said, "No Blake?" Her curiosity really would kill her one day. She could hear her mother's voice screaming from the back of her mind, *Leave well enough alone!*

"No." Suzanne looked at her glass. "I told him we were having a girls' night." Both women looked over to the table of husbands before looking at one another once again. Marty tried to school her expression, to wipe her face free of any obvious intrigue or surprise. "I'm weird about him being around my—*our* friends." Suzanne sighed in resignation and gulped her beer like it was a marathon runner's first bottle of water at the finish line.

Marty nodded noncommittally. She really didn't know what to say to that. If she had been seeing someone new, she'd probably feel the same way, but if she really cared for the person it really wouldn't matter. "Is it because he's a man or because they're *our* friends?" Marty dared to ask.

"Neither." Suzanne stared into the distance for a moment before changing her answer. "Both? Maybe? They all know I'm bisexual, so they won't care that I'm with a man, but I still feel like they're judging me."

"It doesn't really matter, you know that, right?" Marty looked steadily into her eyes and spoke more to herself than to Suzanne. "It doesn't matter what they think. All that matters is that you're happy." A silence passed between them. Marty looked at the lines etched into Suzanne's forehead and wondered for a moment whether she really was happy.

"You were never fazed by my sexuality."

"Why would I be?" Marty asked. "You're gorgeous and sexy. I knew I'd have to fight people off to be with you. I didn't care whether I fought men, women, or both. All that mattered to me was winning!"

Suzanne looked away from Marty with a laugh. "This is so weird."

"What?" Marty grinned. Suzanne's laughter was infectious.

"Being here with you, but not *with* you." Suzanne winced.

"Oh, yeah." Marty scratched at the back of her neck. She thought it best not to tell her she had just had a similar conversation with Annmarie, right after being caught checking Suzanne out.

Truth be told, the situation was even more bizarre than Marty was willing to admit at first. After Abigail's birth, their late-night outings and time spent with friends dwindled, but they were completely inseparable when they were out. Marty looked around at the familiar faces and noticed how couples naturally did that, especially married parents. This was their time to be free. She watched as Charlotte snuggled up to her husband and slid her hand into his back pocket. Off in a quiet corner, Carol had Teresa casually pinned against the wall, engaging in an intimate conversation.

"Were we that sickening?" Marty started at Suzanne's voice. "I mean, I know we were bad, but—"

"We were worse." Marty knew Suzanne was ready to argue. "You always had your hands on me."

"Yeah, well, you used to tell me you loved me even if I was just going to the bathroom!" Suzanne nearly scoffed. Marty felt a pang of lovesickness, and judging by the uncomfortable shuffle Suzanne performed, she'd noticed it as well. This wasn't a safe topic.

"Let's just agree that we were awful." Marty expected a smart remark in response, but Suzanne swallowed another shot and finished off her beer.

"Forget that." Suzanne made a show of slamming the empty glass onto the bar's glistening surface. "Let's dance." She threw her head back in the direction of the small, cramped makeshift dance floor. She obviously wasn't willing to allow Marty a say because she gripped her hand and dragged her along.

"I don't think we should," Marty said. After what had nearly happened on the boat, it wouldn't exactly be prudent to put themselves in a similar position. *Would it? Wait. Why am I trying to talk myself out of this?*

"Come on, Marty! I haven't been out in so long, and you know how much I love to dance." She batted her lashes, and Marty's resistance was gone.

Suzanne's wide eyes were full of so much excitement, Marty had no choice but to grip her hand a little tighter and make a show of twirling her. Suzanne's gleeful laugh lit something inside Marty could've sworn deserted her long ago. She released Suzanne's hand and allowed herself to fully enjoy the moment she found herself in.

Suzanne performed slow, hypnotic rolls to the tempo of the blaring music. Marty moved in time, but all she could think of was that Suzanne was so close. Marty knew exactly how it would feel to press herself against her ex-lover's back, what her hair would smell like, and how the base of her neck was probably already damp from exertion. Marty stepped forward. If Suzanne wanted to dance with her, all she had to do was step back. And she did.

Marty bit back the small moan she felt build at the contact between her hips and Suzanne's backside. The natural instinct and synchronization between them all came flooding back. They swayed and shuffled back and forth, grinding their hips together seductively. Marty and Suzanne had been a couple long enough to know exactly which dance moves would be flirty and which would nearly incinerate their dancing partner.

Marty felt something shift in Suzanne during one particular song. She had reached back and grabbed Marty's hips with a nearly painful grip, causing her ass to grind just a little harder into her crotch. A jolt of pleasure ripped through Marty, and she wanted more pressure. She *needed* more pressure, and she could tell by the way Suzanne's arms flexed that she was willing. Marty wrapped her arms around Suzanne's waist and flattened her palms against her taut abdomen. She pulled Suzanne in so her back was flush against Marty's breasts. Marty pressed her cheek against Suzanne's ear and felt how hot she was. She looked down at the little beads of perspiration forming in her cleavage.

Marty wanted to taste that sweat.

She turned her head slightly and pressed her soft lips to the reddened shell of Suzanne's ear. She was ready to state her wants and demands, but reality stopped her.

"I've got to get going." Marty all but pushed Suzanne away and made a beeline for the door. Just as she stepped out into the fresh air, someone grabbed her wrist. When she spun around, she faced a glassy-eyed Suzanne.

"I'm sorry," Suzanne said. Her chin started to quiver, weakening Marty's resolve.

"You have nothing to be sorry for." Marty reached out and fixed a few mussed strands of blond hair that fell on Suzanne's forehead. Marty watched as her ex blinked slowly at her. "Come on, let me drive you home."

"You don't have to," Suzanne protested weakly.

"You're a lightweight and had two shots with a lager chaser. You may not be feeling drunk yet, but you definitely need a ride." She pressed her hand gently to the small of Suzanne's back and led her in the direction of her car. Marty opened the passenger side door and waited for Suzanne to get comfortable in the worn seat before closing it. She took a deep breath of comforting, humid night air before getting behind the steering wheel.

"You have all of your things?" Marty looked Suzanne over as she shifted in the passenger seat. Suzanne nodded.

"I'm sorry for dancing with you like that." The words were out of Suzanne's mouth before Marty even had the chance to start the car. "I just don't know how to…"

"We don't know how to dance without touching each other. I know." Marty smiled what she hoped was a comforting smile before putting her key in the ignition and starting the car. It seemed to start the sky above them as well; lightning weaved throughout fluffy clouds.

"Is it supposed to rain?" Suzanne leaned forward and looked up through the windshield. A fat droplet splashed against the glass, answering her question. A rumble of thunder echoed in the distance, and the screen of Marty's phone flashed from the console between them.

"It's a coastal flood warning." Marty glanced once at the words punctuated with a red exclamation point and back to Suzanne. "Let's get you home. Where am I heading?" Marty watched as Suzanne's drowsy face contorted with confusion. "I have no idea where you live now."

"Oh, I'm renting a small house in Spring Lake Heights for now. Just head in that direction, and I'll direct you once we get closer." Suzanne looked out the window, and Marty followed the directions.

The car ride had grown awkward. Their easy conversation in the bar or even the casual talks they shared over the phone during the past weeks seemed to elude them. Marty wanted to ask if Blake was renting the home as well or if he lived somewhere else, and if they were currently house hunting as any other soon-to-be married couple would. Should she offer to help them?

That would be awkward, Marty thought. She squinted at the disappearing road before them. The rain was coming down in sheets, but she knew the roads well enough to avoid large puddles. Should she mention some listings far from Point Pleasant to ensure she wouldn't run into them hand in hand at a local market looking through the fresh produce? *That would be deceptive yet incredibly beneficial to my survival.* Marty was about to suggest it, but Suzanne spoke first.

"How do you know about Tess's guacamole skills?" she said in a voice so delicate, so lacy thin, Marty wasn't sure she heard her correctly.

"What?" *What does guacamole have to do with anything?* Marty leaned over as far as her seat belt would allow in order to hear Suzanne more clearly above the pitter-patter of heavy rain.

"At the barbecue, you were raving about how good Tess's guacamole was. I was curious as to how you knew." Suzanne started biting at her thumbnail, something she did every time she got nervous. That clued Marty in to exactly how many layers this question truly had. It was loaded.

Marty took a deep breath and tightened her grip on the steering wheel. Something about her question dug its way beneath her skin. Tess had always been a small thorn in the paw of their marriage. Marty had reassured Suzanne she wasn't interested in Tess, but her jealousy seemed to be alive and well, even though their marriage was anything but. Maybe that was why Marty found her hackles rising.

What was Suzanne really asking? If she had decided to move on with Tess? Seek comfort in the other woman just like she had already done with Blake? Or was she asking if that comfort had been sought out well before their marriage ended?

Marty took another deep breath to calm herself. "When Abigail passed, a few of the neighbors made it a habit to stop by and check on me, especially since they knew about the divorce." Marty shrugged slightly, no longer being ashamed of others' perceptions of her being helpless without Suzanne. "They always brought food, and Tess made guacamole once. I complimented it, so she kept bringing it around." The explanation received nothing more than a nod in response. "There's nothing going on between us," she added in spite of herself.

"That's none of my business." Suzanne spoke mostly to her lap. The car was stopped at a red light as the pouring rain pounded around them.

"No, it's not, but it's what you wanted to know." The light turned green.

"Take the next right and follow it down to the end. Just stop there, I'm on the corner." Suzanne put an end to the former conversation. "Thanks again for the ride. I would've been fine, though."

Marty frowned when she realized they had arrived at the end of the street. She wanted to talk more, explain more, but she knew the timing wasn't right.

"You're welcome." Marty steered the car to the side of the road and put it in park. "Let me know if you need a ride to get to your car tomorrow."

"Thanks." Suzanne reached for the door handle and started to make her getaway.

Against her better judgment, Marty reached out and grabbed Suzanne's hand to keep her in place. Marty felt the diamond ring that wasn't hers impressed on her palm.

"Suzanne." Marty wasn't entirely sure what she was going to say, but she needed Suzanne to know her heart always belonged to her. "I've never—"

Suzanne kissed her, tangling her hands in Marty's hair as she tugged it and Marty moaned. Marty bit down on Suzanne's lower lip, and she soothed whatever discomfort she caused with a healing swipe of her tongue. The taste of Suzanne reminded her of a happiness she'd once lived. A happiness that was no longer hers. Marty knew it was the liquor talking. It would be a mistake to regret the next morning, Marty was sure of that. She pulled away.

Suzanne apologized for the second time that evening, but her apology died in a storm of raindrops as she ran from the car and into the darkness that swallowed the quiet neighborhood whole.

Until...

"This home is being sold 'as is' because the owners are expected to move into their new home in Florida by the end of this month," Marty said to the young couple standing behind her as she slid the key into the lock. "It's in good condition, so don't let that intimidate you." She pushed the front door open and encouraged her clients to step inside.

"Why are they moving?" the taller of the two men asked. Gary and Jacob were the kind of clients Marty loved to work with. They had a short list of "must haves" and an open mind regarding everything else. Gary asked the questions while Jacob quietly surveyed the structural details.

"They're older and retired. It just seems to be the natural progression of life in this area." They both gave her puzzled looks. "People tend to run away from the winter," she said. "I happen to enjoy the cold very much, but maybe that'll change in another twenty years." She chuckled brightly, and they seemed to relax.

"I love snow," Jacob said as he stepped beyond the front door and looked up into the high ceilings of the foyer. "Nice entryway." Gary followed closely.

Marty rubbed her palms together in hopes of warding off the early November chill. Autumn in New Jersey was just about as misleading as springtime was. Some mornings all you needed was a light sweater, but by lunchtime you wished you'd packed a down parka. Today was one of those days.

"Clean lines." Marty looked over to where Jacob's voice came from. He was checking out a clean, glass-enclosed gas fireplace.

"When was the house built?" Gary asked from the center of the great room.

"It's fairly new construction—1999—so I'm sure you'll get a sense of some of the more modern elements like bigger closets and a full-sized pantry in the kitchen." Marty pointed in the direction of a fully updated kitchen, where stainless steel appliances and granite countertops did the rest of the talking.

"I love stainless!" Gary gawked and Marty watched as Jacob's stoic façade fell away into the familiar, softened delightful look of true love.

"They come with the house." Marty was a top real estate agent because she answered questions before they were spoken. "There's plenty of room in the backyard if you ever decide to—" Suzanne's unique ringtone cut Marty's suggestion short. "Gentlemen, why don't you look around while I take this?" She answered quickly and skipped a polite greeting.

"I'm at a showing right now. I really can't—"

"I'm on my way to the hospital with Abigail."

"What?" Marty's eyes flew open as she checked her surroundings for no real reason before checking the time: a little past noon. "What's going on? Is it you? Is it Abby? Are you okay?"

"We're fine," Suzanne said in an even tone. But Marty heard the underlying unease wrapped around those two words. She listened closely as Suzanne took a deep breath before continuing. "Abby got a really bad nosebleed."

"A nosebleed?" Marty chuckled quietly as she asked the question. Suzanne was always the more protective and paranoid of the two, so she wasn't too surprised to hear she was taking their six-year-old to the hospital over a nosebleed. "She'll be fine," she said casually. "Just plug it up with some toilet paper. I used to get them all the time."

"Marty!" Suzanne yelled loud enough to make Marty pull the phone away from her ear.

"What?"

"She's been bleeding for an hour, she's been bleeding a lot." Her whisper was more frightening than her bellow. Marty knew that whisper. Suzanne was scared.

"Jersey Shore hospital or Brick?"

"Jersey Shore."

"Let me just close up, and I'll be right there." Marty knew Suzanne's silence meant her head was spinning with possibilities. "Everything will be okay."

"Just hurry."

"I love you." She was so on edge, she nearly jumped out of her skin when Jacob approached from behind.

"I'm sorry!"

She needed to get away from this house and next to her baby girl. "I'm sorry, Jacob, but I'm going to have to cut your tour short."

"Is everything okay?" Gary sidled up next to his husband and looked on with concern.

"I have a family emergency." Marty swallowed thickly. "I'll call you tomorrow, and we'll take it from there." She was already ushering them from the property and to their car. She was grateful they had decided to drive separately that afternoon.

"Not a problem," Jacob said. "I hope everything is okay."

"Thank you." Marty walked back to her car. The wind was blowing against her, sharper and more frigid than before, matching the fear in her chest.

❖

For Suzanne, keeping her eyes on her family was a matter of survival. She watched as Marty tickled Abigail's ten little toes over and over from baby to big and back again. The giggles that filled the room were as close to a sedative as Suzanne could get even though she was surrounded by cabinets full of them. At least she figured that was what filled the shelves in the small hospital room.

"So basically what I'm trying to tell you is that all the piggies went to the market because roast beef is delicious!" Marty tickled their daughter, her voice bouncing throughout the white room. Suzanne found solace in Abigail's smile.

Suzanne's newest mantra began: *Focus on the good thoughts, throw away the bad.* She looked at Marty and took in the way sunbeams barely made it through industrial blinds to illuminate her green eyes. *Focus on the good thoughts, throw away the bad. This is just a small bump along the very long road of parenthood. She probably just needs to eat more iron or protein or vitamin B. Focus on the good thoughts, throw away—*

"For Abigail Dempsey?"

Suzanne stood so quickly at the unexpected bellow of the nurse's voice, she felt dizzy. "Yes?"

"Yes." Marty stepped forward and Suzanne was grateful for her authoritative quirks. She didn't mind standing just behind her wife.

"The doctor will be right in to see you." The young nurse looked everywhere but at the nervous parents before her. Suzanne noticed the evasive action right away. "I'm going to take Abigail down to the reception desk for a lollipop, if that's all right with you both?" Her smile was bright but stiff as she looked at Abigail, who was squirming on the exam table.

"She can stay—"

"It's fine." Suzanne interrupted Marty and gripped her wrist slightly.

"Come on, Abigail."

Abigail was quick to hop to her feet and follow the nurse.

"This isn't good." Suzanne's thoughts left her head and came out from her lips unknowingly.

"What do you mean?"

"They took a lot of blood, the doctor wants to talk to us alone, and the nurse wouldn't even look at us." Suzanne crossed her arms over her chest. The bulky sweater she wore did little to ward off the chill fear brought to her skin and bones.

"It's probably just a formality." Marty walked toward Suzanne slowly and placed her hands on Suzanne's rigid shoulders. "I need you to believe everything will be okay."

Suzanne looked up at Marty, curious of her phrasing. Each passing second they had been in the emergency room, Marty had managed to keep Abby smiling, but once Abby left, Marty's confidence disappeared.

"Oh, sweetheart." Suzanne pulled Marty into a hug, relishing her comforting heat. The sound of a clearing throat pulled them apart. Suzanne took a deep breath as Marty wiped away a tear.

"I'm sorry." The doctor spoke quietly as he shifted uncomfortably in his worn loafers hidden slightly by baggy navy blue scrubs.

"Hey, this is your hospital, not ours." Suzanne forced her best smile. "No need for apologies."

"Okay, well." The older gentleman shuffled over to a rolling stool that looked almost as aged as he did and sat with the force that accompanied fatigue.

Suzanne stood in front of Marty and leaned back against her. She didn't trust her legs alone to support herself. "We took a look at some of Abigail's blood test results, the ones we could expedite anyway. Her blood platelet counts are concerning."

"What? Why?" Marty said. Suzanne felt Marty grip her waist.

"They're low, very low." The doctor looked between the mothers. "Has Abigail been bruising easily or have you noticed any more bruises than usual?"

"She's a kid!" Suzanne couldn't remain calm any longer. Her voice was now high and shaky. "Kids are constantly getting hurt between athletics and recess at school and rough housing at home. I don't think twice about bruises."

"There's been more." Suzanne spun around at the meek sound of Marty's voice. She eyed her wife angrily and curiously. Why had she never said anything? Marty looked Suzanne in the eye sadly, and then she turned her attention back to the doctor. "I didn't think much of it because she's a rambunctious six-year-old," Marty said with a small smile. "But I think, maybe, since the summer she's been having a few more bruises than I've been used to seeing."

"Why wouldn't you mention that to me?" Suzanne asked.

"I didn't think of it at the time."

"What about bleeding?" The doctor interrupted the women, clearly wanting the conversation to move forward.

Suzanne took a deep breath and looked around the room. "Her gums…" she whispered.

"I'm sorry?" the doctor said.

Suzanne looked at him. "Her gums have been bleeding when she brushes her teeth. I just kept telling her to ease up. You know kids—" She stopped mid-sentence and stared blankly at the wall, blinking rapidly. Her breathing fell shallow. "What's wrong with our baby?"

"Mrs. Dempsey, I—"

"What have we been writing off as childhood naïveté or innocence or childish misbehavior?" Suzanne's question was sharp and loud, and it broke down the polite wall the emergency room doctor was hiding behind like a sledgehammer.

"These symptoms could be indicative of many things, but I would like for you to follow up with a pediatric oncologist in Pennsylvania. His name is Dr. Jeffrey Fox, and he's one of the best."

"An oncologist?" Marty sagged against the exam table.

"We already made a phone call. He's expecting you tomorrow morning." The doctor stood and placed his hand on Marty's shoulder. "Nothing is confirmed, but when test results come back like this, you want a specialist to take a look at it right away." He looked at Suzanne again. "The receptionist will give you all the office information when you leave. Give them a call just to confirm for tomorrow. Take care." He squeezed Marty's shoulder and left.

Suzanne stood in the center of the room with her arms wrapped around her midsection. Just that morning, she'd been planning out their Thanksgiving menu. Everything had changed in an afternoon.

In the next twenty-four hours, Suzanne would realize she had nothing left to be thankful for.

CHAPTER TWELVE

Marty may have been a laid-back realtor, but she was neither flighty nor forgetful. It had to be here somewhere. She rifled through her large satchel purse, a slew of expletives following every handful of empty gum wrappers and old receipts she clawed out from the bottom. She distinctly remembered putting the business card in her purse. She needed that card. Important information about her contact for a multimillion-dollar beach house her latest clients were interested in was on it. Yes, Marty could easily Google the information, but she continued her search out of principle. When had she become so careless?

"Are you okay over there? I've heard the alphabet being spelled out with curse words for the past fifteen minutes." Charlotte chuckled as she took a sip of her afternoon tea.

"I'm fine," Marty said through a clenched jaw.

"Listen, Marty." Charlotte stepped closer to her friend's desk and leaned slightly on the corner. Marty never looked up. "I know it's usually Annmarie's job to be nosy, but you've not been yourself ever since we all went out."

"I said I'm fine." Marty nearly impaled Charlotte with her stare. She backtracked and took a deep breath at Charlotte's wounded look. Charlotte was just doing what she did best: caring. "I really am okay, Charlotte. I promise." Marty smiled the best she could while she lied. "I just haven't been sleeping well, and we all know how grumpy I can be when I'm tired." She wondered if Charlotte believed one word she had just said. She just stood there with narrowed eyes, gently dipping the teabag up and down in her tropical colored mug.

What else could she say? She and Suzanne had a moment the other night that left her feeling guilty and confused and pissed off for the past few days? As the uneasy seconds of silence passed, Marty wondered how she could explain something even she thought was bizarre. She wanted Suzanne back, had plotted to make it happen, but when Suzanne had advanced, Marty had run away with her tail between her legs. Why?

"Fine," Charlotte said. "What are you looking for?" she asked, hovering over Marty.

"A business card for the realtor in charge of the three-story Victorian by the Manasquan Inlet."

"Do you have someone interested?" Charlotte's big eyes lit up.

"I do." Marty stood and dumped the contents of her purse onto her desk. "It's got to be here somewhere. I never lose—" Marty halted everything as she looked down at the small pile before her. Not a breath left her lips, not a hair moved on her head, and her eyes remained unblinking.

"Did you find it?" Charlotte reached out and touched her forearm gently. "Marty?"

Marty fell into her chair, all energy leaving her body. A chill ran down her spine, and she reached out for the small strip of colorful entwined yarn that hung from the edge of the desk.

Best friends forever. Abigail's voice was loud in her head.

"Are you feeling all right?" Charlotte put her tea down. "You're as white as a ghost." She pressed her cool hand against Marty's forehead.

Marty wound the colorful threads around her fingers. Tears filled her eyes, and she sobbed, "Best friends—" She started crying then, hysterical wails that echoed throughout the office.

Charlotte gripped her shaking shoulders. "Marty, sweetheart," she said, her voice racked with panic. "Let's go to the bathroom." Curious and worried eyes were glancing in their direction. Charlotte managed to get Marty to stand and walk very slowly toward the bathroom. Once inside, Marty sat on the toilet with a thud and continued to cry.

"Here." Charlotte tore at the toilet paper roll, unraveling more than a few healthy handfuls before thrusting the wrinkled mess at Marty. "Stay here. I'll be right back."

Charlotte rushed back to Marty's desk. "She's fine!" she called out to the entire office before picking up Marty's cell phone and dialing. "Please pick up, please pick up!"

"Hello?"

"Suzanne!" Relief washed over Charlotte. "It's Charlotte."

"Why are you calling me from Marty's phone?"

"Marty's, well…she's kind of—"

"What, Charlotte? She's what? What happened?"

"She's hysterical," Charlotte finally blurted out. "She found something in her purse that triggered it, and now she's in the bathroom sobbing. I don't even think I could get her to talk if I tried."

"Bring the phone to her." Suzanne's tone was cool, even.

Charlotte rushed back to find Marty worse for wear. Her eye makeup was now messy trails along her cheeks, and her usually clear, mossy green eyes were dulled by swollen red lids. Charlotte thrust the phone into her hands. "You're in good hands now," Charlotte whispered to herself as she backed out of the bathroom.

"Marty? Hey, Marty it's me. Suzanne." The sweet gentle cadence of Suzanne's familiar voice did little to stop Marty's tears, but her sobs became more subdued as she listened. "Charlotte tells me you're having a hard time. Want to tell me about it?"

Marty took a deep breath through her nose. Her stomach was rolling, and she was exhausted all of a sudden. She looked down through watery eyes at the small memento in her hand. The colors blurred together in a distorted rainbow.

"Remember…" Marty cleared her throat, her words barely audible. "Remember when Abigail stayed at the hospital the first time?"

"Of course."

"We stopped at the store and bought her every craft kit and coloring book they had." The sweet sound of Suzanne's laughter eased Marty's tears into a near stop.

"I think we spent close to two hundred dollars that day."

"We picked up one kit." Marty continued while she knew she was able to, "Abigail made about seventy friendship bracelets with it."

"Abby gave us each one of the best ones she made, and then she gave one to every nurse that checked on her and her doctors."

"I took mine off one day for some reason I can't even remember now, and then I couldn't find it. I thought I had lost it." Marty looked down at the small bracelet in wonder. She recalled that night she had begged Suzanne to take hers off and play along as she told Abigail how they had put them someplace special. "I found it, Suzie, I finally found it." Marty's tears started anew.

"I'm so happy you did, baby." The term of endearment Suzanne used wasn't lost on Marty as she sat in elation and stared at her findings. "What are you doing tonight?" Suzanne said abruptly.

"Nothing." Marty wiped her face with the wads of crumpled toilet paper that lay on her lap. A new, easy feeling illuminated in her chest. It felt familiar, like a deserted piece of her was finally settling back into place.

"How about I come over and cook for you? I think now is a good time to go through the things I left at the house." Marty was bewildered by Suzanne's proposition. The last time she had brought up such an idea, Suzanne fled her company. She didn't think Suzanne would be ready to spend that kind of time with her anytime soon, especially not after the other night.

"Sure, I'd really like that." Marty thought for a moment and said. "Suzanne, about the other night—"

"That'll teach me to drink like that again." Suzanne's laugh was tight, artificial in its controlled delivery. "Never again for me, not if I don't want to become like my mother."

"You'll never be like your mother." Marty defended her ex-wife quickly.

"You're right, Angela's cooking skills are lacking." Suzanne laughed again, and the serious conversation was over.

"Stop by around eight? I know it's a little late, but I have some paperwork I want to catch up on when I get home. Lord knows I've wasted enough time crying like a baby in this bathroom." Marty chuckled in embarrassment.

"Sometimes a good cry is exactly what we need." A beat of silence passed before Suzanne spoke again. "I'll see you at eight, Marty."

"See you then." They hung up and Marty left the bathroom completely unlike how she had entered it. Her radiant smile was filled with anticipation.

Their Daughter Grew Sick

The car ride really wiped her out." Suzanne said in a weak voice. Marty thought she had to be exhausted as well. They stood together in the doorway of Abigail's room and watched as her chest moved in a peaceful rhythm. The long drive back from Pennsylvania had taken its toll on everyone.

"I'm sure the weeks in the hospital didn't help." Marty spoke without thinking and regretted the words the moment Suzanne rolled her shoulders.

"You don't think I know that?" Suzanne's whisper was harsh. "After everything Abby went through, you think I'm mostly concerned about her sitting in a car?"

"That's not what I..." Marty closed her eyes and sighed deeply as Suzanne stormed off in the direction of their room.

It had been like this from the start. Tense days and silent nights were the new normal. Each and every time she tried to talk to Suzanne, she'd get the same response: "Our daughter is sick, what do you think is wrong!" Every conversation they had over the past six weeks revolved around treatments and side effects.

Whenever Marty tried to talk to Suzanne about another matter, she was shot down and reprimanded for thinking beyond what their daughter was going through. She'd always walk away guiltily, wondering what was so wrong with being concerned for themselves too. Weren't two young mothers with a daughter battling leukemia allowed a modicum of sympathy for themselves?

Marty turned and walked down the hall to their bedroom. Suzanne was already changed and beneath the covers. As Marty changed into her night clothes, she considered their life now. She knew Suzanne was scared. She was terrified too, but was it too much to ask for them to experience this terror together?

"What would you like to do this weekend?" Marty tried, not wanting to go to bed with this habitual tension between them for another night.

"Whatever Abigail wants to do."

"Is there anything you've been wanting to do with Abby? Anywhere you've been wanting to go?" Marty climbed under the covers carefully. She didn't want to disturb Suzanne if she was comfortable. Suzanne turned and looked at her, her blue eyes a shade lighter than earlier. That usually meant the anger was gone, and all that remained was fatigue.

"I've been wanting to take her to that horse farm in Howell for some time now." Suzanne's response lacked excitement, but her words weren't clipped or aggressive. Marty would take what she could get.

"We can do that." Marty reached for the book she had been trying to read for over two weeks. The children's cancer floor at the University Hospital was a hard place to concentrate even when you had nothing to do but read. "We don't have to be back at the hospital until Monday afternoon, and the doctor said there's no reason for Abby to limit herself as long as she felt up to it. Let's take her."

"I was there, Marty. I know exactly what the doctor said."

"Suzie, please." Marty dropped the book on her lap and looked at her wife. "I'm not looking to fight or argue. You're taking everything I'm saying out of context."

"Well, excuse me!" Suzanne sat up straight and Marty's head fell. "Maybe you need to be more careful with how you say things to your obviously dense wife!"

Marty shook her head in time with her quickened heartbeat. "I just want to have a nice weekend with my family." Her eyes started to glisten. She knew the tears had been prepped and ready since they left the hospital, but she tried her best to remain strong.

"Just a normal weekend with my girls." She reached out across the patterned comforter and grabbed Suzanne's hand. She didn't grip back. When Marty didn't receive a response, she played the short conversation back to herself over and over again like she did with all their recent spats. She forced herself to hear Suzanne's request one more time.

"Unless you want to take Abigail yourself?"

Suzanne pulled her hand back and folded her arms over her chest. She didn't answer Marty, which was a clear answer in and of itself.

"That's fine, you know. Take her if you'd like. We've always been good about spending alone time with her, and that shouldn't change now." Marty replaced her book on the nightstand and switched off her lamp.

She lay back and stared at the ceiling. Her eyes were wide open and her mind was far from tired even though her body was exhausted. Hundreds of thoughts floated around in her head, but she didn't want to push Suzanne. She'd have to be patient with both Abigail's healing and Suzanne's coping.

A half hour passed before Suzanne finally settled again. A soft sigh sounded out into the darkness, and Marty took stock of the positive. They were home in their own bed, which might be a small comfort along this troublesome road they were traveling, but was a comfort nonetheless. *We're a strong family*, Marty reminded herself. As her eyes started to droop, she moved to her side and reached out for her wife. Suzanne stirred momentarily before pulling herself away from Marty and scooting closer to the edge of bed. Marty opened her eyes and looked at the ruffled blond hair on the back of her wife's head.

For the first time in their marriage, Marty started to doubt that strength.

CHAPTER THIRTEEN

Marty buzzed around the house at a frantic pace. She kept reminding herself that not too long ago she had shared the space with Suzanne, and whatever prep work she was doing was unnecessary. But she wanted everything to be perfect. She made sure the throw blanket Suzanne loved to wrap around herself while watching television was across the back of the couch. Marty took out the crystal tumbler glass Suzanne always chose to drink out of, whether it was juice, soda, or wine. She even had a favorite fork with a bent prong Marty placed on the counter with the napkins. She wanted Suzanne to drown in the comforts of her former home, even if she was only able to share them with her for one night.

Once she arrived home from work, Marty showered immediately. She washed away the emotional turmoil that still clung to her after her breakdown. She dried off quickly and dressed carefully for the evening ahead. Marty chose tight, dark wash jeans and a loose fitting T-shirt that dipped low in the front. With her chestnut curls secured atop her head in a haphazard bun, she gave off a comfortable casual air while still accentuating her natural physical appeal. She recalled all the times over the years when Suzanne would compliment her for a look that required little to no effort. Marty knew how much Suzanne enjoyed this laid-back version of her.

Everything was set and in place by time the doorbell rang at eight o'clock. Marty approached the door slowly, not wanting to appear too eager. When she opened the door to a smiling Suzanne, Marty's stomach flipped and filled with a pleasant warmth.

"Hi!"

"Hey, Suzie." Marty was almost breathless. Though she had seen Suzanne multiple times recently, a new tension vibrated between them. Marty hoped this was a positive shift. Thanks either to their fumbling kiss after the bar or their earlier conversation, she felt a refreshed closeness to Suzanne. She anxiously toyed with the loose ends of the bracelet on her right wrist.

"I brought wine." Suzanne looked at the label on the bottle, then up at Marty through her long lashes. "Although I'm not sure if you'll trust me with alcohol around you ever again." She smirked devilishly.

"We'll see about that." Marty's chuckle was warm and inviting, the humor easing her racing mind. "Come in." She stepped aside to allow Suzanne inside. "I'll get the corkscrew." They walked together toward the kitchen, and Suzanne set the bag she was carrying on the counter.

"So, what're we having?" Marty opened the bottle of wine and looked at Suzanne expectantly. A slight blush colored her cheeks, and Marty decided then that Suzanne was more beautiful than ever. She took in the way Suzanne's simple burgundy tank top clung to her flat abdomen and her denim cut-off shorts hugged her full thighs. Marty took a deep, controlled breath.

"Would you think terrible things of me if I brought supplies for you to make your famous chicken Marsala?" Suzanne looked sheepishly to the glass sliding door. Marty laughed deeply. "I know you had a rough day, but I've been craving—"

"I'll happily make my chicken Marsala for you if you help me."

"Deal." Suzanne's face lit up. "Where do you want me, chef?" Marty's heart started to thud at Suzanne's flirtatious tone. It seemed so natural to kiss that victorious grin off Suzanne's gorgeous face.

"You're on chicken duty," Marty said, turning away from the temptation.

"Still don't like touching raw chicken?" Suzanne said before washing her hands.

"Who does?" Marty looked at Suzanne with disgust and offered the bag containing the packaged poultry.

The two women worked together in a perfectly choreographed preparation dance. They had worked well together for the barbecue, but this was different. Neither could figure why, but the intimacy of it all had a certain effect on their moves and interactions. No expected guests could barge in and break down the delicate atmosphere. Suzanne and Marty were just together in the kitchen, performing a task they had done so many times before.

They spoke very little and instead concentrated on dinner. Marty had a feeling Suzanne wanted to ask about what had happened that afternoon, if she was okay and if incidents like that happened often. When the silence between them became lengthy, Suzanne would open her mouth slightly, her rosebud lips starting to form a word, before she'd stop and frown at whatever thought she was holding at the moment.

"Suzie?" Marty said quietly as she started to place portions of steaming food onto ceramic plates.

"Hmm?"

"I'm okay." Marty was amused by Suzanne's surprised expression. "I mean, today was a first." She looked down at the thin bracelet secured around her wrist, took the delicate, frayed edges between her fingertips, and regarded their texture thoughtfully. "Like you said, maybe I just needed a good cry."

"Stop doing that." Suzanne shook her head roughly before taking the plates from Marty and moving them to the kitchen table.

"Doing what?" Marty asked incredulously. She took her seat across from Suzanne and watched her pick up the bent fork.

"Knowing what I'm thinking." Suzanne stabbed at her dinner. "It's creepy.

Marty laughed heartily. Though Suzanne's face was fixed in a stern facade, Marty saw around it easily. "I can't help I know you so well."

"You can try," Suzanne teased through a mouthful of tender chicken.

"That's like asking me to forget basic mathematics or the fifty states."

"Most people don't even know all fifty states."

"I'm not most people." Marty teased back casually before starting on her own dinner. She couldn't remember the last time she made chicken Marsala, one of the few dishes she had mastered over the years.

Chitchat about their respective days and jobs filled the silence that fell between large and small bites of savory decadence. They deposited their silverware on their empty plates and sat back and groaned at their tendency to overindulge. Marty washed, Suzanne dried, and all too quickly they found themselves standing outside the door to Abigail's bedroom.

"This isn't going to be easy," Suzanne said.

"I know, but I can't keep putting it off." Marty opened the door wide and stepped into the small room she found solace in every evening. "I don't want it to turn into a sort of sad museum."

"Have you changed your mind about keeping this room as is?"

"No!" Marty nearly squeaked. She cleared the emotion from her throat before continuing. "I actually want to spread some of her things throughout the house, especially in the living room and my office. It gets lonely sometimes, and I figure if I have Abby's things around I'll feel like she's still with me."

"Oh, Marty…"

"And I'm sure you'd like to have some of her things at your place." Marty swatted at a runaway tear. "I'm sure Blake won't mind."

"I wouldn't care even if he did." Suzanne spoke with an obvious fire in her tone.

"I'm just saying that when you two get married—"

"We're taking our time with that." Suzanne's shoulders fell, and she turned to look at a colorful drawing on the wall. "He's ready to marry me tomorrow, but I need time." Marty caught a small shiver running along Suzanne's body. She wondered if she should check the thermostat.

"Can't say I blame the guy. I couldn't wait to marry you. And I knew I was going to the moment I met you." Suzanne's shoulders shook slightly with laughter. Marty took a deep breath through her nose and changed the subject. "I kept all her blankets in the—"

"We were good parents, right?" Suzanne turned and looked to Marty with watery eyes. Marty froze. "I have all of these memories, you know? They're happy ones, and even some of the sad ones make me smile." Suzanne approached Marty and folded her arms across her chest. Marty was familiar with the subconscious action. She had observed it hundreds of times over the years, but it still affected her. When Suzanne was feeling weak or small or vulnerable, she'd wrap herself up in her own halfhearted embrace and then be engulfed by Marty's arms in the next instant.

Marty struggled to refrain from doing what came naturally.

"You were a wonderful mother, and even though Abby is no longer with us, you're still a mother. One of the best." Marty reached out and gripped Suzanne's forearm, a touch that was both safe and comforting.

"You were too."

"Yeah right!" Marty's bark of laughter was bitter and raw. She released Suzanne and stepped away quickly. She sat on the edge of Abigail's bed and came to rest with her elbows on her knees, staring off to the far wall, her eyes distant and empty. "I could've given her more, done better by her," she said just above a whisper.

"We gave her everything we could." Suzanne sat beside Marty on the twin-sized bed.

"That's not true," Marty said angrily. "If I hadn't—" Marty couldn't bring herself to say the words. A teardrop ran along the bridge of her nose and hung to the tip. "The last year of her life could've been happier, and maybe she would've lived longer if it were." Marty's composure fell away. She broke down into relentless tears, and Suzanne quickly pulled her into a hug.

Suzanne held her tightly. "None of this is your fault," she

whispered. "What happened between us did not lessen the quality of Abby's life, I promise you."

Marty wanted to argue. She wanted to scream and yell and tell Suzanne that she couldn't promise her that. But she didn't have the energy. She barely had the energy to cry anymore, but her body mustered up the strength and the tears continued. She heard a faint sniffle come from Suzanne, and just as she was about to apologize, Suzanne kissed her warm forehead. And then her temple and prominent cheekbone. Marty closed her eyes and relished the feel of soft skin touching along her wet eyelids and cheeks. When Suzanne's kisses came to a halt at the corner of her mouth, Marty froze.

She didn't dare turn away or advance.

Finally and ever so slowly, Suzanne enveloped Marty's lips fully with her own. Marty sighed in pleasure and relief, finally feeling at home. This was a kiss of desire and affection, not fueled by alcohol or incident. The kiss was gentle and welcoming, sweet and pure in ways Marty was sure she wasn't worthy of. It was a baptism of sorts. Troublesome sins surfaced and were washed away, leaving Marty's heart and mind clear.

Marty leaned forward and took Suzanne in her arms as she deepened the kiss. She was seeking and demanding in her advance. Her lips continued relentlessly as she sucked and nibbled Suzanne's plump lower lip. Marty kissed Suzanne deeply, her tongue tasting lost love and fruity wine. Marty framed her love's face in her hands and let her kisses become shallower. She ran the tip of her tongue along Suzanne's Cupid's bow and swallowed the moan it elicited. She reached down to the hem of Suzanne's tank top and ran the tips of her thumbs beneath the fabric. The skin-on-skin contact seemed to break the spell.

"I'm sorry." Suzanne pulled away and touched her fingers to her lips. Her eyes didn't meet Marty's.

"Stop being sorry."

"I shouldn't have done that. Not the other night or tonight." Suzanne stood and started for the door. Marty grabbed her wrist and held her in place.

"You should've never *stopped*," Marty said. "We should have never stopped."

"Marty…"

"I love you, Suzie." Marty's lips curled into a lopsided, watery grin. "I always have, and I always will. There will never be anyone else for me." Marty ran the pad of her thumb along the soft skin on the inside of Suzanne's wrist. "I'd much rather live a lonely life than spend a day with someone that isn't you." Marty took Suzanne's stunned silence as encouragement to continue. She looked into her shimmering sapphire eyes. "You and I were just meant to be together. It's so painfully obvious. Don't you see?" Marty took a tentative step forward and closed the distance between their bodies.

"I felt so alone," she continued. "I felt like I failed you, and I couldn't help our daughter. I let a moment of weakness ruin my life." Her voice broke, her apology coming out in a whimper. "I am so sorry. I've never known regret like this. Losing Abigail and cheating on you has made me feel like my heart has been torn to pieces. But what's left still beats for you." Marty's chin quivered. "That guilt will be with me until I die." She reached up to cup Suzanne's cheek and brushed away a tear.

"I don't expect forgiveness from you, but I would do anything for another chance." Marty leaned in for a kiss and was met with emptiness. Suzanne pulled back.

"I can't." Marty watched as Suzanne looked her in the eyes and denied her. Her stomach churned. "I can't do this to Blake."

"You're not like me," Marty scoffed. The pain searing throughout her chest was a mixture of anger and despair.

"That's not what I meant."

"I get it, and I don't blame you. Blake's a great guy." Defeated, Marty left the room with a meek nod and made her way down the stairs. Just the short break from Suzanne's deep gaze gave her a chance to collect herself. It only took a minute for Suzanne to join her by the front door. "I do want you in my life. I guess I just wasn't ready." An odd sense of numbness overtook Marty as she smiled hollowly. "We'll try again sometime." She opened the door and stepped aside. "Good night, Suzanne."

Suzanne's head tilted to the side as she scrutinized Marty. She looked so full of questions and arguments, but instead of speaking, she walked wordlessly through the door and out to her car.

They Grew Angry and Tired

The beat-up Subaru continued to circle the parking garage, going up and up toward the few empty spots left. Marty cursed to herself quietly. No matter how early she agreed to meet with clients, she always found herself arriving at the hospital during the afternoon rush. She'd most likely wind up on the roof again. She parked in a hurry and rushed in the direction of the aged parking garage elevators, clutching her long wool coat to her body in an attempt to keep the whipping winter breeze from cutting through her. By the time she made it into the elevator, her hair was disheveled and partially stuck to her pale pink lipstick. The metal doors reflected the dark hollows of her eyes. She couldn't hide them with makeup anymore. She pressed the button for ground level.

The past four weeks of treatments had been hard on everyone, especially Abigail. Three times a week she had been put through the wringer. By the time Friday rolled around, if she showed no signs of a fever and her numbers were promising, she was allowed to go home for two days. Two days where Suzanne and Marty did everything to make her comfortable and happy, but did very little of it together. Christmastime renewed Marty's hopes of feeling like a family again, not just two women standing beside their daughter as she fought an invisible villain.

Marty walked briskly from the parking garage into the hospital. She greeted the security guard with the same pleasantries as usual. She maneuvered the well-known path to and up the elevators. The pediatric ward was just as busy as the rest of the hospital in the early afternoon, but the patients were decidedly more pleasant. When Marty turned the corner, she spotted her wife immediately. Suzanne was standing just outside of Abigail's room with her arms folded and her toe tapping. She continued forward with a deep breath and decided to make an attempt to cheer her wife up.

"Sorry I'm running so late." Marty kissed Suzanne's cheek briefly. "Although I'm not too sorry because you're still beautiful even when you're annoyed with me."

"Dr. Fox wants to talk to us." Those seven words inflicted so much fear.

Marty followed Suzanne as she hurried along to where Dr. Fox was waiting for them at the nurse's station.

"Good afternoon, Marty." The kind doctor held out his hand, and Marty readily took it.

"What's going on?" Suzanne cut through the formal greetings. Marty could tell her patience was waning.

"Nothing much, and that's the problem." The doctor regarded both women with warm, gentle eyes. "We're not seeing an improvement in Abby's numbers." A commotion erupted from behind the counter. Several nurses retrieved papers that had scattered across the floor.

"Sorry about that," Dr. Fox said. "We've had a change of staff, and some of the new nurses are still trying to figure things out."

"What about Abigail's numbers?" Marty cared very little about the hospital staff floundering about. She was actually surprised by how quiet Suzanne was being. As a matter of fact, Suzanne seemed frozen.

"It's not unusual for there to be little change. Some kids just require two or three rounds of treatments." Marty opened her mouth to speak, but the doctor continued before she could. "The reason why I'm bringing it up now is because I've just read about an experimental treatment."

"We're not experimenting on our daughter!" Suzanne snapped back to herself and at the doctor.

"It's all approved by the necessary medical boards, I assure you. I would never suggest you try something I didn't stand behind one hundred percent," Dr. Fox said. "But most insurance plans still consider it experimental because it hasn't been brought into loop of standard treatments, so they don't cover it in full."

"But you do think it'll work for Abby?" Marty asked hopefully.

"My professional opinion is yes. It's very similar to how we've been treating her except there's different dosages and a new, more active—"

"We'll do it," Marty said eagerly. "I trust you to do what's best for Abby."

"Marty, wait." Suzanne regarded Dr. Fox through narrowed eyes. "Our insurance won't cover it?"

"No, not completely. Maybe fifty percent at best."

"It doesn't matter." Marty wanted to sign whatever paperwork needed her signature to get started.

"Can we have a minute?" Marty felt Suzanne grip her wrist tightly and tug her into a small waiting room just off the nurse's station. "What are you doing?" Suzanne whispered sharply.

"What do you mean what am I doing? I'm doing what's best for our daughter."

"Insurance won't help us." Suzanne started to worry at her thumbnail.

"Don't worry about the money," Marty said with her head held high. "I have three beach properties aimed to close by mid-January, and if we need more than what we have I could sell the boat or put a reverse mortgage on the house. We need to do what's best for Abigail, and Dr. Fox said that this is it."

"You shouldn't have agreed so quickly. We should have made that decision together."

"Together?" Marty looked at her wife, flabbergasted. All of the hurt, anger, and despair built up inside Marty finally detonated. "None of this has been done together!" A nurse stopped, and Marty took a calming breath before speaking again.

"The last thing we did together was agree to take Abby to this hospital. Ever since then, we've been nothing more to one another than someone to carpool with and stand next to when shit starts to get too real. So please, Suzie, tell me again about how the decision to take the next step with Abby's treatments needed to be done together." Marty's eyes burned as she watched Suzanne struggle to dispute her. Ultimately, she remained quiet. "I need a coffee." Marty turned away and walked slowly to the elevators. The cafeteria was on the opposite side of the hospital, and the long walk would do her good.

She had managed to keep her fear reined in for so long. Holding back that anxiety kept Marty from lashing out, but she had reached her boiling point. She had promised Suzanne years ago that she'd work on her anger, and she wasn't about to break that promise now. Yes, a long walk would serve her well.

The elevator ding signaled her arrival on the ground floor. Marty walked around and past strangers. In times like this, she often tried to imagine what brought the other people there. Sick grandparents, broken bones, and emergency surgeries, she was sure. She stood behind an elderly gentleman as she waited for her beverage. *Why me?* she wondered. *Why Abigail? Why my family?*

"Excuse me? Are you in line?"

"I'm sorry, what?"

"Are you in line? I'm desperate for a tea, but not desperate enough to be rude and cut in front of you if you were waiting." The woman's smile grew a fraction, displaying perfectly aligned white teeth that contrasted sharply with her deep mahogany skin.

"Yes, I am, but please," Marty stepped back and waved to the space in front of where she was standing, "go right ahead." The other woman eyed Marty briefly before counting the few other patrons that had lined up in the meantime.

"Thank you." She took Marty's former place. "I'm loath to admit this, but this is the kindest thing anyone has done for me in a while."

"It's nothing." Marty was flustered and suddenly feeling very shy, odd for her. "I'd hate to stand between a woman and her tea." Marty's nose twitched at the woodsy scent of the other woman's perfume. "Sandalwood?" she wondered more to herself, but the word got out.

"Yes," the stranger said. "Good nose."

"An ex-girlfriend of mine used to wear it. I guess I'll never forget it." Marty blushed at the unintentional confession. She felt the other woman staring, her skin prickled under the sharp scrutiny.

"Yvonne." She introduced herself with an extended feminine hand and waited for Marty to do the same. Marty took her hand. Yvonne was tall and gorgeous, with sharp features and short cropped black hair that highlighted her pronounced cheekbones.

"Marty." They shook in greeting and Yvonne held Marty's hand until it was her turn to order.

"I blame my ex-girlfriend for my tea addiction." Yvonne giggled. Marty found the sound delicate and therapeutic. "That among many things. If you have some time, I'll tell you about how I blame my one ex for my high arches." Yvonne lifted her right foot playfully.

Marty looked at her watch and recalled the unaffected look in Suzanne's eyes when she'd arrived earlier in the afternoon. When she looked back at Yvonne, her smile was unrestrained. Why shouldn't Marty indulge in conversation for a few minutes? She subconsciously ran her thumb across the cool metal of her wedding band.

"I have some time."

CHAPTER FOURTEEN

The night was getting darker. Crickets and katydids called out proudly into the clear, still night. The cloudless evening did not match the storm raging within Suzanne's psyche and heart. She drove and she drove, helplessly lost and scatterbrained as she raced toward the water. Suzanne needed the soothing roll of the waves to slow down her troublesome thoughts. She tightened her grip on the steering wheel as she thought about Marty's wounded green eyes.

Moments earlier, she had finished a tense phone call with Blake. Their five-minute conversation had been weighted down by pointed questions and vague answers. She had gone to Marty's for dinner, yes. No, she wasn't home yet. She wasn't sure when she would be home, and Suzanne was less than happy with Blake's entitlement. Blake had hung up on her.

How had such an innocent evening turned out this way? Suzanne's laughter sounded odd and out of place in the vehicle's quiet cabin. She knew better than to assume an evening with Marty would be innocent, especially when the level of intimacy they shared within her former home was overwhelming and felt so, *so* good.

When she had heard Marty crying into the phone earlier that afternoon, she didn't know how to handle it, but what really scrambled her thoughts was how much she felt in that moment. She was engulfed by the need to heal this wounded woman. Suzanne wanted nothing more than to be next to Marty and hold her close until the tears had stopped, whispering soothing reassurances that somehow everything would be okay. She could say those words to

Marty even if she didn't fully believe them herself. Suzanne turned right at the next red light.

What am I doing? She was happily with Blake now. *Am I happy?* She slowed the car as it approached a stop sign. He was wonderful to her and treated her so well. She *should* be happy. Blake had been incredibly supportive during the divorce and Abigail's death. He seemed to know just what Suzanne needed every step along the way. They even had a past they could retreat to when the present became too heavy to bear. But what about now? What about during the clear light of an average day? Blake was kind and gentle, he had his moments of humor, and he was handsome in a wholesome, conventional way. He didn't ignite her the way Marty did. Suzanne sighed heavily, pulled the car to the side of the road, and cut the engine in resignation. How many times was she going to have to give herself the same pep talk before she realized she didn't love the man?

Suzanne threw her car door open and stepped out, moving like a woman in a hypnotic trance. So many thoughts she had numbed herself to shuffled about, fighting for her consideration and acceptance. She raced up the path, her breath coming in short puffs.

The key was where it always was, just under the lip of the clay planter to the right of the front door. She let herself in silently, the smell of dinner still lingering in the air. She removed her shoes and left them by the door before going upstairs. The house was shrouded in darkness except for a small flameless candle that flickered on a table at the top of the stairs. She arrived at the top without making a sound and tiptoed to the bedroom. Her heart was thundering in her ears so loudly each beat was followed by a ring.

The door to Marty's bedroom was ajar. Marty was sleeping on her side, the bedsheets draped delicately over her bare shoulder. The moonlight cut through the windows brightly enough to highlight Marty's skin. Suzanne froze. She took a moment to listen to her gut, question her actions, but all she could hear was her heart telling her to move forward.

Suzanne stripped, desperate to feel Marty's skin on her own.

She slid between the covers and pressed her length against Marty. Marty's skin was just as soft and warm as she remembered. Suzanne took a shuddering breath as Marty began to stir.

"Wha—?"

"Shh…" Suzanne wrapped her arm around Marty's waist and fanned her fingers across her abdomen. She sat up slightly on her other elbow and nibbled Marty's exposed ear. "I miss you," Suzanne said breathily.

"Suzie?" She turned on her back, and Suzanne smiled brightly at her.

"I couldn't go home. I tried." She laughed in embarrassment. "Then I told myself I'd go sit by the water and think." Suzanne traced a line from Marty's stomach to between her breasts. "But I came back." She raked her short nails along Marty's chest. "I came back to you."

"You came back to me," Marty whispered with wonder. She brought her hand up to touch Suzanne's cheek delicately, as if she were testing the reality of a dream.

Suzanne leaned down and captured Marty's lips in a fevered kiss. The fire they had stoked earlier still burned between them. Suzanne knew it always would. No amount of sorrow or anger could end her feelings, her desire and need. She kissed Marty with renewed devotion. Gone was the apprehensive voice inside that told her no and reminded her how Marty had hurt her. They had hurt each other. She knew that now.

Suzanne lay fully atop Marty, whimpering at the feel of their bodies pressed together. Breast to breast, pelvis to pelvis, and mouth to mouth, Suzanne continued to kiss Marty, slowing to a more languid, peaceful pace. She had no need to hurry. This moment wasn't getting away from them. The sun was long from rising. Not even the most obsessive of clients would call Marty at this time, and Suzanne's phone had been turned off the moment Blake hung up on her.

No interruptions, just Suzanne and Marty in bed reviving a love that had seemed lost but remained all along.

"I love you." Suzanne felt Marty's words against her mouth and in her heart.

Suzanne started rolling her hip rhythmically, coaxing Marty's thighs apart. She hissed with pleasure when she felt Marty's wet center press against her shaven mound. The way Marty reacted to her touch had always been a weakness of hers. Suzanne increased the pressure of her seductive circles against Marty's most sensitive spots. Marty bit down on Suzanne's shoulder and released a strangled moan.

"Wait, stop," Marty said, but Suzanne was determined and growing frenzied with passion. In a swift motion, Marty flipped Suzanne on her back. Suzanne's blue eyes widened in shock and embarrassment.

"I'm so sorry, Marty, I—"

"No, no, no." Marty peppered Suzanne's face with small kisses, and Suzanne started to relax. The tension melted from her features and shoulders. Marty wasn't stopping. She wasn't rejecting her or changing her mind. Marty simply smiled down at her. Suzanne nuzzled into Marty's palm when it came up to her cheek. "How is it possible that you're more beautiful to me now than ever before?"

Suzanne knew this wasn't some smooth pillow-talking line Marty was using—she truly meant it. Suzanne grew uncomfortable under the attention.

"You don't know what you've got until it's gone?" Her attempt at a joke to ease the moment fell flat, and so did Marty's face. Suzanne was quick to amend herself. "I had forgotten how beautiful you make me feel." Suzanne laced her fingers into Marty's and guided her hand away from her cheek and down to her breast. "I'm here." She kissed Marty deeply, finding the taste she had missed so dearly.

Suzanne ran her hands along the length of Marty's back and down to her small buttocks. She gripped them firmly before retracing her steps. Up and down and around again, Suzanne relished the feel of Marty's silken skin. Marty shivered against Suzanne and kissed along her neck and down to her chest. Marty enveloped Suzanne's dusky nipple with her warm mouth, her tongue trailing around the pebbled flesh before she nipped at it. Suzanne called out, the fire in her body turning into a blaze of uncontrollable proportions.

"Marty, please," Suzanne begged and whimpered. She was about to go insane feeling Marty's fingers on her heated skin but never leading to where she needed them most. "I need—I want…"

"Shh…I know what you want, but you're going to have to be patient." Suzanne felt the ghost of a touch along her inner thigh. Her pussy clenched. "I've been waiting so long for this moment, and I didn't think I'd ever have it again." Marty kissed the peak of one breast and then the other. "Now that I have you, I plan on enjoying it."

The little light illuminating the room was just enough for Suzanne to see Marty's teasing smirk. In that moment, she hated herself for ever believing she loved Marty any less than with her whole heart. She let go of that hate and focused on the adoration that filled her chest.

"I love you, Marty." Suzanne sat up slightly and kissed her. "I love you so much, and because of that, I won't kill you for torturing me." She moved her hand stealthily beneath the blanket. "But I do not plan on playing fair." Suzanne entered Marty swiftly and easily with two fingers. She was so wet and ready for her, Suzanne felt Marty's inner muscles responding immediately.

"Shit!" Marty's arms gave out, and her full weight came down on Suzanne, who delighted in it. She slid in and out of Marty, her palm pressed just so against her hardened clit. Marty searched for the edge of the covers with her right hand.

Within seconds, Marty filled Suzanne with three fingers. "Oh God! Marty!" Her wail echoed in the bedroom. Both women moved their hips in time. Neither was in a hurry to reach their shared ecstasy, but their bodies didn't understand the desire to move slow and relish such wonderful pleasure.

Suzanne was the first to start shaking. The rush of blood coursing through her veins and between her legs was intense. She gripped the damp curls at the back of Marty's neck and tried to focus on how soft and warm Marty felt in her palm.

"I'm so close," Marty warned.

"Me too, baby, me too." Suzanne clenched her jaw and started to whine as warmth flooded her body. "Come with me." Those three words were all the permission they needed.

Together their bodies ignited in release. Marty called out to Suzanne desperately, her green eyes open and focused on Suzanne's face for as long as possible. Once the tremors of pleasure had subsided, Marty moved off Suzanne slightly, her wet hand resting on her stomach. Suzanne's fingers remained in Marty even as their heartbeats returned to normal.

A single tear ran down the side of Suzanne's face as a feeling of coming home filled her and lulled her into a peaceful sleep.

❖

When Marty awoke in the morning, she cursed the sun. Although she hadn't looked at the clock yet, it felt too early. She stretched languidly and enjoyed the tightness in her muscles as she moved. Each twinge of pain was a physical reminder of the night before. She looked to her side and sighed at the empty space. Suzanne's absence wasn't a surprise to her. Suzanne often struggled with emotional moments—good or bad. She just hoped Suzanne recognized this as a good one.

Marty got up and dressed in her most sinfully comfortable clothes before brushing her teeth and using the bathroom. She left the bedroom while saying a silent prayer she had something worth eating for breakfast. A sniffle coming from Abigail's bedroom caught her attention. She peeked in and found Suzanne sitting on Abigail's bed. She was dressed in one of Marty's oldest Princeton T-shirts, and the letter written to Marty was set on her lap. She leaned against the doorway.

"She was smart."

Marty's soft comment startled Suzanne. The blonde wiped away a tear. "Too smart!" She laughed lightly and folded the letter.

Marty walked into the room and sat beside her. Minutes ticked by in comfortable silence.

"She told me about the time the two of you were bird

watching." Marty watched Suzanne's brow furrow as she searched her mind for the memory. "You said you wished I was there. And then I found this." Marty picked up the paper and turned it over several times in her hands. It should feel weighty because of its significance, but it was nothing more than ordinary. "This is what made me call you after the funeral. I actually found it right after you left and after my mom scolded me for my behavior." She shook her head at the not-too-distant memory. "I was destroyed—I lost you, and I had just buried my daughter." Marty's chin quivered, and she took a steadying breath. "It was like Abby just knew." Suzanne took Marty's hand and rubbed it between her own. "I wouldn't give up on us, not after this. Anything you would've given me I would've taken. Friendship or more." She looked down at their joined hands.

Marty thought back through the struggles they had overcame to get here. She still had so much to ask and discuss, but she needed to know what was next, and she needed to apologize. She had to explain herself and tell Suzanne what had happened that night.

"Are you mine again?" she asked shyly. Her eyes never met Suzanne's.

"I always was." Suzanne leaned in for a kiss, but Marty pulled back.

"We need to talk about that night and what had happened between us."

"I don't want to."

"*I* need to, Suzie." Marty looked to Suzanne with pleading eyes. "We needed to have this conversation back then, but I couldn't talk to you. Things are different now, and I don't want any questions between us, no skeletons in the closet. If everything is out in the open, we can have a fresh start. And maybe," Marty shrugged weakly, "maybe you can trust me again?"

Suzanne took a shuddering breath. "Okay, but I need coffee first, and then maybe I should tell you more about Blake too."

Marty swallowed hard. She was ready to tell Suzanne about her moments of weakness, but was she ready to hear about Suzanne's?

At First They Grew Distant

H ey, how are you?" Blake said.
"Tired," Suzanne admitted, her eyes fixed on the gray clouds outside the large windows of the hospital.

"I'm heading in now to start my shift. I could bring you lunch…" The silence was a question in itself. "Or I could treat you to the usual cafeteria fare. I know how much you love their dry turkey on stale wheat bread."

Suzanne laughed weakly before declining the offer. "Marty will be here soon. I think she plans on spending most of the day for once. She moved around a few appointments or canceled a meeting. Something like that."

"Oh." Blake's disappointment was evident, which made Suzanne smile again. They had grown close again during Abigail's hospitalization. He comforted her, and having an old friend floating around made her feel less lonely. "That's really good."

"Yeah, I suppose it is," Suzanne said unenthusiastically. "Abigail misses her." She looked at the clock and sighed. Marty would be there shortly, and so would the newfound tension that surrounded them.

"Suzie, what's going on?" Blake asked through the sound of wind whipping around his phone.

"Nothing. I'm just tired."

"Don't lie to me."

Suzanne took a deep breath. "Do you have a little time before your shift starts?"

"I have twenty minutes to spare for the mother of my favorite patient."

"I'll meet you at the benches out front. I could use some air." Suzanne stopped to tell Abby she'd be right back and made her way outside. In just a few minutes, she was standing outside, hugging herself enough to ward off the bitter damp chill that accompanied gloomy winter days. She zipped her down jacket as she approached Blake, who had already found a vacant bench.

"Hi." She sat beside him.

"Hey," Blake said with a wide smile. "It's cold today!" He made a show of shivering.

"The fresh air feels good." Suzanne inhaled deeply and allowed the clean air to burn her lungs.

"So…" Blake started.

Suzanne appreciated the gentle encouragement, but she wasn't entirely sure where to begin.

"Remember senior year when we were paired with Tammy and Michael for that physics lab?" she asked while she watched cars drive past the hospital.

"Vaguely."

"Tammy and Michael had dated for two years at that point and broke up about a week before we had to work on that lab."

"That's right. It was an awkward lab to be part of. They wouldn't talk to each other, and when they had to, it would almost always end up in a fight, even if we were discussing the laws of motion."

Suzanne looked at Blake, smiling and scratching his beard so casually, oblivious to what he had just said. Her chin started to quiver. "We're Tammy and Michael."

"What?" Blake's face screwed up. Suzanne laughed at his confusion in spite of her tears.

"Marty and I. I feel like Tammy and Michael. I feel bad for every doctor and nurse that has to be around us both. And don't even think about telling me we're not! The first time I saw you in the hospital was right after a very loud argument and my wife storming off."

"Hey, come on." Blake placed his hand on Suzanne's forearm. She liked the feeling, the warmth of the comfort. "We see this all the time. Things like this, *tragedies* like this, are hard for parents to handle. Please don't worry about what the staff may be thinking. Focus on your family." Blake spoke with such a confident softness to his voice that Suzanne was inclined to do as he said. "And you'll always have me. Don't forget that." Blake entwined his fingers with hers.

Suzanne sat and considered his words. After so many years apart, she still trusted him. He had always been a steadfast and honest presence in her life. She'd once loved this man, and it was easy to remember all the reasons why. Suzanne's phone beeped. She read the short message and put the device back into her pocket. Marty was parking, and the anxiety Suzanne had grown accustomed to carrying tightened its grip around her heart again.

"I think it's time to head back inside." Suzanne pulled her hand away.

"Why haven't you told Marty that you know me?" Blake said. He looked over to Suzanne, his eyes shining slightly.

Suzanne shook her head. "I don't know," she said. Suzanne didn't know why. Every time she'd go to formally introduce the two, she'd freeze. Maybe she was selfish and wanted to hold on a little long to this connection that didn't involve her wife. Maybe she was afraid of Marty having a negative reaction to her resuscitating a friendship with an ex. Maybe it was all of the above. "I guess I just don't want to add any fuel to the fire right now." She shrugged, appearing more nonchalant than she felt.

"Okay." Blake seemed to accept her reasoning. "I'll see you inside." He stood and walked into the hospital.

Suzanne stood still, thinking about what he'd said.

"Hey!" Marty's familiar voice bellowed over the nearby traffic. Suzanne turned and greeted her with a small smile. Marty jogged to be at her side. "What are you doing out here? It's freezing!" Marty kissed Suzanne lightly.

"I needed fresh air." Suzanne grimaced at how dismissive and curt she sounded. Marty hadn't done anything, and her ire was already rising. This emotional push and pull was taxing, and she absolutely hated how Marty was still smiling at her.

"I brought lunch and a new coloring book for Abby. This one is loaded with animals." Marty held up an oversized shopping bag. "Come on." She gripped Suzanne's hand and started to lead them inside. "At least you kept your hand warm for me." Marty's joke and warm smile evoked an icy chill through Suzanne.

She thought of Blake and wondered if now would be the time to tell Marty about him and their past. She tried to speak, but nothing more than a defeated sigh came out. Suzanne's mouth turned up into a forced smile. "Abigail will love it."

CHAPTER FIFTEEN

A nd just like that, you fell back in love with him?" Marty asked. "No, of course not." Suzanne sipped her coffee. "Enough about Blake. Hurry up and tell me your side before I change my mind."

"You're not still in love with him, right?"

"No." Suzanne laughed lightly. "I loved him. I still love him for who he is, but I'm not *in love* with him. Not like I am with you." Suzanne leaned forward and kissed Marty gently. The softness of her helped calm Marty's racing heart. "Now talk."

Marty grimaced at Suzanne's demand. She looked away and began to gather her thoughts, transfixed as she watched the steam dance above Suzanne's coffee cup. They sat side by side on the couch, talking casually about Blake until now. As sickened as she felt at even the smallest mention of a close connection between him and Suzanne, it was the easier topic to tackle. She was so unsure how to start the conversation she insisted they needed to have. Every memory came flooding back from the past several months, each more vivid than the last.

"Some people cut themselves in order to feel during times of deep sadness or depression." Her voice sounded hollow as it carried across the space between her and Suzanne. "I did a lot of reading on the topic after you left and after Abigail died."

"Did you ever…?" Suzanne's curious eyes shined in the dim morning light.

"That night, that woman—it was my own fucked up version of self-harm." Marty thought she'd never be able to look Suzanne in the eye if they had this discussion, but now she felt as if that connection was her lifeline. "After a while, I felt completely numb to everything around me. I just kept working because I felt in control when I did. When I was with you and Abigail, I felt no control at all." Marty shook her head. "You were slipping away, Abby was slipping away, my whole life was slipping away, and I couldn't do anything about it. I put on a smile and just went through the motions."

"Marty, I am so—"

"I'm not done." Marty took a shaky breath. "I met Yvonne in the hospital cafeteria the day we had that fight about insurance and changing treatments. We talked for a bit. She turned out to be a therapist, so I thought there was no harm in sharing some of problems with her."

"You could've talked to me." Suzanne gripped Marty's hand.

"No, I couldn't, not then," Marty said solemnly. "But I can now. We talked almost every day after that, and I became sort of addicted to the attention and the normalcy of it all. I need you to believe me when I tell you I didn't see it as anything more than a friendship then." Marty held Suzanne's hand tightly. "Nothing happened until she asked me to show her a house."

"The night I found you?"

Marty nodded. "She kissed me, and I didn't stop her because I actually *felt* something. Not emotionally, but physically, and that took my mind away from my sick child and my failing marriage." Marty's breath was becoming ragged as she fought back tears. "I was so afraid." She started to sob and fell against Suzanne's side.

Suzanne soothed Marty gently, raking her fingers through her tangled hair and brushing the tears from her cheeks. Marty was terrified telling this story would destroy this delicate thing they'd made from the wreckage of their marriage, but her fears were erased the moment Suzanne kissed her quivering lips.

"I love you, Marty, and I am so sorry for what you went through," Suzanne said as she cradled Marty's red cheeks in her palms. "I'm sorry for shutting you out and making you feel so alone."

"My mistake isn't your fault." Marty cleared her throat, allowing her voice to regain some of its strength.

"It's not, but I played a part in our life getting to that point. I am so sorry for that." Suzanne wiped away a tear of her own.

"I'm sorry too. For everything I did and didn't do. It really sucks we had to get to this point for all the mistakes and bad choices to become so clear." Marty pulled back from Suzanne and laughed mirthlessly. "We're some pair, aren't we?"

"We are indeed." Suzanne smiled briefly before her expression clouded over. "We also have something in common now."

"What's that?" Marty eyed her curiously.

"The day we had that argument at the hospital was the day I ran into Blake for the first time."

"Where was I?"

"Getting coffee," Suzanne said.

One cup of coffee. One decision made out of anger and fear had ultimately derailed her marriage.

"Don't do that," Suzanne said as she pushed against Marty's shoulder.

"Do what?"

"Analyze this." Suzanne looked out the window. "In a fucked up situation like ours, I have to believe everything happens for a reason. What reason? I'll never know or fully understand, but I need to believe that."

Marty pulled Suzanne against her and buried her nose in her fragrant blond hair. "I've stopped trying to understand any of this," she whispered into Suzanne's hair. She waited a moment, steeling herself, preparing herself for the answer to her next question. "How long before you and Blake became more…?"

"A month before our divorce was finalized," Suzanne sighed. "I was so hurt and scared. He offered me comfort right away, and I think at first I thought moving on was the best kind of revenge." Marty winced. "But then I started to realize I needed the company, so I mistook that for a greater feeling than it was." Suzanne wiped her nose. "I see now I basically used the man, but quiet nights alone? I don't think, I couldn't—"

"I know." Marty wrapped her arms around Suzanne and held her tight. "Believe me, I know."

"I'm sorry you had to go through this alone." They sat silently for a few moments, just taking in each other's presence. "Come on," Suzanne said as she sat up. "Let me make you breakfast." She stood and walked to the kitchen with Marty close behind.

They set out preparing a simple breakfast together. Suzanne cooked as Marty set the table and prepared more coffee. The late morning was quiet and bright with possibilities and promise. Marty couldn't help herself as she stole glances at Suzanne, smiling as she cooked. Life, against all odds, was starting to feel almost normal again. For the first time in months, Marty was starting to believe she could be happy once more.

She moved quietly, her socks barely scuffing against the wood of the floor, and she pressed the length of her body against Suzanne's. "I missed you so much." She whispered directly into her ear, and Suzanne shivered.

"We've slept together," Suzanne blurted out awkwardly as she flipped a pancake. When she turned around slowly, Marty could see the fear in her eyes.

"What?"

"I know I should feel more 'tit for tat' about it, like it's okay, but..." Suzanne swallowed. "Blake and I, we've been *intimate*."

"No." Marty held up her hand to stop her lover's explanation. "As far as I'm concerned, you've told him you won't be ready until you're married again. That's why he was so eager to put that ring on your finger."

"Not quite," Suzanne said with a smile. "It was actually after a pregnancy scare that I started to realize how much I still loved you."

"P-pregnancy scare?" Marty felt the color drain from her face.

"It was silly. Carla actually helped me through that crisis." Suzanne rolled her eyes. "When I realized how scared I was at just the thought of being pregnant with Blake's child, I thought long and hard about why."

"Well?" Marty said, her mind still reeling.

"Because *you're* my family. I can't imagine raising a child with anyone else." Suzanne took a deep breath and blinked her moist eyes a few times.

Marty wrapped her arms around Suzanne and held her close. She dared to break the silence. "What now?"

Suzanne swallowed audibly. "Dammit." She started stacking pancakes on the plate Marty held out. "Why can't this just be easy?"

"Nothing has been easy since that beautiful November day you called me while you were rushing Abby to the hospital."

"You're right." Suzanne picked up two coffee mugs, and they walked together to the table. "First, we eat. Second, we make believe there's nothing outside of this house for us to worry about for a little longer. Third, I talk to Blake tonight."

Marty's heart swelled with joy. Her body tingled with exhilaration at the idea of focusing solely on them until she had to be at work in the afternoon, but knowing Suzanne had plans to spend the evening with Blake twisted her stomach. The unlikelihood of Suzanne spending another night with her became obvious.

Marty almost kicked herself for assuming so much so quickly. Suzanne always needed a little extra time. Why should this be any different? Marty took a bite of her breakfast and almost choked. *What if Blake puts up a fight?* Suzanne now knew every detail that had led to Marty's affair. Would it be so hard for a good man to convince her that Marty wasn't a good woman? After what she had done, Marty couldn't even consider herself good enough.

When Marty closed her eyes in order to calm her panic, she thought about the night she'd watched Suzanne walk away. She knew for sure she'd never survive that again.

And Then They Grew Apart

Marty spun a quarter on its edge for the tenth time, losing herself to the blurred sphere. Listings piled up in front of her, a grocery list sat off to the side, and several clients' numbers were scrawled on Post-its and stuck around the perimeter of her phone. She was busy and keeping busy. Anything to free her mind of the constant nagging thoughts. They had both agreed to the more aggressive and experimental treatments for their daughter, and Abigail had just finished her induction phase of chemotherapy. This was when they were supposed to be announcing her remission, but Dr. Fox hadn't. What he had done, however, was reassure the mothers the next phase had a much better rate of success now that they were getting aggressive. These empty assurances did little to assuage Marty's sickening worry, and the cold space between her and Suzanne at night didn't help.

But they were home now. They'd arrived the day before and were given a few months away from the hospital for Abigail's body to repair what it could before it was all broken down again. At one time, Marty would have felt hopeful, but now she was just exhausted and terrified. Every conversation with Suzanne turned into a fight, every dinner was spent in silence, and Abigail rarely felt up to anything more than lying in bed and watching a movie.

Every time Marty closed her eyes, she was haunted by the sunken features of Abigail's tiny face. She felt like a horrible mother, thinking about herself and her own fears while her daughter was the one suffering the most. She felt selfish and despicable. She couldn't stop the twist in her gut every time she heard her child heave or the resentful burning in her chest when Suzanne would leave the room. Marty felt like everything was unraveling around her, and she had no idea how to stop it.

Her phone signaled a new message.

Missed you at the cafeteria today.

Marty smiled wistfully at the bright screen. *I'd say I missed the cafeteria today too, but I make better coffee.*

You'll have to make me a cup sometime.

Marty stared at the screen. From the first day she had spoken to Yvonne, their conversations had been flirty but innocent. At times, she caught herself wondering if Yvonne was interested in something more, but she always chalked those thoughts up to an active imagination. She was married and vocal about it. Yvonne knew about Abigail and the challenges she'd been facing lately. She was a good friend, and lucky for Marty, a therapist by day. Before she came up with a response, Yvonne messaged her again.

If you're free tonight, and feel free to say no, I was wondering if you were available to show me those properties you were telling me about.

Sure. Marty responded quickly and too eagerly, but she chose to ignore the excitement she felt. *Meet me at seven?*

I'll be there.

Marty typed out the address information and sent it. She went back to work with renewed energy. The afternoon passed quickly, and it was just after six when Annmarie sat beside her.

"Hey,"

"Hey!" Marty spun in her chair to look at her friend. "How was your day?"

"After five showings, the Andersons finally put in an offer."

"Which house?"

"The one on Oak Terrace."

"Didn't you show them that one weeks ago?"

"Yes."

"And then about forty more since?"

"That's the one."

"Ouch! Those kind of clients are the worst."

"Hey, at least they put in an offer. How are your numbers recently?"

"Not too good." Marty scratched the back of her neck and rolled her shoulders. "I think I put too much pressure on myself. I don't know what the cost is going to be for this round of treatment, so I'm trying to sell, sell, and sell." She let out a long breath. "I'm having a hard time connecting with clients like I used to because all I see is dollar signs." She felt terrible putting all of this on Annmarie, but she had been such a good friend since the beginning.

"I know this sounds impossible, but just try to relax when it comes to work." Annmarie placed her hand on Marty's. "This always came naturally to you." Marty nodded. "How is Abigail? Happy to be home, I bet."

"She is very happy to be home. We all are." Marty finished her sentence quietly, with a less confident voice.

"How are you and Suzanne holding up? She's hard to get a hold of these days."

Marty didn't know how to answer the question. "We're doing our best," she said. "Suzanne's just busy."

"Send her my love, and remember, if either of you need *anything*, don't hesitate to ask."

"Of course." Marty offered a meek smile. "Thank you."

Annmarie stood. "Are you almost done for the day?"

"I'm showing the house on Princeton at seven."

"That's a little late."

"It's for a friend." Marty shoved some papers into her leather purse and stood. Just as she was about to say good-bye, her desk phone rang. "Hello?" she answered.

"Marty." Suzanne sounded exhausted. "While you're at the store, can you also get some antacids? Abigail's stomach is still a little off."

"Sure." Marty held the receiver against her ear with her shoulder while she scrawled the added item to the list.

"Don't forget it," Suzanne added.

"I won't. I wrote it down."

"You always write things down and then forget them."

"Suzie, if I say I won't forget it, then I won't forget it."

"Don't talk to me like that when you're at work." Suzanne's voice started to rise. "People can hear you."

"There's nobody around!" Annmarie eyed Marty curiously. Marty shook her head.

"That's right, you seem to be the only realtor around that spends more time at the office than with your family."

"Please don't start this now, Suzanne."

"When will you be home?"

"I'm heading out for a showing now, so I don't know, nine maybe." Marty's estimate was met with silence, but she could hear her wife stewing loud and clear. The tense silence came to an end when Suzanne offered a curt good-bye and hung up.

Marty shot Annmarie an embarrassed look. "Good night, Annmarie."

❖

"Are all of your conversations like that?" Carla asked her sister while she helped peel potatoes.

"Like what?" Suzanne knew exactly what Carla was asking, but she didn't want to answer her.

"So tense. Jeez, Suzanne, who are you?" Carla looked over her shoulder to make sure Abigail was immersed in whatever nonsense was playing on the television screen. "You two are acting like complete strangers. Strangers that don't even like each other!"

"I don't know what you're talking about—"

"That's bullshit and you know it!" At Suzanne's motion to keep it down, Carla apologized and continued. "All you do is fight with her."

"Oh, *I'm* the one that's fighting?" Suzanne crossed her arms over her chest.

"Yeah, you are. I've watched the way Marty acts around you. It's like the poor woman is walking on eggshells that are on fire!"

"Oh please!" Suzanne scoffed.

"I'm not saying she's a saint, and I know that what the two of you are going through is hard."

"Impossible."

"It's horrible and impossible, and I can't even begin to imagine what it's like, which is why I don't understand why you're fighting the only other person who gets what you're going through."

Suzanne let Carla's words sink in slowly and deeply. Just as each and every word registered, she looked at her sister with watery eyes and said what had been festering in her heart and mind since the diagnosis. "This is my fault, and every time I look at her or even think about her I feel guilty." Suzanne bit at her lip to keep it from quivering. "I lost one baby and then I give her a sick one? Carla, how could she still love me? How could she not blame me for this?" Suzanne had to look away from Carla's sympathetic gaze.

"Have you told her this?"

"No."

"Why not?"

"I'm scared to." Suzanne swallowed thickly. "What if it's true? What if she doesn't love me anymore? What if she hates me?"

Carla took her into her open arms and rubbed soothing circles on her back. "You need to tell her. Can you call her?"

"She's showing a house, I can't."

"I got an idea." Carla punctuated her announcement with a cheerful clap. "Find out where the house is and go surprise her." Suzanne eyed her doubtfully. "Look, I've got everything under control here. I'll feed your kid and we'll watch all of her favorite movies while you're gone. Go, explain yourself, make things better."

"Okay."

"Okay?"

"Yeah," Suzanne hugged her sister again before reaching for her keys. "Okay."

❖

"I know you're a north Jersey girl, but you have to admit this is a nice house."

"It is, definitely." Yvonne agreed readily.

Marty locked up the front door and led the way back down the ornate block walkway toward their cars. "I'm confident in saying it has everything you're looking for."

"Marty?"

"Yeah?" Marty turned to find Yvonne standing still with a serious expression weighing on her gorgeous features. "Everything okay?"

"That's actually what I was about to ask you." Yvonne's small smile was wide enough to shine brilliantly.

"Why?"

"You haven't been saying much." Yvonne laughed lightly. "Yes, you've been talking, but not really *talking*. I try to separate the therapist in me from any of my personal relationships. I don't like to push people, but I can't with you. Not anymore."

She could talk to Annmarie, but not openly and completely since she was friends with Suzanne as well. Now that someone was willing to listen, Marty knew she needed to voice what had been on her mind.

"I think my marriage is in trouble and even if—" Marty stopped. She closed her eyes and took a breath. "Even *when* Abigail survives all of this, I don't know if we will." Saying the words made her feel guilty.

"This is a hard thing for couples to go through together." Yvonne stepped up to her.

The winter night was clear and bitter. Every star was alive in the sky and puffs of their breath made small clouds around them. Marty hugged herself.

"We're not…" she said, barely above a whisper.

"Not what?" Yvonne reached out and gripped Marty's forearm.

Marty stared at the contact for a moment before speaking. "We're not in this together." Frigid silence settled between them. Marty watched as the mist her words created drifted away in the wind.

"You told me something, now may I tell you something?"

"Of course." Marty clenched her jaw, fighting against a shiver.

"I don't want this house."

Marty laughed, but then she realized Yvonne was serious.

"I asked you to show me a house because I missed you."

"Yvonne, I—" Marty stopped protesting when she felt Yvonne's full lips against her own. Yvonne gripped the front of her jacket and pulled her closer. Marty kissed back without hesitation.

Marty didn't stop to think about what she was doing. She was feeling *everything* instead. She felt the cold air surrounding her and the way her body was heating up in spite of it. She felt Yvonne caress her cheek and down the side of her neck. She felt Yvonne break their kiss and whisper against her moist mouth.

"Let's move this to my car, yeah?"

Marty nodded and followed Yvonne with a lusty stumble.

❖

"Four thirty-two, four thirty-two," Suzanne repeated to herself as she traveled down the length of Princeton Road. She finally spotted the number, but not Marty's car, so she pulled up to the curb on the opposite side of the street from the home.

The impressive house sat on a corner piece of property and was dark. Not a light on in the place. Suzanne got out of her car and crossed the street. She cursed quietly and resigned herself to the fact that she had just missed her. Marty would probably be home before her now, curious as to where she ran off to and why Carla was sitting alone with Abigail. She kicked at a pebble on the ground and was about to turn back when the flash of brake lights around the corner caught her eye. She noticed two cars parked down the small side road. One she didn't recognize, but the other was definitely Marty's.

She approached the running vehicle, dread bubbling in the depths of her stomach despite the voice in her head telling her not to assume anything. *Don't think the worst, it's her client.* She noticed the steamed-up windows as she got closer, and the rapid movements within them.

Suzanne stood outside the car and counted to three before pulling on the door handle. Marty sat with her legs spread wide open and another woman's hand between them.

CHAPTER SIXTEEN

"I need to ask you something," Marty said from the bedroom doorway. She was leaning casually against the wooden frame, but her insides were a shaky mess.

They had finished breakfast and indulged in a long, hot shower together, cleansing and kissing and reaffirming their love for each other. But now the reality of the day had set in, and they had begun to ready themselves for what came next. Marty got dressed for work, and Suzanne pulled on the clothing she had discarded the night before. Once they walked out the door, everything would change.

"What's that?" Suzanne paused momentarily as she dressed.

"Why were you there that night?" Marty had replayed the memory over and over countless times since it had happened, but this was the first time she had ever asked that. Her focus had always been on the pain and embarrassment, on her own stupidity.

"I was coming to surprise you." Suzanne buttoned her pants. "I wanted to apologize for being terrible and I wanted to tell you I love you."

"I really messed up that surprise, didn't I?" Marty laughed mirthlessly. She didn't want the morning's mood to decline. She'd asked her question and she'd gotten her answer. She'd wallow in how unfair it all is later. "So…"

"So," Suzanne echoed as she ran her palms over the wrinkles in her pants.

• 213 •

"Will I—do you think…" Marty stopped and laughed. "I feel like we just had our first sleepover."

"You weren't this awkward after our first sleepover."

"True." Marty kept her eyes on her clasped hands. "Will I see you tonight?"

"I'm not sure, probably not." Suzanne slid into her shoes. "But I'll call you after I talk to Blake, and then we'll see what tomorrow brings?"

"Okay." Marty's heart sank. She winced when she heard how little she sounded. But how was she supposed to control herself when she was about to say good-bye to the person that finally made her house feel more like a home than it had in a long time?

"Hey." Suzanne wrapped her arms around Marty's waist and looked up into hopeful green eyes. "I just have to do this one thing, and then we can focus on us, on what to do next, and how to heal." Marty framed Suzanne's face with her hands, and Suzanne's smile widened.

Marty traced Suzanne's furrowed brow with her index finger. "Do you think that's true? Do you think we can heal after everything?"

"Not completely," Suzanne said. "But we have a better chance together. I know that." She laid her head against Marty's chest.

Marty inhaled her scent and relished its calming quality. "When will you see Blake?"

"I already messaged him to come over after his shift ends at six, so soon after that."

"When did you message him?"

"When you were searching for this," she said, gripping Marty's backside. "I love you in pencil skirts."

"I know." Marty kissed Suzanne's full lips. "I wanted to make sure you'd be thinking of me all day."

"Mission accomplished. Ready?"

Marty looked around to make sure she wasn't forgetting anything. "Ready."

They walked downstairs together hand in hand. Marty saw Suzanne to her car and kissed her soundly, pressing her against the door and rubbing her thigh between her legs. When she pulled back, Suzanne was nearly cross-eyed.

"*Wow...*"

"I'm making up for lost time." Marty winked as she went to her own car. "Call me as soon as you can. I'll be at the office until about eight, so if I don't answer right away, keep calling until I do." Marty flashed Suzanne a charming smile before getting into her car. Despite her bravado, Marty still worried this reconciliation was too good to be true. She shook off the thought and grabbed her phone. Telling someone could help her believe the reality and quell her fears.

"Hello?"

"Hey, Mom, guess what." Marty smiled. "Abby was right."

❖

"Please say something," Suzanne said for the third time during ten painfully quiet minutes. Blake's eyes were still fixed on the wall opposite them. He had barely gotten through the door before she launched into her long-winded explanation and apology. She told him about her mistakes and regrets, but she knew she was married to the love of her life. She still loved Marty and would forever.

"I don't have anything to say," he finally mumbled.

"You have to have *something* to say. You can't hear all of that and not have anything to say to me."

"I could say a lot of things, Suzie. Dammit!" Blake stood abruptly and started to pace. Suzanne wiped her clammy palms on her jeans. She was preparing for whatever fight was about to happen. "I get a message from my fiancée this morning saying she wants to see me, and I'm the idiot that thinks it's a good thing!"

"You're not an idiot."

"Aren't I? Think about it. All this time I really thought I had you, that I had a chance to be with you." He looked down at Suzanne as she sat nervously. "I asked you if I had anything to worry about. I gave you chance after chance to tell me you didn't want to be with me."

"I know, but you need to believe me when I say that I didn't expect this."

"I don't want to believe you." He looked at Suzanne with his jaw set like cement. "But I do because I know you." Blake's shoulders sagged. "You'd be too scared to let yourself continue to willingly love someone who hurt you. You'd be blinded by it, actually. Kind of like how I was blinded by an everlasting schoolboy crush that got me into this position."

"I didn't exactly stop you," Suzanne said.

"But I can't blame you, can I?" He shook his head before wiping his eyes, then looked back to Suzanne and smiled sadly. "I can't blame you for any of this."

"I *am* to blame."

"No, you're really not. Your child was sick and your wife cheated on you. I'm sorry. You weren't in the best place, and I took advantage of that." Suzanne's mouth fell open. "I didn't realize it at the time, of course. I'm not a dick!" He chuckled halfheartedly.

"Blake, I really am so sorry." Suzanne hoped that, in time, Blake would also believe they were meant to meet again.

"I know," he said. "I won't lie and say something macho, making believe this doesn't hurt, because it does. But I am thankful for the time I had with you."

"That is the least macho thing you could've said." Suzanne wiped away a tear.

"I know. Any chance it'll convince you I've been the one all along?" He smirked playfully. Suzanne shook her head. "Didn't think so. It's always been Marty. I thought maybe I could fill her shoes, be good enough and make you happy. If I'm being completely honest, deep down I knew that would be impossible."

Suzanne eyed him curiously. "You barely know her, and you met her when we were at our worst."

"Some things are still obvious. Every day I'm surrounded by parents trying to do their best, like they're trying to win at a card game with the worst possible hand. But kids? They talk a lot." Blake shifted toward Suzanne. "Abigail talked about all the things you and Marty had done with her and for her. She was a happy kid." Blake's eyes started to glisten. "Happy parents make happy children. It really is as simple as that." He cleared his throat roughly. "Plus, anyone with eyes could see just how much Marty loves you. God, it used to make me so jealous!" Blake laughed, and Suzanne joined in.

After the teasing fell away, an awkward shift took place in the silence between them.

"I guess I should go." Blake walked to the front door, grabbing the duffel bag he had optimistically packed that day.

Suzanne followed closely and wrapped her arms around him for one final hug, hoping he'd sense her eternal gratitude in that one small gesture.

"Thank you for everything," she said after opening the door.

"Marty is very lucky. She better not mess things up again."

"She won't," Suzanne said with certainty. "We were both to blame for our marriage failing, you know. She was just the one who fell apart first."

Blake nodded and kissed Suzanne on the cheek. He lingered for a moment, the scratch of his stubble chafing her skin.

"Good-bye, Suzie."

"Bye, Blake."

Once Blake had walked away, Suzanne closed the door to her apartment. Her hand remained on the doorknob and she released a steady breath. Her eyes closed. She was ready to reclaim the life that was hers. How could going back to someone feel so much like going forward?

The End

Suzanne lost count of the number of times she'd paced the living room. The ten-minute drive back home was a blur of anger and tears. She wondered how she even made it home safely. When she walked through the front door, she saw Abigail sleeping on the sofa. The peaceful look on her face filled Suzanne with an odd sense of calm resignation and determination. Abigail. Her daughter was her sole focus now, as it should be.

Carla was at Suzanne's side the moment she noticed her puffy eyes and wet cheeks, but Suzanne wasn't ready to explain, just move forward.

"Would it be okay with you if I came to stay with you for a bit?" Suzanne said, squirming under her sister's scrutiny. "Just a week or so, I promise."

"Of course it's okay, but what about—"

"Help me get Abigail to bed." Suzanne started to wake her daughter gently. She wanted her to be back asleep by the time Marty got home. Above all, she wanted Carla out of the house before she clued into what had happened. She'd tell her in time. "And I'll probably be over sometime tonight." Suzanne scooped up Abigail and carried her up the stairs.

Carla didn't say anything, but Suzanne knew she'd have to explain later. *One hurdle at a time*, Suzanne told herself as she said good-bye to her sister. As she watched Carla leave, she noticed Marty's car in the driveway, headlights off and idling. Carla shot Suzanne a curious look before getting into her own car and driving away. Suzanne knew Marty was either waiting for Carla to leave or she was scared of Suzanne. *Probably both.* She went inside.

Marty didn't come in for another fifteen minutes. Her shoulders were slumped and her features drawn. Suzanne could tell she had been crying as well, but she didn't feel any sympathy for her. Suzanne sat resolute on the couch, her hands folded on her lap and shoulders squared.

"Suzanne, I'm—"

"Don't."

"What?"

"Don't, just don't. There's nothing you can say, not now."

"At least let me explain!"

"Explain what? *How* you decided to have an affair or *why* you decided to have sex with another woman?" Suzanne felt her ire rise and she tamped it down. She had a plan, and getting emotional wasn't part of it. She need to make a swift, clean break if she wanted Abigail's life to be mostly undisturbed. "No. No explanations." She stood and walked to the door. She bundled her thick winter jacket up and grabbed the duffel bag she had waiting.

"Please, Suzanne!" Marty reached out and grabbed Suzanne's wrist. "Please?" Her eyes welled with tears, and Suzanne felt her resolve waver for a moment, but this wasn't about two women and their marriage. Their situation was so much bigger than that.

"No." Suzanne spoke around a lump in her throat. "My lawyers will be in touch. Please, Marty, don't make this difficult. We need to think about Abigail, not you or me or *this*." She motioned between the two of them.

Marty let her wrist go. "Lawyers?" she said, her voice shaky and wilted.

"I don't want anything from you." Suzanne hoisted the bag onto her shoulder and turned the doorknob. She looked back to Marty. "We need to focus on our daughter from now on." She opened the door and walked to her car. Marty didn't follow at first. Each word had to hit her separately before she sprang into motion.

"Wait!" Marty called out. "We can fix this." She ran out into the driveway. "I'm sorry. I'm so incredibly stupid and sorry and it meant nothing more than—"

"Marty, stop!" Suzanne raised her hand in the air. "*You* did this, and now all I'm asking of you is to think and act in the best interest of that little girl upstairs." She pointed to Abigail's window, took a deep breath, and looked into Marty's watery eyes, and waited until she saw comprehension through the pain. "I'll see you at her next appointment. Other than that, I'll be by to pick her up. Any other schedules will be discussed between our lawyers." Suzanne climbed into her car and started it.

Marty watched as the car crawled its way into the street and sped away from the house. The fight and all the energy she had moments before drained from her body, and fatigue filled her limbs. She fell to the ground. Her knees ached as the cold asphalt dug into her skin. Tears streamed down her cheeks, and her muffled wails carried out into the frigid night.

CHAPTER SEVENTEEN

Charlotte placed the extravagant floral display on Marty's desk, smiling. "Something you want to tell me?"

"What?" Marty didn't look up from the computer screen at first. When Charlotte remained silent, she finally looked over, her eyes wide with surprise.

"Do we have an admirer?" Charlotte plucked the small card from in between the stems and handed it to Marty.

Marty snatched it away and opened it. She scanned the small message and grinned widely. "They're from my mother."

"That was sweet of Denise. She's such a gem. What's the occasion?"

"I had some good news."

"Such as?" Charlotte asked and propping herself on the edge of Marty's desk.

"Suzanne and I…" Marty paused and chose her next words carefully. She didn't want to jinx their future even though last night their reconnection had felt anything but tentative and fragile. "We're reconciling."

"Oh, Marty!" Charlotte clapped.

"Quiet, please!"

"I wish Annmarie was here! She'd be so happy."

"She'll know soon enough, I'm sure. Listen, Charlotte, don't say anything to anybody. It's new and we're still figuring things out."

"When did this happen?"

"Last night." Marty's smirk was full of implication.

"*Oh.*"

"It's still complicated."

"You may say that, but your smile lets me know just how simple it really is." Charlotte pushed herself off Marty's desk and hugged her. "I'm so happy for you! You two need each other now more than ever." Marty was ready to agree vehemently, but Charlotte ran off to answer her ringing phone.

Marty sat back, stared at her mother's small gift, and decided to call and thank her. She pulled her phone from her purse and froze when she saw she had one message from Suzanne.

Won't be able to come over tonight. I'll call you later.

Marty's heart and hopes sank. There weren't enough lines to read between so her imagination started to spiral out of control. She typed out her reply:

Is everything okay?

Yes. What time will you be home?

The answer was immediate. *Seven.*

Talk then. Marty's stomach started to turn.

❖

Suzanne rushed about frantically, making sure everything was in place and just so. This was why she was rarely spontaneous—the anxiety that came along with getting everything perfect at a moment's notice was unbearable. With everything set, she waited. Marty was a half hour late. Maybe she should call her. Maybe her decision to *not* call at seven like she said she would was a terrible idea. Maybe Marty was thinking she had changed her mind.

"Suzie? Are you here? I saw your car out front." Marty stepped through the front door.

"Kitchen!" Suzanne wiped her hands on her thighs and surveyed the room one last time. *This is why I hate being on either end of surprises!*

"Hey, I thought you were—" Marty stopped at the threshold

of the room, holding her bag and the bouquet of flowers Denise had sent.

"I wanted to surprise you." Suzanne started to wring her hands together nervously. "Flowers?"

"From my mom," Marty said, looking at the table. Suzanne had lit candles and set out the good bowls for a lovely dinner of cold cereal, a container of milk chilling on ice. "Mini-Wheats?"

"Yes. Here, let me take these and you have a seat." Suzanne took the flowers and led Marty to the table.

"Read the card," Marty said.

Suzanne took out the note after setting the vase down. "'To my girls, now you can start to mend together again. Love, Mom.' That's so sweet, but how did she know?"

"I may have called her this morning." Marty shrugged guiltily. "So, anyway, what's all this about?"

"It's about me loving you and wanting to set things right after all." Suzanne sat beside Marty and took a deep breath. She reached for Marty's hand and held it on the tabletop. "Marty, I know I can be difficult and withdrawn and distant, but since day one, you've managed to break through all of my bullshit. Because of that, because of you, I've become a better person. When Abigail got sick, I struggled with this guilt that was eating me up inside. Every day it chipped away at me until I didn't even recognize myself."

"Guilt? For what?"

"For our baby being sick, for having to go through all of that."

"That wasn't your fault."

"I lost one baby, and then Abigail." Suzanne's throat tightened. She bit at her bottom lip when it started trembling. "When I looked at you and I saw the sadness in your eyes, I started to hate myself for the pain I had caused you."

"Suzanne, I don't blame you. Abby, the first baby, none of that is your fault." Marty tightened her grip. "As impossible as it is to accept, it was Abby's time." Marty looked at the chair Abigail usually occupied during their meals. She let out a whoosh of air, a cry mixed with laughter when she saw Ripley staring back at her.

"I wanted it to feel like she was here."

"It does. God, it always feels like she's still here."

"I hope so, and I hope that never fades." She scooted closer to Marty and pulled their bodies together. They stayed like that for long minutes, Suzanne relishing the easy closeness she felt to not just Marty, but Abigail as well. She sat back. Her nerves were still jittery, but she knew it was now or never.

"Marty, I need to ask you a question."

"Yeah, sure, what's up?" Marty wiped away her tears.

"If I wear this," Suzanne raised her left hand and wiggled her ring finger, showing off her wedding band, "will you wear this?" She held up Marty's wedding band.

"How did you…"

"You put it in the same place you always did when you took it off." Marty kissed her the moment she stopped talking, practically wrestling the gold band from her before she slid it back onto her finger. Suzanne was struck by how complete Marty looked in that moment, with her ring and her smile in place.

"I'm still intrigued by your dinner choice, though."

"We shared a bowl of Mini-Wheats at four in the morning the night you proposed to me." Suzanne watched as it all came together in Marty's mind. She wasn't just asking for them to wear their rings again, she was asking for it all again. "You asked me the first time, so I think it's only fitting for me to—"

"Yes! When?"

"Martha Dempsey," Suzanne continued, undeterred by Marty's predictable interruption, "will you marry me again and give me back the life I loved?"

"Yes! When?" Marty repeated, this time more loudly.

"As soon as possible?"

"Yes." Marty kissed Suzanne, gently whispering the same words over and over against her lips. "Yes, yes, yes…"

"I love you so much, and I'm so sorry for walking away."

"And I'm sorry for not making you fight and for being so weak and stupid during our worst time. This time, Suzie, I promise I'll do better."

"Me too, Marty, I promise."

The two women kissed again, slowly pulling each other into a loving embrace that reunited their hearts as well as their souls. The world around them stopped and fell into place. Suzanne and Marty spent that night and every night after repeating and renewing their vow to each other—for better or for worse, until death did they part.

One Year Later

H ow are you not even the slightest bit nervous?" Suzanne asked Marty as she finished folding her last napkin.

"I'm just not."

A year had passed since their reconciliation, a year filled with familiar challenges and new risks. They had remarried quickly on a perfect winter's day, standing in the county courthouse with Denise and Charlotte as their witnesses. They ended the day with hot chocolate in bed, wrapped in one another for added warmth.

"You're the jittery one, not me." Marty elbowed her wife playfully, but Suzanne was less than amused.

"I can't help that I worry!"

"I know, and I love you all the more for it." Suzanne relaxed when Marty kissed her cheek. "You keep us balanced."

Since they had reconnected, the world around the two women seemed a bit easier to handle. They had gone to counseling together and spoke openly about their grief and sadness. When Abigail's birthday rolled around, Marty had to force Suzanne out of bed and into the shower. They made a trip to the cemetery, ate Abigail's favorite foods all day, and watched her favorite movies. When it came time for bed, Marty was reluctant to leave their daughter's room, so they slept soundly on the cramped twin bed. In the middle of the night, when Suzanne woke to her wife's hushed tears, they had come to a surprising decision together.

"Why did we invite so many people?"

"Because it's called a party for a reason."

"I think we went a bit overboard." Suzanne looked around their house. Every free corner was filled with balloons of all colors, and banners hung in every entryway. "I'm afraid it's too cheerful."

"Hey." Marty wrapped her arms around Suzanne's waist. Suzanne fell into the comfort immediately. "We've talked about this in therapy. We're allowed to have this. We're allowed to be happy and excited." Marty ran her hands along Suzanne's back.

"I know, and no matter how sad I feel, I'm still happy because I love you and you love me."

"I do."

"And you look stunning today," she said as she fingered the strap of Marty's simple sundress. "Have I told you that yet?"

"Nope," Marty said with an exaggerated pop.

Suzanne wrapped her arms around Marty's waist gently. "Well, you're gorgeous. Absolutely breathtaking." Suzanne stood on her toes and planted a firm, enticing kiss on Marty's plump lips.

"You're not so bad yourself, even if you are still in your pajamas." Marty tugged playfully on the drawstring of Suzanne's flannel sleep pants.

"I should go change, huh?"

"We still have forty minutes before anyone will show up." Marty felt beneath the hem of Suzanne's T-shirt. "What do you say I help you?"

Suzanne's abdominal muscles quivered as Marty skimmed her fingertips along her ribs. "I think we'd be late for our own party."

"Remember when you told me that you'd do anything for me or get me anything I need?" Suzanne nodded. "I need you." Marty kissed Suzanne's cheek and then just below her ear. She whispered, "Just a taste."

"I suppose. I mean, it wouldn't be right for me to deny my wife, especially when she's—" The doorbell rang, effectively extinguishing the growing flame between Marty and Suzanne. Marty growled in disappointment, but Suzanne laughed. "You get that while I change." Suzanne kissed Marty's pout chastely and made her way for the stairs.

She was no more than five stairs up when she heard Marty. "Angela?" Suzanne froze. She hadn't spoken to her mother since their less-than-ideal family dinner over a year ago, and she was all the happier for it. She steeled her nerves with a deep breath and turned back the way she came.

"Mother? What are you doing here?" Angela was standing in the doorway beside an uncomfortable-looking Marty. With a simple look, Suzanne let Marty know she could run away. And she did. "How did you…"

"Carla has kept me up to date with any important news."

"Is Carla with you?"

"No, I'm sorry. It's just me."

"That's not what I—"

"Yes it is. Now, please drop the formalities. I came here for a reason, and I'd like to get right to it."

Suzanne swallowed harshly. "Sure, come in."

"I thought you were having a party."

"We are."

"And this is how you're dressed?"

"I, uh," Suzanne heard Marty's quiet laughter in the kitchen. Somehow, the gentle sound helped calm her. "I was just about to change, actually. Would you mind coming upstairs while I do that? Our guests are close friends, but not *that* close." Suzanne walked up the stairs and Angela followed. She made quick work of changing in the master bathroom while her mother sat stiffly on their bed.

"You haven't spoken to me in over a year," Angela said.

"You haven't made an effort to reach out to me, either."

"Suzanne, I come from a world where children seek out their parents, not the other way around."

"And I come from a world where you defend what's right." Suzanne's rebuttal was heated but controlled. She stepped out from the bathroom and crossed her arms over her chest.

"Carla told me about the conversation you had that night, and I think about everything that was said a lot."

Suzanne wanted to tell her that their last dinner rarely crossed her mind, but she kept that to herself.

"Finding out through a third party your daughter got remarried was a bit of a wake-up call."

"Well, when your behavior was so outstanding at my first wedding…"

"I'm here to apologize. You were right, I never gave Martha a fair chance, nor did I acknowledge your marriage properly."

"Why? Suzanne asked. "Why now?"

"Your father actually sat me down one day and lectured me for quite a while on the importance of family. He helped me see that your happiness is all that matters." Angela paused for a moment and looked at a family portrait that sat on the dresser. "I wasn't there for you when you needed a mother. I let my own stubbornness keep me from helping my own daughter through a terrible time." Angela's voice cracked, causing Suzanne to grow uncomfortable. Emotional, sober displays from her mother were rare. "I'm very sorry for that."

"I can't just forgive you like that." Suzanne spoke firmly and honestly, even if her voice was shaking.

"I know. I don't expect you to, but I will earn your forgiveness. Starting today." Angela stood and advanced upon her daughter. Suzanne's eyes widened in shock when Angela hugged her. She was even more shocked to find she was hugging her mother back. The clearing of a throat startled them apart.

"I'm sorry to interrupt, but we have guests on their way and I think I'm just making things worse down there."

"Marty," Angela called out. Suzanne stared at her as if she were extraterrestrial. "While I have you here, I'd like to invite you both over for dinner next weekend. Carla and Daniel will be there, and I'd love for you both to come so we can have the whole family together for once. Now come on, you don't want your guests walking into a disaster area." Angela left the room and two flabbergasted women behind.

Suzanne looked at Marty, who asked, "What was that?"

"I have no idea." Suzanne shook her head. They joined Angela in the kitchen, a new ease filling the room as they continued to set out foods and decorations in happy silence.

"So," Angela said as she put out the last of the plates, "what will it be this time? A grandson or another granddaughter?" Suzanne stopped what she was doing, block of cheese in one hand and a sleeve of crackers in the other.

"How…?" Marty's question hung in the air, and she stared at Suzanne. "I thought we weren't telling anyone."

"I didn't!" Suzanne vehemently denied. "I didn't even tell Carla!" Angela chuckled. Suzanne watched as her mother approached Marty and placed her hand on the slight baby bump hardly visible beneath her dress.

"I'd have thought for sure that the two of you would know by now." She patted her unborn grandchild lightly. "Some things, a mother just knows." Suzanne and Marty shared a tear-filled smile.

"We're doing a pregnancy announcement and gender reveal today. That's why we're having this party."

"Oh, how lovely!" Angela clapped. "Do either of you know yet?"

"No," Marty said. "We had the nurse put the result in a sealed envelope with the sonogram print out. We'll open it later and find out along with everyone else."

"I'm so happy for you both." Angela looked between the two women.

"We're happy too." Suzanne gripped Marty's hand and drew her close. She snuggled into her wife just as the doorbell rang.

"I'll get that!" Angela announced uneasily.

"I think she's a little uncomfortable." Marty chortled.

"I don't care." Suzanne kissed Marty quickly. "I like having my hands on you."

"And I love having your hands on me." Marty kissed Suzanne once before pulling away from her. "But we're throwing a party now. Maybe later, I'll let you put your hands all over this rapidly growing body of mine."

"Like you'd be able to stop me." Suzanne smiled salaciously and laughed as Marty fanned herself before leaving the room to greet their guests.

Suzanne stood back and took a deep breath. After everything, after the challenges and tears, she'd managed to be happy again after all. *They* had managed to be happy again after all. She looked at the plain white envelope that taunted her from the countertop. Soon enough, she'd find out if they were having a boy or another daughter to love unconditionally. After everything they'd been through, Suzanne found herself realizing she'd still be happy either way. She'd handle whatever life threw at her next, because she had Marty to face it with. If the short time she had with Abigail had taught her anything, it was that there is light in darkness, happiness in sadness, and life in death.

About the Author

M. Ullrich has always called New Jersey home and currently resides by the beach with her wife and three boisterous felines. After many years of regarding her writing as just a hobby, the gentle yet persistent words of encouragement from her wife pushed M. Ullrich to take a leap into the world of publishing. Much to her delight and amazement, that world embraced her back.

By day, M. Ullrich works full-time in the optical field and spends most of her days off working on her writing. When her pen isn't furiously trying to capture her imagination (a rare occasion), she enjoys being a complete entertainer. Whether she's telling an elaborate story or a joke or getting up in front of a crowd to sing and dance her way through her latest karaoke selection, M. Ullrich will do just about anything to make others smile. She also happens to be fluent in three languages: English, sarcasm, and TV/movie quotes.

Books Available From Bold Strokes Books

Camp Rewind by Meghan O'Brien. A summer camp for grown-ups becomes the site of an unlikely romance between a shy, introverted divorcee and one of the Internet's most infamous cultural critics—who attends undercover. (978-1-62639-793-4)

Cross Purposes by Gina L. Dartt. In pursuit of a lost Acadian treasure, three women must work out not only the clues, but also the complicated tangle of emotion and attraction developing between them. (978-1-62639-713-2)

Imperfect Truth by C.A. Popovich. Can an imperfect truth stand in the way of love? (978-1-62639-787-3)

Life in Death by M. Ullrich. Sometimes the devastating end is your only chance for a new beginning. (978-1-62639-773-6)

Love on Liberty by MJ Williamz. Hearts collide when politics clash. (978-1-62639-639-5)

Serious Potential by Maggie Cummings. Pro golfer Tracy Allen plans to forget her ex during a visit to Bay West, a lesbian condo community in NYC, but when she meets Dr. Jennifer Betsy, she gets more than she bargained for. (978-1-62639-633-3)

Taste by Kris Bryant. Accomplished chef Taryn has walked away from her promising career in the city's top restaurant to devote her life to her six-year-old daughter and is content until Ki Blake comes along. (978-1-62639-718-7)

The Second Wave by Jean Copeland. Can star-crossed lovers have a second chance after decades apart, or does the love of a lifetime only happen once? (978-1-62639-830-6)

Valley of Fire by Missouri Vaun. Taken captive in a desert outpost after their small aircraft is hijacked, Ava and her captivating passenger discover things about each other and themselves that will change them both forever. (978-1-62639-496-4)

Basic Training of the Heart by Jaycie Morrison. In 1944, socialite Elizabeth Carlton joins the Women's Army Corps to escape family expectations and love's disappointments. Can Sergeant Gale Rains get her through Basic Training with their hearts intact? (978-1-62639-818-4)

Believing in Blue by Maggie Morton. Growing up gay in a small town has been hard, but it can't compare to the next challenge Wren—with her new, sky-blue wings—faces: saving two entire worlds. (978-1-62639-691-3)

Coils by Barbara Ann Wright. A modern young woman follows her aunt into the Greek Underworld and makes a pact with Medusa to win her freedom by killing a hero of legend. (978-1-62639-598-5)

Courting the Countess by Jenny Frame. When relationship-phobic Lady Henrietta Knight starts to care about housekeeper Annie Brannigan and her daughter, can she overcome her fears and promise Annie the forever that she demands? (978-1-62639-785-9)

Dapper by Jenny Frame. Amelia Honey meets the mysterious Byron De Brek and is faced with her darkest fantasies, but will her strict moral upbringing stop her from exploring what she truly wants? (978-1-62639-898-6)

Delayed Gratification: The Honeymoon by Meghan O'Brien. A dream European honeymoon turns into a winter storm nightmare involving a delayed flight, a ditched rental car, and eventually, a surprisingly happy ending. (978-1-62639-766-8)

For Money or Love by Heather Blackmore. Jessica Spaulding must choose between ignoring the truth to keep everything she has, and doing the right thing only to lose it all—including the woman she loves. (978-1-62639-756-9)

Hooked by Jaime Maddox. With the help of sexy Detective Mac Calabrese, Dr. Jessica Benson is working hard to overcome her past, but they may not be enough to stop a murderer. (978-1-62639-689-0)

Twisted Screams by Sheri Lewis Wohl. Reluctant psychic Lorna Dutton doesn't want to forgive, but if she doesn't do just that, an innocent woman will die. (978-1-62639-647-0)

Lands End by Jackie D. Public relations superstar Amy Kline is dealing with a media nightmare, and the last thing she expects is for restaurateur Lena Michaels to change everything, but she will. (978-1-62639-739-2)

A Class Act by Tammy Hayes. Buttoned-up college professor Dr. Margaret Parks doesn't know what she's getting herself into when she agrees to one date with her student Rory Morgan, who is fifteen years her junior. (978-1-62639-701-9)

Bitter Root by Laydin Michaels. Small town chef Adi Bergeron is hiding something, and Griffith McNaulty is going to find out what it is even if it gets her killed. (978-1-62639-656-2)

Capturing Forever by Erin Dutton. When family pulls Jacqueline and Casey back together, will the lessons learned in eight years apart be enough to mend the mistakes of the past? (978-1-62639-631-9)

Deception by VK Powell. DEA Agent Colby Vincent and Attorney Adena Weber are embroiled in a drug investigation involving homeless veterans and an attraction that could destroy them both. (978-1-62639-596-1)

Dyre: A Knight of Spirit and Shadows by Rachel E. Bailey. With the abduction of her queen, werewolf-bodyguard Des must follow the kidnappers' trail to Europe, where her queen—and a battle unlike any Des has ever waged—awaits her. (978-1-62639-664-7)

First Position by Melissa Brayden. Love and rivalry take center stage for Anastasia Mikhelson and Natalie Frederico in one of the most prestigious ballet companies in the nation. (978-1-62639-602-9)

Best Laid Plans by Jan Gayle. Nicky and Lauren are meant for each other, but Nicky's haunting past and Lauren's societal fears threaten to derail all possibilities of a relationship. (978-1-62639-658-6)

Exchange by CF Frizzell. When Shay Maguire rode into rural Montana, she never expected to meet the woman of her dreams—or to learn Mel Baker was held hostage by legal agreement to her right-wing father. (978-1-62639-679-1)